IS IT A CRIMINAL'S DEEPEST FEAR
THAT'S AT THE HEART OF HIS CRIMES?

Jaguar Addams understands the criminal mind. A survivor
of the Killing Times and the Year of the Serials, Jaguar is
a Teacher on Planetoid Three, the newest and most ad-
vanced of the off-Earth prisons. She is also an empath—
capable of telepathically entering the minds of criminals
and leading them back on a virtual journey to the heart of
their greatest fears.

Her newest case is assassin Clare Rilasco, who has just
murdered the Governor of Colorado and, it seems, allowed
herself to be caught. Whomever she's hiding from, their
wrath must be more punishing than the prison on Planetoid
Three and the terrifying treatment of . . .

the fear principle

the fear principle

B. A. CHEPAITIS

ACE BOOKS, NEW YORK

This book is an Ace original edition
and has never been previously published.

THE FEAR PRINCIPLE

An Ace Book / published by arrangement with
the author

PRINTING HISTORY
Ace edition / January 1998

All rights reserved.
Copyright © 1998 by B. A. Chepaitis.
Cover art by Finn Winterson.
This book may not be reproduced in whole or in part,
by mimeograph or any other means, without permission.
For information address:
The Berkley Publishing Group,
a member of Penguin Putnam Inc.,
200 Madison Avenue, New York, NY 10016.

The Putnam Berkley World Wide Web site address is
http://www.berkley.com

Make sure to check out *PB Plug*,
the science fiction/fantasy newsletter, at
http://www.pbplug.com

ISBN: 0-441-00497-0

ACE®
Ace Books are published by
The Berkley Publishing Group,
a member of Penguin Putnam Inc.,
200 Madison Avenue, New York, NY 10016.
ACE and the "A" design are trademarks
belonging to Charter Communications, Inc.

PRINTED IN THE UNITED STATES OF AMERICA

10 9 8 7 6 5 4 3 2 1

To Edward Palmer Bancroft
   The boat who carried me to this shore.

the fear principle

"In morals, what begins in fear usually ends in wickedness. Fear . . . as a . . . motive, is the beginning of all evil."
—Anna Jameson

the fear principle

prologue

SHE WATCHED THE TWO MEN CARRY THE LIMP BODY of a third man into her darkened apartment.

"Where've you been?" she asked. "I expected you an hour ago."

The balding man shrugged his heavy shoulders. "We had to wait, too," he said.

"All right," she said. "You're here. That's all that matters."

She looked around her living room and seemed to consider for a moment. "Put him there." She motioned with her long, graceful hand toward the couch. They lowered him carefully and stood, waiting for further instructions. She walked to the couch, bent over his unconscious form, and pulled up his eyelid.

"What did they give him—rezonine?"

"Yup. He won't be up for a while."

"I guess. He's got an implant?"

"Left leg. Paralytic, but not neuralgic."

"Okay. That's good enough. Thanks."

The balding man shuffled his feet, then spoke. "Um . . . Dr. Addams. We're supposed to get a report from you on how you plan to proceed with the prisoner."

She looked up at him, eyes cold and knifelike. "I've sent

my initial report to my supervisor. If anyone else cares to read it, they can get it from him.''

The man took a step back and ducked his head down.

His companion, who was young and blond and exuded confidence, cleared his throat and spoke. ''Look, we didn't mean anything by it. The Board guy—Dinardo—he said get it from you while we're here.''

Her expression didn't shift one molecule as she repeated, ''I've sent my initial report to my supervisor. If anyone else cares to read it, they can get it from him.''

''Okay, Dr. Addams,'' the young man said. ''I'll tell them you said so.'' He touched his companion on the arm and they left her, still musing over the man on her couch.

The two men walked in silence to the elevator, pressed the call button, and waited. As it hummed up the four flights toward them, the young man whispered to his co-worker, ''She's not so bad to work with, really. I don't blame her for getting pissed off. The Board's always on her about some shit or other.''

''Yeah. I know. I worked with her before. She's fair. Only I'm damn glad I'm not that guy in there. I'd hate to be *her* prisoner.''

The young man looked back toward her apartment and nodded vigorously.

''Ain't that the truth,'' he said.

Supervisor Alex Dzarny was about to open Jaguar Addams's initial assignment report on prisoner Adrian Graff when the telecom came through that Clare Rilasco had arrived on the Planetoid to begin her sentence.

''Testers've got her?'' he asked Rachel, the team member who was in charge of research for the assignment.

''She was tested on Planetoid Two. They recommended one of our programs,'' Rachel replied.

Alex tapped a finger against his desk. He wondered what the testers would make of this woman, sentenced to the Planetoid prison system for assassinating Gregory Patricks, the Governor of Colorado. A simple enough crime, but in her case a few strings were attached, such as the inability of anybody to find out whom she was working for, and the two attempts that had been made on her life since her arrest.

"Where is she?" he asked.

"The tank."

"Be right there," he said, and flipped the telecom off. He picked up her preassignment file and made his way toward the holding rooms of the building, choosing the stairs over the elevators because he wanted the walk as time to think.

The Planetoid prison programs were based on the premise that crime grew out of fear, and that prisoners needed to be put in a situation where they would face their core fear and overcome it—or, as sometimes happened, be overcome by it. The system had less than two decades of history, but they had, so far, a spectacularly low recidivism rate. Eighty-seven percent of their prisoners returned to Earth and committed no more crimes. Two percent were like Rachel—prisoners who remained on the Planetoid to work as team members or Teachers. The others either relapsed or didn't make it through their programs. These latter were cremated, and their dust mingled with the dust of the stars.

Nobody complained about that. In the chaos that followed the Killing Times, the public was happy enough to have a new system that was both effective and, more important, invisible. Take the worst criminals and put them on a Planetoid that circles the earth as a rim of light dimmed by all but the darkest phases of the moon. Nobody even bothered to lift their eyes and look for it in the sky. People on the home planet didn't want to see, or know. A Board of Governors was established to create procedural rules, and all they asked was that the system remain invisible to the good people of the home planet who funded them.

Alex often questioned the absence of checks and balances in their system, the secrecy of it, and the potential for corruption, but he also knew that the criminals who came to them had already refused all other treatments and signed away all legal rights.

The Planetoids took the incorrigibles.

They took them and gave them to testers, who surveyed them in a variety of ways for their principal and corollary fears. Prisoners were then turned over to Teachers, who developed programs to guide the criminal toward his or her fear, into the heart of it, and, with any luck, out through the other side.

Now it was his job to decide which Teacher would work with the newest arrival on Planetoid Three, Clare Rilasco.

He ran his palm over the code ID key for the holding-room door, and it opened to his print. On the other side, a guard looked up from reading a *Playboy* magazine and quickly closed it, pushed it aside.

Alex ignored the move. "Rilasco with you?" he asked.

"She's inside, sir. Do you want to—"

"I do."

The guard punched a series of codes into the inner lock, and the door swung open.

Alex took one step inside, and stopped short.

Clare Rilasco turned toward him, her alabaster-smooth face and large violet eyes framed in corn-silk hair, the softly rounded contours of her body held as easy as blue in the sky. She observed Alex's response, and he imagined it wasn't an unusual one, because she tilted her head at him as if to say, Yes, I know, I'm beautiful. You'll have to forgive me for it, and then we can be friends. Then she lifted her hand and curved it in welcome.

"I hope you aren't another tester," she said to him gently. "I don't like the way they treated me."

Alex swallowed whatever breath he had left, and let a shiver run down his spine and out his legs. "No," he said. "I'm Supervisor Dzarny. I'm just here to get acquainted."

She stood and pushed back her plastic chair, walked

across the otherwise unfurnished room with her welcoming hand extended to him.

Her movements were fluid, and she showed no signs of tension as she carried her beauty closer and closer to him. He pushed his hand out and met her, determined to control at least some part of these proceedings. As her hand touched his he determined also to keep it brief.

"Actually," she said, "I'm surprised at how easy it's been so far. I'd heard so many things about the Planetoid system—how cruel and harsh it was. I expected whips and chains."

"We're not that medieval, or that Catholic," Alex said, smiling.

"I'm glad. Do you know what happens to me next?"

"That's partly what I'm here to decide, Ms. Rilasco."

"Please—call me Clare. Everyone does."

Alex shook his head. "I'm not everyone," he reminded her. Her tone and manner could easily make this into an afternoon's formal business meeting, or a social tea. He could see how she managed to escape accusation previous to this, though at her trial she claimed to have over a hundred dead men to her name, and some of those men powerful public figures.

When she gave her testimony she had surprised everyone—including her legal representative—by saying that Governor Patricks was the last in a long line of hit jobs. She had no objection when the legal representative for Colorado called her a professional assassin. She liked being called professional.

She declined to identify any of the people she worked for. When she was hired for a job, she was expected to keep it in confidence, and her clients paid her well to do so.

Investigation hadn't revealed anything to link the Patricks murder to anyone beyond her, which made Alex assume she had the backing of an organization accustomed to covering their tracks. At her sentencing, the judge had

expressed the hope that Planetoid treatment would convince
her to reveal the ultimate perpetrator of such a heinous
crime. Both press and politicians had picked up on the
theme, and the case had become a publicity circus. Now
the Board that governed Planetoid operations was in high
twitch about it, certain that public opinion of Planetoid ef-
ficacy rested or fell with the Rilasco case.

They hoped that her testing run would provide some lead
back to the contractor of the hit on Patricks, but Clare
showed anomalies from the start. She was close to flat line
on her neurophysiologicals, with the limbic region showing
no response at all. The testers panicked about this, then
discovered that the machines were reading them, not her.
They couldn't get a read on Clare no matter what they tried.

She was too far under the reactivity curve for standard
personality and emotive testing as well, and since the tests
were set up so that first results determined second choices,
the testers didn't even know what to do with her next.

In the end, they'd slapped down a diagnosis and program
recommendation based on previous understanding of assassins' test results. Alex had a feeling that wouldn't apply to
her either.

Now he'd have to find someone who could not only work
with the slippery surface of this cool and beautiful woman,
but could also extract information indicating a connection
between Clare and her unknown employer. It would have
to be extracted because she wasn't about to give it away.

He stood and considered her, and she returned his gaze
with equanimity.

"Well," she said, after some time. "Now what? Do you
frisk me? Hit me?" She tilted her head at him quizzically.
"Rape me?" she asked, her voice dropping in pitch.

"None of the above," he said. Then he breathed in
deeply, releasing air slowly, his eyes staying with her as he
turned his hands palm out to touch the air around her.

The testers' report was deficient, but there were other
ways of understanding prisoners. They might not be offi-

cially approved ways, but they were utilized on Planetoid Three, and Alex was among the Supervisors who knew how to use them.

He ran the palm of his hands over the space surrounding her, touching the edges of that bubble called the human energy field. She stood very still inside the electric hum his hands created, not asking any questions, not moving at all.

He would keep his touch light for now. Like flicking fishline over water, to see if anything was jumping beneath the surface. He'd have nothing he could immediately translate into words, but later he would sit with the feel of her energy as it moved around and through her, making decisions based on knowledge gathered in his skin and his bones.

He lowered his hands, and she smiled at him.

"Are you an empath?" she asked.

He said nothing.

"I know about the empathic arts," she continued. "You'd be surprised what I know."

"What you know," Alex said, "is what we're going to find out before you leave. That's why you're here."

Her full lips curled into a smile. "I understand," she said. "That's your job. And my job is to make sure you fail."

Alex left her with the last word and returned to his office to scan his compufiles on various Teachers, to see who would be best suited for the assignment. He sensed that the case was more complex than the mirror-smooth surface of this woman indicated, and might call for a nontraditional approach.

He went through his mental list of possibilities and came up with the names of four experienced men and women, each of whom had worked with professional assassins. Any one of them would make sense for this case, and two of them were free. Perhaps a male-female team, he thought. Teresa and Rion would work well together, and they were always willing to try out the unknown, ad-lib. They'd create something interesting for Clare.

In spite of this, his hand moved from his computer and reached across his desk for the hard-copy file with Jaguar's name on it.

Jaguar Addams had been working for him for three years, but it was almost nine years since she had shown up in his office, very young, with no experience, but enough ego to balance out the deficit.

"I'm going to be a Teacher," she said. "I want you to tell me how I start."

She said Nick Lyola, one of Alex's Teachers, sent her here because he knew she was interested in working for the Planetoid system. She'd been looking around, learning about the system, about the job of Teacher as it was applied on Planetoid Three.

"I understand there's room for new people," she'd said, "and I'm ready to work."

He would have laughed, except for the look in her eyes, old, deep, and dangerous as the sea. She was serious. He would be, too. He explained to her that Teachers had to have higher degrees. Masters, and preferably doctorates in the philosophies or humanities. Most Teachers were hired from the home-planet criminal-justice system, and they had to be over twenty-five. Jaguar had brushed all these conditions away with a graceful sweep of her hand.

"That's bound to change," she said. "Actually, ex-prisoners are probably the most qualified for the job. A higher degree won't train you for this."

"You're almost right," he told her. "Yes, prisoners are probably the most qualified but the Board of Governors won't let us hire them except as team members to help the Teachers out. As far as the degree, well, nothing prepares you for this work, except the discipline it takes to know yourself from the inside out. University is a pretty good place to start learning that."

He watched her when he said this, to see if she understood at all what he meant.

Jaguar had knit her brow and studied her hands. "I understand the premise," she said. "See who you are. Be what you see."

The words surprised him. Ritual words. The words of the empath. He looked once more at her eyes and saw they were impenetrable. Empath, he thought. Practiced. Sure of her arts. She noticed his study of her, and she nodded at him. How much, he wondered, did she know about him?

"You'll have to get yourself back to school, then reapply. You have family who can help?"

She shook her head. "They were killed in the Serials."

Of course. Many of the people who applied for work on the Planetoids wanted to get away from the memory of that time. They'd lost families, friends, homes, and hope. For some, just the mention of Manhattan or Los Angeles brought on flashbacks. The larger cities in North America had been the hardest hit, and he assumed Jaguar came from one of them.

"New York?" he'd asked her.

"Manhattan," she replied.

His army unit had been in Manhattan, cleaning up the aftermath. Manhattan and Los Angeles had taken the worst of the devastation.

That may have been why he did what he did next. Compassion for survivors, and his knowledge that luck—nothing more—had kept him safe. He'd emerged from the Killing Times without personal loss, without injury or trauma.

He had told her about various scholarship opportunities and sent her on her way. Then he called in some favors, found out where she had landed, and arranged to pay the remainder of her tuition without her knowing about it. When she graduated and was hired as a Teacher, he kept track of her. Her first assignment had been on Planetoid One, but she hadn't lasted long there. Planetoid One, the

first of the prison colonies, was too confining for as un-
domesticated a creature as she was. When she was kicked
off, he'd made arrangements to have her transferred to his
zone instead of fired altogether. She still didn't know any
of this. Not even now that she was Dr. Addams, under his
supervision.

He'd had opportunities over the past three years to regret
his decision, but never to doubt the depth of talent and
passion she brought to her job. She would go way out of
bounds, was immune to direction if she didn't want to take
it, had no sense of the politics of her work, but her success
rate was the highest on the Planetoid.

He ran his hand over her file, thinking.

She'd never worked with an assassin before.

She was on the Graff assignment.

She was less experienced than the other Teachers he was
considering.

She was not suited for a high-profile case like Rilasco.

But his hand wouldn't leave her file alone, so he opened
it, and scanned the initial report for her current case, a con
man brought in on his third charge of felony fraud and
willful negligence leading to wrongful death.

As he scanned, his face grew darker, his night-sky eyes
narrowing.

"Oh Christ, Jaguar," he said to the report. "You've
changed the whole damn thing. Now what're you doing to
Graff?"

1

HE WAS RUNNING. SOMETHING HAD HAPPENED TO HIS cell bubble. A power outage, or short circuit, and he was running now, while he had the chance, the slick soles of his prisoner's shoes finding precarious purchase on the ancient marble floors of the courtroom.

Running, and the courtroom crowd was jeering at him, pointing at him and laughing. They were laughing and he looked down, saw that his clothes were falling off him, becoming rags. He was running, almost naked, running from the guards, but his feet wouldn't go anymore.

"Wait," he yelled at the swarm of people that gathered around him. "Wait. This is my old dream. I really did escape. I did."

But they only continued to laugh, a circle of jeering faces growing tighter and tighter around him, as he, naked and alone, grew smaller and smaller, skin hanging in wrinkled folds around his bones.

He woke with a start, his body jerking upright. His vision blurred, sharpened, clouded, and unclouded.

The first thing he saw clearly was her eyes.

Sea green, washed with tawny sun and glittering silicon crystals of burnished sand.

The rest of her face came slowly into focus, with its smooth amber skin framed by silken walnut hair that seemed to have been dipped, here and there, in molten gold. She stood looking down at him, her eyes holding him still while he regained clarity.

When he tried to stand she pushed him down again.

"Going somewhere?" she asked, her voice husky and low.

"I—" he said, "I'm—where?"

"Toronto," she said, "city of. Canada." She sat down on the arm of the couch and reached toward the end table, picking up a pack of cigarettes. She pulled one out for herself and offered him the pack.

"Smoke?"

He shook his head, watched while she lit hers and sucked in smoke. She turned her sea eyes to him.

"That's right," she said, in answer to his unasked question. "Smoking's illegal in the city zones, Canada and United States. So, figure it out."

He tried to get his brain to work. He had been arrested, he knew that. That wasn't just the dream. It was real, this time. He was arrested, and convicted, and was being sentenced when something happened to his cell bubble, and he ran. Then—a large and annoying blank.

He looked around, his gaze touching on the crucial points of the room. He could see the tops of other buildings out the window. He was up high, in the smallish living room of an apartment. Pretty well furnished. Nothing too new or fancy. Just a regulation telecommunicator rather than the newer, more expensive holophone. Security cameras in the corners, nice thick throw rugs over wood flooring—must be an older place to have wood floors. A desk with computer inset, a shelf full of disk books that he couldn't see the titles of, and a rocking chair. Very old bentwood, with a caned seat and back. A valuable antique, he thought.

Then, on a small table near the rocking chair, a clay bowl filled with dried herbs, a red feather and a dark one resting next to it with a few small stones, and what looked like an animal skull.

He prided himself on being able to size someone up by the contents of their rooms. Whoever this woman was, she was not rich. She was not inclined to be flashy. She had a sense of history. This much he could tell. But why was she allowed to smoke?

He turned his gaze from her possessions to her. She was watching him watch her as she breathed out rings of smoke that sailed across the room over his head. Her shirt looked like silk—vintage, maybe—a deep red floaty thing over matching silk pants, also floaty. She wore one earring, the sign of artists, but he couldn't tell what kind. Anyway, artists weren't exempt from the smoking ban, though they'd lobbied hard for it.

Older people, those over sixty-five with a history of the addiction, were allowed to continue. Looking at her, it was obvious this was not her disclaimer. So what else got you an exemption? Doctor's orders for those deemed chronically unstable biochemically, since it had been discovered that cigarettes regulated depressive episodes with remarkable efficiency.

She could be crazy, he thought, but she didn't look depressed. What else? There was, of course, the exemption for law-enforcement officials who served in certain high-risk capacities, but she wouldn't be that. Would she?

He narrowed his eyes at her, and the corners of her mouth twisted up into a smile.

"That's right," she said. "I'm a cop."

He pressed his arms into the side of the couch, prepared to propel himself up and out. She laughed.

"Just checking," she said, "to see if you're awake."

"Then you're . . . not a cop?"

"Actually, I am. I'm the cop who flipped the power grid so your bubble would crash and you could run."

"You helped me escape?"

She inclined her head graciously in acknowledgment, her

hair falling like waves of silk around her shoulders.

"Why?"

"I thought you were kind of cute, and I know how to without getting caught, so I went ahead."

"That's bullshit," he said.

She smiled back and took a deep drag off her cigarette. "Bullshit," she murmured. "Don't you ever wonder how something as solid and inevitable as bullshit became a metaphor for a deliberate illusion?"

He pushed himself to sitting up, swung his legs down, and planted them firmly on the floor. As he did so a sharp stabbing pain ran across his eyes, forcing him to lower his head into his hands. She waited while he groaned at length.

"You took a spill," she said. "When I grabbed you."

Flashes of events went on and off in his mind. Memory began to return. But he didn't remember taking a spill. As he remembered, someone grabbed him, he swung, and whoever it was responded in kind, knocking the back of his head into the side of a brick building.

"You hit me," he said, taking his hands from his face and glaring at her.

"You *missed* me," she said. "Good swing, though." She tamped her cigarette out in a clay ashtray painted in pictographs of wildcats and snakes, then said apologetically, "I thought I was about to lose you, and I went through a lot of trouble to get you, so I took the necessary measures."

"What the hell," he hissed, "is going on here. Who are you, and what do you want with me?"

"I'm Jaguar Addams," she said, running a finger along his shoulder, "and you're *my* prisoner now."

He snorted derisively, brought up a hand, and rubbed the back of his neck, shrugging her off in the process. This was not a fun game, even if the player was cute.

"You named after the Explorer series?" he asked.

Lots of children bore the burden of names such as Onyx and Zarathustra, after one or another of the probes that had been sent out to establish Planetoid colonies in the years of the Serials. Adrian had always thought it ironic that it took the Killing Times to resurrect the dying space program, but he had to admit that NASA worked fast once kicked back into life. There had been eight probes sent out in the first run. This was the first time he'd heard of someone named after the Jaguar probe.

"Actually," she said, "I wasn't named after the Explorers. I was born before they went out. Not after the old British car, either. Or the football team."

"Then what?" he asked when he saw she was unwilling to say more on her own.

She shrugged. "The big cats. They're extinct, too. Except in zoos. I guess you could say I'm the only wild one left. Would you like a cup of tea? I have some fine herbals. Could help your headache."

"I don't want tea," he said, pushing himself forward and staring at her hard. Whatever her game was, he wanted to have some say in the rules. "I want you to tell me why you helped me escape, and why I'm in Toronto, and what you plan on doing with me next."

She leaned back against the edge of the couch, crossed her left leg over her right, and swung it back and forth. "Naughty boy," she said. "How rude of you to question the hospitality of your hostess, and we've only so recently been introduced. Have you never read your Lalê Davidson regarding the rules governing behavior between hostess and guest? You should particularly refer to Chapter Seven, in the *Etiquette of Crime*."

"Thank you for helping me escape," he said with mock courtesy. "Will that do?"

"Not at all. Actually, in almost every tradition except the New Serakones, I own you. Your life is mine. If it pleases me to offer you something, I offer. You then accept gratefully. I've offered you tea. What do you say?"

He stared at her dumbly. Maybe she wasn't a cop. Maybe she was one of the crazies after all. She let some minutes pass in silence, then she slid gracefully off the arm of the couch and went over to him, stood in front of him, and lifted his chin with the long fingers of her right hand.

"I'm a cop," she said, as if answering his thoughts. The tone of her voice was less playful, more intense, though what emotion the intensity implied was beyond his reckoning. "I'm a cop on extended leave. Ever hear of the crazy clause?"

He shook his head.

"If you're a cop, and your superiors think your job is driving you crazy, then you get extended leave. Compassionate leave, they call it. You get full pay for the first year, and then they cut it down, little by little, until you have nothing except whatever pension you've managed to accumulate. Every month you get tested to see if you're done being crazy for the time being. In fact, I have to go in in the morning, when they'll pass any number of sensors over my tortured neural pathways, ask any number of discourteous questions, and then fret over any number of statistical surveys to see if I'm fit for service yet."

She paused, then jerked his chin up higher. "When you look at me, what do you see? Take your time," she added. "Impetuosity can mar judgment unless it's based on a sound intuitive system. People who've just escaped the Planetoids rarely have that." She let go of his chin and dropped to the floor, where she sat looking placidly up at him.

"What do you see?" she asked again.

He stared at her hard, trying to penetrate her focused gaze with his own. At first, he thought he had done it, but as the minutes passed he realized that her eyes would let you in only to swallow you whole. They were a great green sea, salty and deep, filled with complicated eddies and whirlpools that would drag you down and down to a place where the water weighed in tons above your head, pressing you into an endless suffocating sand.

"You're incredibly beautiful," he said, surprising himself.

She threw her head back and laughed.

"At least," she said, "you're learning how to compliment the hostess."

He took in a good lungful of air, shook off the feeling of slow confusion, and leaned back on the couch.

She stood up and stretched, putting a hand against her lower back. "You think *that* was a workout. I've been dragging your deadweight body around all morning. You're not a little man, I'll say that for you."

"I try to keep fit," he said.

She nodded. "Mm," she said, "I know you do. Because keeping fit means that when the old dreams of running and shrinking start, you can remember they're just phantasms. Just ghouls from your childhood panting after you. Nothing of substance, as long as you're substantial."

She grinned at his wide-eyed shock.

"Oh, I know all about you, Adrian Graff. You're a con man of the first degree, convicted of selling illegal drugs as medicine to a bunch of losers dying of ImmunoSerum Disorder, or ISD as it's called in the fast-food world. Convicted, and sentenced to the Planetoids. Unlike you and most of the rest of the apathetic public, I know what goes on at the Planetoids and how little chance you stood of ever coming back. I also know that you're very good at making money, and I'm a cop approaching the end of her first year of compassionate leave. In short, I need money, and you know how to make it, so I want you to make some for me. End of speech. Any questions?"

He contemplated her face, which seemed calm and in charge of itself. She wasn't desperate. And the idea made a lot of sense to him. In fact, he had to give her credit for using what she knew best to make a living. She might be crazy, but it would suit him just fine to play along with her at least until he got his bearings and figured out what to do next.

"How much money do you want?" he asked.

"A lot. Enough to keep me in cigarettes for the rest of my life."

"Keep smoking them, that won't be very long."

"Yes, Mother. Then please just give me half a million, and I won't bother you ever again. I promise, cross my heart and hope to swallow a sword."

Half a million. He could have just handed her the money and been on his way, if the state hadn't confiscated all his accounts. He could do it in a few weeks in New York, or L.A., or even Denver. People were willing to pay a lot for very little when hope was the commodity. But here? He didn't know Toronto. Hadn't ever even visited the damn city. Didn't have any sense of its character or know the streets or the people or the problems, and in his line you had to know all this in depth, as if they were part of your genetic code.

And even if he had the money, he saw no reason to hand it over to her. He thought fast, sifting through the pros and cons of the situation. Getting to know a new city, a whole new world in which to ply his trade, and she seemed savvy enough to guide him. Certainly playing games with her was better than the alternative he'd been facing just a few hours before.

But half a million? He shook his head.

"Oh, okay then," she said, pouting a little, "make it two hundred and fifty thousand, and we'll call it even. Not a bad price to pay for your life, is it?"

"It'll take time," he said. "I have to get to know the city."

"I can help you with that," she said. "In fact, I have a few leads for you right off the bat. I didn't go into this blind, after all."

"No. You don't seem that type. But . . ."

"But what?"

"How do I know you'll let me go when you've got what

you want?'' he asked. "And why shouldn't I just skip out now?"

"Two good questions. I knew you weren't as stupid as everyone said you were."

"Thanks for the vote of confidence. What're the answers?"

"About me letting you go when you're done—you don't know, dearest. You won't know until it happens, or doesn't. In fact, why don't you assume that I'd just as soon kill you as . . . well, you know."

He shifted again, thinking maybe he should try the door, and as the thought crossed his mind he felt a tingle running up the inside of his legs. He raised his eyes to her.

"That's right," she said. "That's the answer to question number two. There's an implant in your leg. You can't get very far without it hurting like hell, and if you keep trying, you'll just fall down and lie on the ground until I come get you. Right now it's set for a very short range. Later, if it seems okay, I'll give you a longer leash. Trust me, baby?"

"About as far as you trust me," he said.

"Good. That's good. Then we understand each other. But you know, there are benefits to your tenure with me." She slipped her silk blouse over her head, let it slide to the floor.

"At least," she said as she let her hand drop into his lap, "I like to play with my food."

"So," he said, "I see."

The pressure of her body against his pushed him prone onto the couch. The scent of something fresh and wild, like the rampaging mint that ranged the unkempt lawns of old suburbia, reached him, pulling him into an ocean of no known depth. He let all effort leave him while she swarmed up him as if she were the last crashing wave of an incoming tide.

The banks of computer screens buzzed, hummed, and spoke in soothingly neutered tones under the artificial sunlight that bathed the subbasement of the building. Each screen was in use, and Alex had to wait his turn behind two other people who also wanted access to the Teachers' files.

He leaned against a wall that was painted a color everyone referred to as therapy green, a color that supposedly was both calming and fortifying to the psyche. Alex sniffed the air to see if they were still piping in the herbal concoction someone had decided was the exact right combination of stimulation and relaxation so that the people stuffed in here working all day wouldn't go mad and kill each other.

When he first heard about the aromatic infusion, he'd questioned a Board Governor, who blinked at him as if he was questioning the pope and said, "Of course it's effective. It was tested on postal workers."

Alex leaned, and tried not to tap his feet impatiently as he waited. He hadn't chosen a Teacher for Clare and pressure was on him for a decision. He wanted to check through the files of Teachers not under his supervision to see if he could borrow one. The general files would be incomplete, of course, but he could learn enough to narrow down the field, and then he could consult with the appropriate Supervisor on availability and advisability.

After reading the full report from Jaguar's current case, he'd decided not to use her. She had altered Adrian Graff's program radically, against the advice of the testers, and against the specific injunction by the Governors' Board that she stick to protocol or face a reprimand, He'd have to talk to her about it, though he was sure she'd have a reasonable explanation for her changes. She always did. And she was usually right. But that didn't save him from having to run interference between her and the Board. To put her on the Rilasco case, which was already twisting their torques, would be foolish.

It was too bad, he thought. With her capacity for the empathic arts and her willingness to use them, he was curious to see what she'd do with Clare, how she would proceed to get below her glasslike surface.

"Lost in thought, or lost in line?" a voice asked him, and he turned abruptly to find himself staring into the grin of Nick Lyola.

Alex took a step back. Nick never did have a clear idea of physical boundaries. He was always getting in faces, which Alex chalked up to the years he'd spent on NYPD as a homicide detective.

"Hello, Nick," he said, then gazed around the room. "You here for business?"

This room had the files for Teachers, and was generally only used by Supervisors or personnel checking records for insurance, pension, employment history, and so on. Teachers most often had reason to use the home-planet file banks, located on the other side of the building.

"Returning my temporary access code. I had a few things to look up on someone."

He shifted on his feet and leaned heavily into the wall with his shoulder, bringing his narrow face closer to Alex's. He was a tall man, almost as tall as Alex, and his bright blue eyes didn't have to look up much to meet Alex's. Still, he squinted as if he was looking into a bright light, and Alex noted that there were dark circles under his eyes, a sagging around his mouth from his tendency to grin with one side of it.

Getting a little old, Alex thought. Or maybe he's just tired. His last case—one he'd been on with Jaguar—hadn't gone well. The prisoner, a repeat offender pedophile, had committed suicide after an attempt was made at emphatic contact. Jaguar's attempt. Something went wrong, she said. Nothing to do with Nick, or her. Just a lousy case. It happened now and then.

But the two cases preceding that one, which Nick had handled alone, ended up with another prisoner death, and a prisoner who had to be sent on to another Teacher. Something wasn't right.

Nick reached out his hand, index finger pointed, and jabbed Alex playfully in the chest, grinning his one-sided grin. "I'm glad I found you here," he said. "I understand you're reviewing the Rilasco woman for assignment."

"News," Alex said, "travels fast."

"Small Planetoid," Nick replied. "You got her covered yet?"

"I'm still looking."

Alex supposed Nick wanted a high-profile assignment to climb back on top of his professional mountain. He had passed on the job of Supervisor when it was offered to him years ago, saying he'd rather be the best Teacher he could be than a lousy administrator. And he was a very good Teacher, too. He believed in the no-frills approach, and abjured the high-tech toys offered for neural access, for dream-pattern interruption, for any number of physical and emotional stresses that could be created to bring fear up from under. He stuck to basics, and for him a clear sense of the multitudinous kinds of evils humans could perpetrate against each other was basic. Nick was good because he understood all the ways a person could lose their soul. He knew the criminals he worked with, could anticipate what they'd do, think, resist, or respond to, as if they occupied his own flesh.

Alex suspected he had some natural ability in the emphatic arts, but if he was practicing them, he kept it carefully hidden. His skill, his understanding of fear and violence, didn't seem to be a matter of communication or touch. It lived strictly within his own skin, and it served him well in his job. But Alex still couldn't bring himself to like him.

He repeatedly tried to convince himself that his dislike was a matter of differing styles rather than anything wrong with the man or his work. After all, he had a success rate second only to Jaguar's, and a loss-to-death rate almost lower than hers as well. Granted, he was known to have a short fuse, an intolerance of arrogance, his own way of working. But he'd been with the Planetoid system since its inception, working on Planetoid One when it was just a bubble dome floating in space, and transferring to the more sophisticated Planetoid Three when it began operations.

It made sense that he'd see himself as first in line for Clare. Still, Alex had the sense of some other agenda, and decided to probe just a little more.

"You interested?" he asked.

"Sure," Nick said. "Who wouldn't be? She's the talk of the town right now. Sounds like a real challenge."

"That's true. You've worked assassins before?"

"Four. All male, but the females are so rare anyway. Or maybe they're just smarter, and don't get caught as much, right?" This said with a playful wink.

Alex wished he could like Nick more, but he just didn't think he could see his way clear to it. That, he reminded himself, was no reason to keep him off a job he might be qualified for. He'd have to come up with something more solid.

"Haven't you got a home leave coming?" he asked. "You've had a couple of rough ones. Maybe you should take it now."

Nick's grin disappeared, and his face looked heavier without it, eyes receding into dark circles, flesh hanging a little loosely around his chin. "The last rough one wasn't mine," he said grimly, "and I got a few things to clear up on that."

Alex raised his eyebrows at him. "Such as?"

"You'll see. I left something on your desk."

"You want to tell me anything more?"

Nick shook his head. "I want you to read it. And you should know, I've talked with the Board, and they're waiting to hear from you."

Now Alex found himself tensing. Teachers going to the Board without discussing the issue with their Supervisor first was power playing. Alex resisted the urge to pick Nick up by his faded blue shirtfront and ask him who the hell he thought he was. Instead, he assumed his iciest tone and said, "What's this about, Nick?"

"It's about Jaguar," he said, and nodded knowingly, as if they belonged to the same secret club. "You'll see."

"Jaguar? What about her?"

"You'll see. I gotta run, but we'll be talking." He winked, gave Alex a thumbs-up, and left.

As Nick left, Alex felt the click and hum of foreknowledge—a brief dip into and out of his capacity for precognition, unexpected and coming without his volition. And perhaps it was at that moment, or perhaps it was when he returned to his office and read Nick's complaints, that he decided to do the worst possible thing and put Jaguar on Clare's case.

2

SUPERVISOR ALEX DZARNY KEPT A NEAT OFFICE.
There were no stains from coffee cups on the neatly or-
ganized surface of his Formica desk, and no piles of disks
leaning off of windowsills and chairs, as there were in some
Supervisors' offices. The white walls had no pinholes, no
yellow corners of old Scotch tape. Just a posterboard map
of the region, and a very small black-and-white reproduc-
tion of a primitive pictograph, framed in ebony. That had
been a gift, given long ago, by the woman who now sat on
the other side of the desk from him.

She was explaining to him, in her balanced, impeccably
lucid way, the reasons for her changes in the Graff assignment. Her subject, Adrian Graff, convicted of larceny fraud,
believed that she had helped him to escape to Toronto, and
had consented to work a few con games for her. She had
set up a program with team members that would result in
the con man being conned, and felt that this program, along
with a few personal touches she would include, would suc-
cessfully lead him to his fears. She anticipated a few weeks'
worth of work. It was, she said, a relatively simple case.
The testers had called his fears accurately except for one.

"Which one?" he asked.

"The tests stopped at a surface fear," she said. "The

report said that the expressed fear was penury, masking a principal fear of impotence. In fact, that's a cover fear.''

"For?" he asked.

"Ordinariness.''

Alex leaned back in his chair and drummed his fingers against his desk. "I'm waiting,'' he said.

"I know. That's not one of the protocol fears. But it's his fear. He's terrified of learning that he's as petty, common, and unimportant as he believes himself to be.''

"Dr. Addams—'' he used her academic title, as he did when he was about to question her logic—"how did you reach this?''

She put her hands on the desk and spread the fingers out, flexing them, clenching them, unclenching them. Alex recognized the gesture. It signified, for her, an attempt to touch the assignment at its core. Generally, her attempts were successful. Often they went against protocol, and sometimes against all codes of behavior allowed the Teachers of Penal Planetoid Three. If she wasn't so good, he knew, she would have been out long ago.

"My subject,'' she said, "wants to avoid ordinariness because his father was an ordinary and tedious drunk who shot his depressed wife and then himself. Adrian wants to be slick, important, so his father's ghost won't stare back at him in the mirror when he's trying to see himself.'' She sighed deeply. "He's wrong, of course. His father's ghost controls everything he does, though he left nothing behind except a half-empty bottle of Jack Daniel's. Or,'' she asked, a corner of her mouth turning up, "should I say it was half-full?''

"I think, in this case, half-empty would be appropriate. How old was he at the time?''

"He was seventeen when the Serials started, and eighteen by the time Dad shot Mom. He sells false hope, because that's all he has to sell. Real hope—well, that's one of his corollary fears. Along with love. I'll use both in his program.''

"Love?" Alex asked. "Not impotence?"

She lifted her shoulders and let them fall. "For Adrian, the one implies the other."

Alex rubbed the tips of his fingers against his temples and thought. Jaguar wouldn't interrupt him, he knew, unless he asked her another question. One of her most valuable traits was her ability to maintain silence. It could be one of her most irritating qualities as well.

"Okay," he said after some time had passed. "Proceed. We'll have to rewrite the protocols, though. Let's make it . . . hmm. Core fear, self-imaging. How's that?"

"It hardly matters, does it? I'll report back when it looks like we're approaching the fear. Maybe two weeks." She stood, picked up her sunglasses from his desk, and put them on. He held out a hand to stop her.

"No, you won't," he said.

She remained standing, one hand resting on top of his desk. After a moment her index finger began to tap lightly on the slick surface.

"Have a seat," he said, and when she pulled her dark glasses down her nose to peer at him over their lenses, he added, "please."

She pushed her shades to the top of her head and curled herself back into her chair. He reached over and took a file folder from the top of his pending bin, and handed it to her. She looked at him inquisitively, turned her eyes to the pages inside, and read. Then she lifted a scowling face back to his.

"Alex," she said, "this is ridiculous. These charges—it wasn't like that."

"Jaguar," he mimicked, "*this* is ridiculous. By now you should know how to avoid this kind of trouble. Nick is well and truly pissed at you," he continued over her protestations, "and if I can't talk him down, he'll bring you before the Board."

"On a charge of—of slander and code breaking? How will he prove that?" she asked.

"Do I dare ask you, at this juncture," Alex returned rather coldly, "how you convinced Adrian that staying with you would be a good thing?"

She raised her chin up and blinked her eyes. "You may or may not. What you dare is up to you, not me," she replied coolly.

"We don't have to argue about this," Alex said.

They both knew that Supervisors and Planetoid Governors would remain willfully blind to the techniques a Teacher chose in a prisoner's program, as long as the Teacher was successful, and used a little discretion in the wording of her final reports. There were rules against unnecessary sexual behavior or the use of the empathic or ritual arts, but these would only be invoked in cases of repeated failure, repeated deaths, or repeated complaints from team members or Supervisors. Jaguar would have no problem skirting the edges of the rules, if only she would learn to be more politic in her interactions with the Bureaucratic body. Or in her interactions with other Teachers, for that matter. Especially with Nick.

Alex always thought that Jaguar and Nick were too much alike to work well as a team. He was surprised when she agreed to partner with him, especially since she'd refused to partner with anyone else. But she'd said yes immediately when she found out Nick had requested her, and they were able to bring a series of complex cases to successful conclusion. She said she understood his style, and where he'd learned it.

There was something more to the relationship than she was willing to share. Some history between them. There was also anger between them, and a consistent wrestling for power, even when they worked well together. And as far as Alex could tell, it had always been like that. What was happening between them now was some old shit, only more of it.

"Nick says you used sex to get him to agree to certain procedures in a case you were working on together," Alex said to her. "He says you seduced him, using empathic arts in a coercive way, and convinced him that your protocol was the right one. When the program failed, you made him take the fall for it."

Jaguar looked at Alex carefully from under half-closed lids. "Am I supposed to waste energy responding to that?" she asked. "Or can I get back to work now?"

"You're supposed to—" Alex started, and then stopped. What did he want from her, anyway? An explanation would be a nice place to start.

"I know what he claims to be angry about. What is it with you?"

She brought her sunglasses down from the top of her head and twirled them, grinning at him. "Maybe he had the right key, but was working on the wrong keyhole."

He pulled in breath, and let it out slowly. She was sitting on something. Something she obviously wasn't going to give him now. The negative side of her capacity for silence, here at its worst.

"Look," she said casually, "if the prisoner couldn't take the heat, it wouldn't be the first time. He was a pedophile. You know what that's like. But I did *not* tickle Nick's funny bone to get him to play my way."

"Then," Alex said, "what did you tickle?"

"Nothing, Alex. Really. Nick wanted to try to get at the prisoner's fear of women through me, and I said no. He said I slept with everyone else, why not with this guy? I told him because it literally wouldn't do a fucking bit of good. He said I better play along or he'd report me, being senior Teacher and all. I told him to go ahead, if he could get his head unstuck from his ass long enough to find a telecom."

"I take it," Alex said, "you're reporting this interaction verbatim."

"And for the record. Also for the record, the conversation was public. At a bar called the Crab Nebula. Seafood a specialty."

"And you didn't sleep with Nick? At all? Ever? For any reason?"

"Yes. Two years ago. For fun. But it wasn't, so I didn't repeat the experience."

"What about the other charge?"

"The empathic coercion?" She turned her eyes full to his. "What makes you think I'd have to bother?" she asked.

Alex nodded. She was right. She wouldn't have to do more than crook a finger to get Nick running to her. And he wasn't the only one. He leaned back in his chair and swiveled, considering what he was about to do and wondering if it was the most foolish thing he'd ever done, or just a close second to hiring her in the first place.

"I'll deal with Nick," he said, "but I want you to deal with Clare Rilasco."

Jaguar startled, and raised an eyebrow at him.

"You know the case?"

"Just what everyone else knows. She's an assassin. Has a whole stableful of dead men to her credit, and got snagged on the last one."

"Gregory Patricks, Governor of Colorado."

Jaguar rolled her eyes. "What he did I wouldn't call governing. Con man with political backing. Selling snake oil."

"I take it you didn't approve of him."

"He cut education funding by half and decided to spend the taxpayers' money to put up casinos so the children of Colorado can all have gainful employment gambling and dancing naked while lonely men masturbate in public. I only wish Rilasco had killed his sidekick, too."

"Your moral stance leaves much to be desired, Jaguar."

"Probably," she said agreeably, "but it's a moot point. I'm on assignment already."

"I know. Adrian's relatively simple—so you say. I want you to start on Clare at the same time. She'll probably take longer, because it's not just a program."

"What, then?"

"You're to find out who ordered the hit."

Jaguar leaned an elbow on his desk and pushed her face close to his.

"You're serious, aren't you? You really want me to do this."

"With your ninety-seven percent success rate, it shouldn't ruffle a hair on your head."

She glared at him briefly, then let it go and leaned back in her chair. "It's ninety-eight percent."

"I beg your pardon," he said, and handed the Rilasco file to her.

He let her read, and gave her time to process the information, along with the idea of working two prisoners at once. It was unusual, he knew, though sometimes it had to happen for lack of Teachers, lack of time. The governing bodies of the Planetoids were more interested in funding new technology for the Planetoids than new people, and Alex had to scramble for workers now and then. In this case, he didn't have a shortage of people. He just wanted Jaguar to do it. She would be suspicious of his motives, he knew. When she raised her eyes from the initial report, they were full of questions.

He nodded, acknowledging them, and asked her simply, "What?"

"Okay," she said. "First, why'd she get caught on this one?"

"Good question."

It was a question Alex himself had asked. Here was a woman who had been working hits for years, and by all accounts had managed to remain both a public figure and invisible at the same time. She'd been seen on the arms of many men, in attendance at political and fashionable public events, and her name was well enough known in the reports of such events. Everyone thought she was just a wealthy socialite, and since her family had money before the Serials, they assumed she'd inherited it when they became victims of an unknown killer.

None of her assignments, as she called them, was connected to her in the remotest way until this last one had snagged her, but good.

"I'm not sure what the answer is, though," he continued. "We know they were having an affair, that she killed him by injecting an air bubble into the femoral artery, and what snared her was the very visible mark left on his groin, along with a pair of her underwear left in his bed."

"Cute," she said. "But pretty far out of character for someone with her experience. Unless she's lying about the other hits. If not, then either she wanted to get caught, or her employers set her up."

"Any of the above is possible. And she's not talking. You'll see when you meet her. What other questions do you have?"

She looked away, somewhere beyond his shoulder and out the window, then brought her cool, clear eyes back to rest on his. "Why me?" she asked.

He expected that one. Knew how to respond. "What possible answers can you generate on your own?" he replied.

She held his eyes steady, without any discernible agitation in her own, as she enumerated. "That you're setting me up to fail by giving me an assignment you know is impossible. That you're hoping we'll kill each other. Or that there's some lesson you want me to learn—perhaps about my moral stance?"

"I don't set up my people, and I don't like exercises in futility," he commented, then waved a hand for her to continue. "Try again."

She brought a finger up to her forehead, let it run smoothly down her nose, and come to rest on her lips.

"Go ahead, Dr. Addams," he said.

"I'm translating an elusive feeling into words. Give me a minute."

"Try saying the words out loud, even if they don't make sense," he suggested.

"Okay," she said, "if that's what you want. My thoughts run along your particular capacities in the empathic arts. You're an adept. You perceive possibilities, and manipulate events toward the end you choose. Are you working within your art, and using me because I fit a specific outcome you've perceived? Will you tell me what that outcome is, or let me work blind? Or," she added, "are you just flying by the seat of your pants."

She *would* see it that way, he thought. She viewed the art of the adept, once called precognition, as manipulative and controlling, and she didn't trust him not to use it against her. No surprise there. He wasn't sure how he felt about some of her choices, either. She had arts he didn't even know how to name yet. Ways of being and doing that she'd learned long ago, in a high desert land. After three years they'd just begun to stalk the edges of trust with each other, sometimes moving closer, sometimes skittering away into their own private jungles of fear.

"Which answer will you choose to act on?" he asked her.

"Which one is most nearly accurate, Supervisor?" she asked in her turn.

He grinned at her. "You must be a fine poker player."

"Try me sometime. But answer my question first."

"I'm flying by the seat of my pants, Jaguar," he said, "and I'll let you know when I'm able to more fully articulate my reasons for choosing you."

"Fair enough. When do I start with Clare?"

"In a few days. She'll be in one of the Fun Houses— House of Mirrors, actually. I'll talk to you when that's settled, and you'll go right in."

She tossed the file folder back onto the desk.

"Something else just occurred to me," she said.

Alex felt himself tense, as if readying himself to hear words he hadn't prepared a response to. "What?"

"Does this have anything to do with Nick?"

He let himself relax. That was an easy one.

"Yes," he said. "It's a classified case, so he won't know your location while you're working on her. You'll be out of his sights and I want you to stay that way as much as possible."

"With pleasure. Anything else?"

"Many many things, but they'll keep."

"Good." She slipped her sunglasses over her eyes, stood and walked as far as his office door.

There, she stopped and spoke, keeping her back to him. "But you know, Alex, the assignment with Nick wasn't an absolute failure. The prisoner's real fear was death—and he did end up facing it."

After Jaguar left, Alex rode the elevator to the basement, intending to pick up the remainder of the background information on Clare Rilasco from Rachel. When the doors opened and he stepped out into the hall, his way was blocked by the bulky frame of Terence Manning, principal record keeper for Planetoid Three.

"Hey," Manning said, "looking for Rachel?"

"Yes, Terence," he said, "and I'll bet you know why." Terence seemed to know everything, and he seemed to know it all at once, as if the air he breathed was permeated with Planetoid news. He supposed that was a good trait in a record keeper, but he found it irritating, like having a conversation with an omniscient narrator.

"Rilasco," he said, jabbing at Alex's arm with his finger. "I know. Got the file today. Jaguar's on it, right? The prelims might be delayed, though. There's about a thousand people want to see them, and I'm headed out to the home planet for a few days. Got some family stuff to take care of." He glanced at his watch, pressed the button that translated Planetoid time to home-planet time, shook his head. "Hope I make it in time."

"We'll manage without you, Terence. You have a good

time, and worry about it when you get back.'' He took a step around him and Terence moved to the side, blocking him.

"Was there something else?" Alex asked.

"Listen." Terence kept his voice low and leaned toward him. "I just wanted to say I'm sorry about Jaguar and Nick. I mean, I'm—well, everyone thought they made a pretty good team, and it's too bad about the trouble they're having. I thought maybe you could tell her that, or maybe if there's something you think I can do to help straighten it out, I'd be glad to."

A bubble of anger rose inside Alex. He didn't want to hear anything else about Nick and Jaguar from anybody, and he certainly didn't want Terence talking about it like it was the romantic tragedy of the decade. And what the hell did he mean when he said everyone thought they made a good team? Who was everyone, and what kind of team did they think Jaguar and Nick made?

"I don't have any idea what you're talking about," he said coolly, "and I don't think you do either."

Terence rolled his eyes and smiled. "Oh, sure. I get it. Private stuff. Don't worry—I'll keep it under my hat. But I wanted you to know I think it's a real shame, after he got her started and all, and I hope they find a way to work it out."

He patted Alex on the shoulder solicitously, and left. Alex stood and watched him go, wondering if everyone else on the Planetoid knew more about Jaguar than he did.

"Where are we going?" Adrian asked, trotting along beside her as they went down Spadina toward Yonge, "and why didn't we take wings?"

She didn't slow, but answered out of the side of her mouth, "I hate those things. Nothing to latch onto."

"That's generally the idea in flying," Adrian said.

He looked around him as she continued walking at a fast clip, her long legs striding out without pause, her mood inscrutable behind narrow mirror shades that wrapped around her eyes.

He had never been to Toronto before, but had always heard it was a clean city, and a polite one. So far he liked it. He made it a point to get a map, learn the streets and the layout, and then, while she was out doing whatever it was she did—getting tested, getting laid, he didn't know— he would walk around, get his bearings, find the best parts of the city to do his work. Conversations with people in coffee shops, at bookstores and newspaper stands taught him a lot.

And Jaguar was helping some, he had to admit. Tomorrow she was going to introduce him to a group called the Ascension Project, people who wanted to increase longevity through meditation, expanded spiritual awareness, and use of herbal synergists. The group was composed of middle-aged business men and women, and sometimes very wealthy older people who were vain of their looks and frightened of their deaths. The Ascension Project programs never asked them to do anything more strenuous, psycho-logically or physically, than sit cross-legged and take deep breaths, but it promised a life span beyond their wildest dreams. Just his kind of hook, and the faster he could bait the hook and make a catch, the sooner he could get out of his attachment to Jaguar. Not that he minded a lot of their interaction. Even now, when she was being insistently dis-tant and moody, the view of her lean body swathed in black leather was a real treat. He hoped to keep in touch once the deal was complete. But he wanted to keep in touch on his terms not hers.

"Where are you taking me?" he asked, walking briskly to keep up with her, trying to figure out how she managed to walk so fast in so much leather and not sweat.

"Another connection. A doctor I know who works with ISD patients. He's got a list of names he's willing to sell for percent of profit. For a little extra, he'll help convince them to buy your snake oil from you."

"Yeah? How much up front?"

"Enough that you better make good, sonny."

She turned and pinched his cheek between her thumb and forefinger, laughing when he pulled away. As he stood and rubbed where she had pinched, she walked ahead, humming to herself.

"Will you slow down?" he yelled to her.

She stopped, and looked at him. "I thought you were in good shape."

"Didn't it seem like it last night?" he said, coming up to her and whispering in her ear.

"Good enough," she said, then thought some more. "I've seen better, but we can work on it."

He grabbed her arm at the elbow and held hard, to keep her from walking away. Last night, he thought she was going to eat him alive, swallow him without chewing once. And she called it good enough.

"What's that supposed to mean?"

She looked down at the hand clutching her elbow, then back up at his face. "Let go," she said softly. A sensation of heat, more direct than sun, spread across the back of his neck, down his shoulders, toward his chest.

He loosened his hold and then dropped his arm to his side.

"Women." She grinned at him. "Can't live with 'em, can't shoot 'em. At least, not since the Serials."

She walked ahead.

He followed, now walking in a more leisurely way. Let her stop and wait for him. He wasn't about to run to keep up with her. It was getting damn hot out, and why should they run? Maniac. That's what she was. She walked ahead very fast, and he strolled behind. She stopped at a corner and waited for him to catch up. When he did, still strolling, he said, "Y'know, I'm gonna need some stuff, too."

"What stuff?"

"Materials. Nothing very expensive. I can make a list,

and you can get them, or you can give me money, and I'll
get them. You pick.''

"I'll give you the money,'' she said. "Just keep the ex-
penses down, all right?''

"My mother,'' he muttered, "you sound like my
mother.''

"What?''

"Nothing. Hey, Jag, after this interview, let's go get
some lunch, okay?''

She wheeled around to face him and stuck a long and
elegant finger in his face. "Don't call me that,'' she
snarled. "Just don't, okay?''

"Man, did you ever get up on the wrong side of today.
What is it with you?''

She lowered her finger and pursed her lips. "Nothing,''
she said. "Just—skip it. Premenstrual, probably.''

"No,'' he said. "I don't want to skip it. I'm tired of
getting my head snapped off for nothing.''

She turned to him. "Do you know what today is?''

"Um—let's see. It's a hot sunny day. Must be June. Not
a lot of traffic, so a Saturday—''

"It's June seventh,'' she interrupted. "Traditional Memorial of the Serials. In Manhattan, there's a vigil. In L.A.,
there's a concert. In Toronto—they're too damn polite to
remember a thing.''

"Well, gee. If I'd known, I'd have made a cake.''

"My family died in the Killing Times,'' she said quietly.
"I watched.''

He shifted uncomfortably from one foot to the other. He
didn't like to talk about the Serials. What was the point? It
was over. Long done. It could never happen again. These
groups that staged memorials, insisted on remembrance
days, were just stupid. If you couldn't let go of that kind
of thing, you were screwed.

"We should keep walking,'' he observed.

Her mouth twitched into an unpleasant half smile.

"Didn't your father kill your mother around then?" she asked.

Adrian felt a wave of anxiety wash over him. He pushed it away and put a smile on his face.

"He probably would have killed her anyway," he said casually. "She was hell to live with."

"Some men," Jaguar responded, speaking slowly and precisely, "turn women into what they hate so that they can hate them. Convenient, isn't it?"

He balled his hands into fists, and hid the fists behind his back. He wasn't going to give her the satisfaction of seeing him angry. He took a moment, brought himself under control.

"I don't have to explain my life to you," he said. "You're not a tester, and it's none of your business. In fact, the only business we have together is business. So let's stick to it."

He stepped forward, off the curb, and a taxi whizzed by, startling him as the driver laid hard on the horn. He jumped back.

"Dammit," he spit out, "I thought people were supposed to be polite here."

"They are," Jaguar observed mildly, "but they don't suffer fools very well."

"What's that supposed to mean?"

"Nothing. Nothing at all. I guess I'm just beginning to wonder how smart you really are." She watched as he raised his tightly pinched face to hers.

This. The moment of vulnerability, when he was using so much energy to hide his emotions, he wouldn't have any left to guard himself from her eyes. This moment was what she'd been working for, and she used it.

She focused hard, held his eyes with hers in close focus, and brushed the surface of his mind with her laughter, the strength of her ego. She allowed her knowledge of him to enter him. She stayed right at the surface, using no words, and no gestures that would frighten him or make him feel too much of who he was. Not yet. Now it was enough to sweep away the surface cobweb of emotions that he used to hide what lay beneath. He wouldn't know what hit him. He would only know that everything felt a little sharper, every word cut a little closer to the bone.

When she was done, she smiled at him. "You like music?" she asked.

He frowned, knit his brows. Something funny here. An old laughter in his head. His mother's voice. The sound of gunshots, smell of smoke and whiskey in the room. What did she ask him?

"I said, do you like music?" she repeated.

She was asking him about music. Had they been talking about that? "Music?" he asked.

"That's what I said. You know, whining guitars and bad sound mixes and incipient deafness. Spelled M-U-S—"

"I know what you mean," he said sharply. "I don't know why you're asking."

She laughed. "There's this band I sing with sometimes. Called Moon Illusion. Friday night we'll be playing out at Silver Bay. Wanna watch? I know how you like to watch."

"Sure," he said, still scowling, "sounds great."

"I'm overwhelmed by your enthusiasm. Look, I'm gonna introduce you to this doctor, and then you're on your own. I have to be somewhere."

Adrian smirked at her. "Hot date?"

She lifted her chin and looked at something in the distance that he couldn't see. "Just a roll in the hay with a big pussycat," she said.

3

''RED THREE ON FOUR OF CLUBS,'' TERENCE said.

The Looker squinted up from his cards to the portly frame of the man who stood next to his booth at the end of the diner. He placed the three carefully at the bottom of the row, and then spoke.

''Where is she?'' he asked.

''She's with Addams. Jaguar Addams.''

He lowered his head and moved an ace up to the top of the row. As he considered his next move he indicated the seat across the booth from him. ''Well,'' he said, ''sit down. We'll need to discuss this.''

''Right. How's the game today?''

The Looker shrugged, and swept the deck into his hands, shuffling. ''I've lost about five hundred, but I'll make it up. That's the way the game goes. Both strategy and luck play a part, and one is nothing without the other.''

Strategy and luck. Terence imagined the Looker knew a lot about both.

When he hired Terence for what he called consultant work, he said he was in research and personnel management for the Division of Intelligence Enforcement, a private corporation that provided research and efficiency analyses for a number of intelligence agencies on a consultancy basis. Their research was techno-toy and applied strategy computer games—lots of psi-capacity work and information gathering for specific projects. The Looker wanted someone on Planetoid Three who could access information from their central files on an as-needed basis, and he wanted to avoid the delays associated with getting this information through the usual channels.

At first, Terence decided to accept this as the truth and not ask a lot of questions. Safer that way. There were many things about the Division of Intelligence Enforcement that he really didn't want as his burden of knowledge. It was enough to know that they were profit-oriented, and paid accordingly, in clean, untraceable bills. With the money from this consultancy work he'd be able to retire in good style.

After he'd signed on and began seeing the kinds of information they wanted, he had second thoughts, but by then it was too late. If the Planetoid Governors found out what he was doing, he'd be in deep shit. If he stopped doing it, he might not be alive long enough to be in deep shit. He'd seen the Looker's research projects, and the kind of personnel he managed, Clare Rilasco among them.

This meeting, arranged quickly and inconveniently for Terence, would probably be about that woman.

He pushed his bulk into the booth and wiggled a finger at a waitress, ordering coffee for himself. He'd just gotten off the air runner that took him from the shuttle station in Florida to this Denver location, and he was feeling space-lagged, groggy. He'd had to arrange special home leave for the trip, and he hoped it was worth it.

Outside the window of the diner, people walked up and down the street, their mouths moving in speech that was probably significant to them, though neither the Looker nor Terence was interested. They had weightier issues at hand.

"Can we have her removed?" the Looker asked.

Terence chose to ignore the possible euphemism of the

word *removed,* but he felt his heart skip into a higher drive. He knew an attempt had been made on Clare's life before she was brought to the Planetoids. It failed, intercepted by her guards. Unfortunately, the hit man had been killed, along with two police officers, in a traffic accident on the way in for questioning. There were no clues as to who had hired him, just as there was no clue as to who hired Clare to kill the Governor.

"Who . . . Clare?" he asked. "If you want an escape—"

"No. Not Clare," the Looker said impatiently. "This Addams woman."

"You mean—from this case?"

"I mean," the Looker said, "from her interaction with Clare, at any cost."

Terence felt acid rising from his stomach to his throat. He'd never done more than pass numbers, names, files. He wanted to keep it that way.

"Many have tried," he said, keeping his voice jovial, joking. "In fact, I could think of a few people who'd volunteer for the job, just for fun. But I didn't sign on to *remove* anyone. I don't do that."

"You do what you're paid for, and you don't ask questions about it. But I wasn't thinking of you, at any rate." He sucked in air through his teeth, made a thoughtful series of clicking sounds with his tongue. "She's difficult," he commented. "An empath. My group doesn't want an empath working with Clare."

His group. The Looker never used the acronym DIE, which he found distasteful. He never used the full name, either. It was always "my group" or "the Division," or "our people." It was the same attachment to secrecy that he had about his name, which Terence never knew. He was the Looker. That was all. Terence thought it was childish, like little boys playing with codes, but he knew the games they played weren't for children. The Division said little, and didn't miss a trick.

They knew Jaguar was an empath. They would know all about every possibility for Clare's Teacher assignment. Although, given Jaguar's reputation, they probably had a pretty thick file on her even before this. And he understood the Looker's concerns about having an empath work the case. They could get in where the testers couldn't. On the Planetoids there was a grudging acceptance of the empathic arts, or at least a willingness not to interfere with their use. On the home planet, the arts still generated suspicion, or aroused terror, or were seen as something practiced only by freaks, misfits, potential ritual killers.

The Looker's research involved technologically generated psi capacities, so Terence knew he didn't have any of those prejudices, but he recognized the potential power of the empath, if left uncontrolled and unmonitored. Monitoring and control were his strong points.

Terence bit back a smile at the thought of the Looker trying to monitor Jaguar. That would be pretty amusing.

"I understand the problem," Terence said, "but it's gonna be tough. Her supervisor's particular about her . . . very protective. And—well, I don't think she's all that removable, once she's got her teeth in something."

"Can we get Clare off the Planetoid?"

"Depends on if you mind a lot of notice. There's lots of eyes watching this one, and she's in a classified location. Security's pretty tight."

"All right. Perhaps the furor will subside and we can consider ways. We'll have to get Addams off the case, though."

"How?" Terence said.

The Looker removed his glasses and held them up to the light, brought them to his mouth and breathed steam on them, then rubbed at them meticulously with the corner of his napkin.

"How many organizations are currently monitoring the Rilasco case?" he asked.

Terence chuckled. "All of them," he said. "NICA's got

a woman there, and so do the regular feds. There's a couple of Colorado state people, and management for the Leadville group. We got a regular Rilasco conference going. Everyone's got something to say about it, calling and asking what'll happen next to the Patricks casino project, to her. It's just a good thing we got a rule against reporters, or they'd be crawling up our butts like fire ants in Alabama.''

"And has she spoken at all—about her employers?"

"Not a wicked word."

"I thought not," the Looker said. He picked up his cards, shuffled, and pulled one. King of spades.

"I'll come to the Planetoids, briefly, and my presence won't be remarked upon as anything unusual. You find someone who can work an e-wave amplifier on her.''

Terence frowned. "A Supertoy?"

From what he understood, there were still some serious problems in using what was commonly called the Supertoy line.

"With two live subjects?" he continued. "I thought—"

The Looker interrupted. "It's in the experimental phases. This will be a good opportunity to gather data and perhaps solve our problem at the same time. Can you find someone to use it? Preferably another empath, and someone she knows. I'd rather not bring any of our people up there."

He cast a suspicious glance out the window and up toward the invisible Planetoid. Terence knew they didn't want to go there if they didn't have to. No matter how cool they all seemed, they didn't like to leave their own turf.

Terence chewed on his lower lip thoughtfully. "There's Nick. I'll bet he'd be glad to have a shot at her. He's got a list of complaints against her already, and Dzarny's covering for her with the Board. But what if it doesn't work?"

"Then we'll determine alternate removal methods. Just go ahead with this for now. And get a recording implant in her."

Terence shook his head. "Not possible. She won't do it

for the Board, or for Dzarny, and I can't get close enough to slip one without her knowing it."

The man snorted. "Never mind. I didn't imagine that the Planetoid was so filled with nervous old men, but since it is—"

"Look," Terence said, "I'm working with her other assignment. Graff. I can get something in him, and then we'll have partial recording anyway."

"All right. Do what you can. Take care of it. Nervous old men," the man said sadly. "You might as well be home dusting furniture and worrying about whether your toilet is composting properly. Be thinking of ways to get Clare back here. Always think ahead."

"I'll work on it."

The Looker leaned across the table and jabbed a manicured finger at him. "Work very hard," he said. "It might be difficult to take care of her where she is, and we would prefer a debriefing with her prior to final disposal of the matter."

He shuffled his cards and laid out a neat row of seven, signaling the end of the interview. "But first, take care of the Addams woman."

"Yeah," Terence said. "Me and about fifty other men who'd like to."

The sun cast long shadows of trees and shrubbery, narrowing and stretching them across the path that wound through the Wildlife Sanctuary where Jaguar walked. She paused briefly in front of the two golden eagles, one missing a leg and the other a wing. They were perched on the tree that grew in the center of their cage, their eyes piercing the netting that surrounded them as they focused on her. When they realized she wasn't dinner, they turned their attention elsewhere.

She saluted them and continued along the path to the gate that separated the public portion of the Sanctuary from the breeding complex. Here she passed her ID in front of the sensor, waited for the green light, then spoke her password.

Panthera Onca.

A simple password, but the entry locks responded to voice wave as well as words, and would open only for those whose patterns matched their index. Besides this security, Jaguar knew that Maria, who directed the breeding program, kept an old but effective shotgun at her side. She didn't want anyone bothering her animals.

Inside the breeding complex, a series of houses had been set up for prisoner programs. Some held regular apartments and provided a base for Teachers whose prisoners needed a normalcy of routine and isolation from the rest of the replica city. There were specialty houses, too, such as the bar and hotel, and the VR site that would be ready for use within the year. Here, also, was the House of Mirrors.

All program facilities were behind another set of gates at the far end of the grounds, away from the animals. This gave Jaguar the opportunity to walk through the complex and visit with Hecate and Chaos, the two jaguars in residence here, while she waited for Rachel to bring her Clare's complete file.

Chaos and Hecate were the only two jaguars in residence on the Planetoid, and perhaps the only hope left of ever reintroducing the species to the wild. No home-planet zoo had had any success with such a program. The most they could get was an *in vitro* process, utilizing an artificial womb for gestation. The breeding procedures they'd developed in these programs included genetic tinkering meant to increase fertility, resistance to pollution-related diseases, and the capacity of the fertilized egg to withstand *in vitro* gestation. But in the process of the splicing and reformulating genetic codes, the wildness had been bred out of the animals, making them more like large domestic cats, and certainly unfit for reintroduction into the wild.

At this Sanctuary, the director had stopped the genetic

tinkering and was letting the cats find out who they were
by themselves.

She took the side path that led to their habitat and
stopped in front of them, wrapping her hands around the
steel bars that enclosed them. Maria had insisted on bars
rather than the wireless laser fencing. She said that if they
were caged, they should be able to see what caged them,
rather than become confused by the visual illusion of freedom.

"Hecate," Jaguar whispered, and the golden-spotted female rolled, stretched herself, claws showing and retracting.
They knew each other well.

"Chaos," she said, and the sleek black male lifted his
massive head, his tail snaking in gracious curves as he
waited to see if she would talk with him. For an empath,
gathering the knowledge of other animals was no more difficult than gathering the thoughts of humans.

There was a beast, and it had a belly. The empathic moment would drop you off there, if you let it.

Jaguar knew this, because she'd met with that beast and
slept quiet and sweet in his belly, danced inside the entrails,
swam in that honeyed stream of warm blood, wanting to
know.

Every night at midnight, the Jaguars were allowed to run
free, hunting down mice and other small rodents for food.
They were just tame enough that a preset signal from Maria
brought them back, willingly, to pace the inside of a cage.

One night Jaguar had been given permission to sit in the
cool, thick scent of their cage while they ran. She watched
their shapes, elusive in the moonlight, skimming the earth,
low to the ground but with the grace of flight. They had
come up to the cage and stared at her, sniffed her as she
sat safe behind their bars.

There was a beast, and it had a belly filled with sweetness
and honeyed dreams of blood and grace in motion. You
could gather the wisdom pooled there, if you were willing
to get quiet and do without words.

Jaguar pressed herself against the cool steel of the bars and curled her gaze toward the black male, who lay on his belly in the pose associated with ancient Egyptian statues of cats, paws forward and head held straight.

She would wait here for Rachel to bring her the complete file on the Rilasco case, and her team member's report for Adrian's case, which she was helping out on. She'd have no time to read through the Rilasco material before she met with Clare, but today was just an introductory day. The information would mean more to her after she'd met the prisoner.

Working two at once, and one of them Clare Rilasco. What was Alex up to this time?

His capacities as an empath made him an interesting Supervisor. Although she knew he didn't often sit in the adept space or call on the waves of knowledge that grew from this art, he would just as frequently be picking up signals in a subliminal way, acting on them instinctively. She assumed that's what he was doing in putting her on the Rilasco assignment, but she wondered if he had a hidden agenda as well.

No. Not *if* there was a hidden agenda. She wondered *what* the agenda would turn out to be.

That was something Nick taught her. There were always hidden agendas. The task was to identify them, and it was always best to assume the worst in doing so.

"When I meet someone," he told her, "the first question I ask myself is what's the worst thing I can imagine that person doing? What I imagine, they'll probably do."

Damn Nick. Now she had to try to determine what his hidden agenda was as well. She couldn't ignore what he'd done for her on the home planet or here. She couldn't ignore whatever it was fate or bad luck or poor judgment that kept them crashing into each other.

She'd slept with him once, pulled by that something into intense lovemaking, wrestling for power with their bodies, continuing as they'd begun, laughing at each other's at-

tempts to win out. Only once, and afterward, she felt
bruised and darkened by the interaction, wanted only to
break the connection between them. But she couldn't.

He started nagging at her about the arts after that. He
wanted her to teach him what she knew, some of the more
complex ways of power that she'd been taught in her Mertec tradition, from her grandparents, and later, from Jake
and One Bird. But what gifts she had she wouldn't share
unless she felt specifically called to do so. With Nick, she
felt specifically enjoined not to teach him a damn thing,
though she couldn't articulate her reasons for that intuition.

Maybe he just seemed too anxious. Too hungry. But apparently he'd already been dabbling in the arts for years—
without ritual, without guidance, without any way to con-
tain or ground the kind of energy that got kicked around
when you touched a wounded psyche.

On their last case, he attempted contact with the prisoner,
denying he'd done so, and denying he'd botched it. Jaguar
had gone in afterward to try to repair the emotional breach
Nick had torn open with his clumsy approach, but it was
too late. She'd shielded him, because she felt culpable for
not helping him when he asked. But that was too late, also.

He'd not only done irreparable damage to the prisoner,
Jaguar suspected he'd come out of the interaction shadowed.

Shadowed empath. Eating the psyches of his prisoners
without knowing how to rid himself of the debris afterward.
Becoming what he ate, his ability to see clouded with the
rage and fear and hate that invaded him from the empathic
contact.

Or maybe he'd been moving toward it all along, the old
pain from the Serials creating a chronic darkness that drew
darkness to it. He'd seen his wife and two children killed
during the Serials, and he bore a scar across his chest, a
bullet wound he'd gotten in trying to save them. When he
made love to Jaguar, he'd taken her hand and pressed it

into the jagged white line of skin as he pressed himself into her.

She could hear him laughing at her, laughing about what the Board would do to her. Nick, laughing and pulling her close. Another male body asking for hers, and she feeling something like longing for that warmth, something like a centrifugal force that pulled her in deeper and deeper. Why did she consent to share his bed, however briefly? For the warmth, the memory of what he'd done for her when she was lost and alone?

Or was it some shadow in her that pulled her to him?

Shadow of the past. She didn't need to attend any of the memorial day events to remember the Serials. Right now, her memory was sucking her back in time at a time when she needed to focus on the present. Jaguar reached into the pocket of her leather vest and felt the crumbled leaves of dried mint, brought them to her face, and breathed in. She emptied her thoughts to a still center, letting the air that entered her lungs carve out a clear space where vision might appear.

She wasn't an adept and had no precognitive capacities, as Alex did, but here, in the presence of the animals whose name she bore, within the watchful gaze of their eyes, she could listen to whatever whispered in her, through her, voices in the wind telling her what she needed to know. In the belly of the beast she couldn't see ahead, but sometimes she could see *through*.

Hecate turned her yellow eyes to the human presence and growled. Jaguar breathed and opened to those eyes, to the dance of the night, to herself.

"I myself, Spirit in Flesh, speak," she said, intoning the ancient Nauhatl that cleared the way to vision, to the clear space.

She felt the hiss of molecular shift and the skin-stretching sense of boundaries splitting. The eyes opened, welcomed her, calling her in. Then, the free fall through nowhere to infinity, internal, but unbounded since it took part in an energy that most people didn't even believe existed. She gasped in the joy of opening herself, being shattered and rewoven within this vast space.

This, without words. Just a touch of fur. Then, the whispers calling to her in voices so old they had no name.

Where is your darkness?

Her darkness. Where? What shadow in her?

Your darkness.

She felt herself moving through the thickness of night, slowly and carefully. Reluctantly. Here. Somewhere inside the slow rise of terror. Inside the past. Inside the Serials.

Here. Where the dead walk.

Manhattan. Here, where she was walking with her grandfather.

She was a ten-year-old, out buying ice cream with her grandfather. They'd just listened to a news pundit saying that serial and ritual killing had risen in North America by 225 percent in the last year. He wanted to rededicate the year, call it the Year of the Serials. Maybe the decade of the killer, too.

That's what I say, people. The Year of the Serials. Maybe we should sell T-shirts, right? Call in and tell me what you say.

But that was just the beginning of the storm.

She stood at an ice-cream vendor's stand, holding her grandfather's hand, listening to his conversation with a child's capacity for absorption in the absence of understanding.

The young man who made her hot fudge sundae complained about the President's decision to cut funding for education programs, social-service programs, arts programs, by 40 percent. He was trying to support his addiction to the theater by selling ice cream from a cart.

President's a nutcase. Out to screw everyone. Not a dime for schools or the arts, but I hear he's hired two new bodyguards. Pentagon funding's stable, and he wants a new division for the CIA.

More talk followed, about the cuts in mental health and homeless housing. The trickle-down theory pissing down on everyone for a third time, even though it had failed miserably the first two times around. Then there was the release of prisoners, their crimes declared to be no longer criminal acts, but acts that required the help of a social-service force cut by almost half.

What're they gonna do, though? They got no more room in the prisons. And you know which prisoners they'll let out? The wrong ones. All the wrong ones. As if we didn't have enough crazies out on the streets as it is. Year of the Serials—Jeesus.

She hadn't understood then, but she remembered. White collar criminals emerged first. Then pedophiles and rapists, serving petty time. After that, those serving time for domestic violence.

Her grandfather had been in a somber mood on the walk home, not talking or singing with her the way he usually did. She'd tugged hard on his leg to get his attention, and he'd looked down at her as if he were looking toward something distant, and unpleasant. She shuddered at his eyes. The way they saw her.

His hand pressed against her forehead, in blessing, perhaps. As if transferring some vision from a world he wouldn't live in long enough to teach her about. His hand on her forehead, and a shock of vision splashed against the back of the eyes. The gleaming walls of a city filled with uncontained rage and despair. This vision, searing and complete. He was a man of the spirit world, a man of quiet in a noisy city. A peaceful man.

Here is your darkness.
Where the dead walk.

The vision shifted, pulled her forward in time, and as she stood alone on a city street, the dead and dying reached for her, scattered like coins on the streets, their hands extended in pleading, in violence. She could smell their death, putrid and chemical, as if they had gone on dying and dying endlessly, their bodies recomposing as fast as they rotted. Dead men, reaching for her.

Your darkness.

She reached to them, feeling their grief pass through her, and then a shock of pain and bright light in her eyes as she was lifted up, lifted by a large hand, and looked into a pair of sharply blue eyes.

Nick.

He picked her up off the ground, held her aloft near his face. She was thirteen, and by then had survived a year and a half on the streets, mostly alone. As he lifted her he laughed, and she scratched at him, at his eyes and face.

Got a tough one, Larry. Wanna help?

Another cop. Not laughing.

Put her down, Nick. Jesus, she's not an assassin.

Never know with these kids. Last one I picked up had a knife, aimed it right for my heart.

Yeah, well, we're supposed to rescue 'em, not torture 'em.

I rescued her. She was about to walk over a live wire.

He rescued her.

This wasn't what she wanted to see. This was all the past. All the past. Nothing to do with Clare or Adrian or the problems with Nick now.

Show me now. Show me today. My darkness today, here, now.

A sense of laughter, light and easy. Voices chiding her, then fading. Her grandfather's voice, teaching her.

You can't force what you see here, Jaguar. You know that.

Voices, fading, and space contracted in on itself to spit her out like old gum onto an empty street.

The vision dissolved, and she took in air, and saw that she was still standing outside the cage, bright sun all around her, the air warm and close against her skin. She sighed, moved her hands against the bars of the jaguar cage. Whatever she'd learned, she didn't know how to use it yet. But at least she'd ended up where she started.

Although the moment of vision could be very still, there was no predicting what the body would do in response to the events of the space. This time, she'd remained motionless; her face pressed into the bars now gone warm under her flesh. The male jaguar sat licking at his mate's ears. She pulled her hands down and saw that the knuckles of her fingers were white, bloodless.

Then she heard a quiet voice behind her.

"Jaguar?" it asked.

Jaguar recognized the tone, and the tenor of concern. She knew who it was. "Hello, Rachel," she replied, without turning around.

"I know it's the Serials memorial. . . ." she said, her voice trailing off.

Jaguar turned around and smiled. "Only on the home planet. Here, it's business as usual. Besides, on the home-planet Toronto there's no memorials," she noted. "They've granted amnesty to all offenders, and rugs to all the dirt so they can sweep it away."

Rachel clucked her tongue, but smiled as well. "You're such a cynic," she said.

"I'm such a realist," Jaguar replied. "You have the new file for me?"

Rachel nodded and moved forward, handing Jaguar a pebble-sized piece of metal. This was the component she would add to her computer to access the rest of the files on Clare Rilasco. She pulled the earring from her left ear and fitted the component neatly in the slot just above the piece of obsidian at the sickle curve of metal.

"Thanks. What do I need to know before I go in?"

"Not too much," Rachel said. "Alex told you she's not here just to rehab, right?"

"I understand the home-planet officials want to know who paid for the hit on Patricks, correct?"

"That's an understatement. NICA, State Bureau of Investigation, all major networks want to know. Apparently even the Division of Intelligence Enforcement is on it.''

"They're busybodies by vocation, anyway. Stupid acronym. DIE—do you suppose that's supposed to be threatening?''

"Probably didn't get it," Rachel said. "They take themselves very seriously, from what I've heard.''

"Because they have to earn their keep," Jaguar commented.

DIE's people were the mercenaries of intelligence, hiring out consultancies on means of improving intelligence operations to a variety of federal agencies. Jaguar assumed, as many others did, that they were actually a branch of NICA, but that the interests of both groups were best served by keeping that connection invisible.

After the Serials, the CIA had changed its name to the National Intelligence Central Agency, reorganizing under a new set of procedural codes established by a nervous Congress and a President determined to clean up a corrupt system. But subsequent administrations weren't as concerned with corruption, and NICA had found ways around the procedural codes pressed upon them in a time of conscience. They'd split into a number of small branches that specialized in different areas of intelligence, and they began hiring outside agencies to assist in their work. Federal regulations for private corporations were very different, and DIE had been born out of that shift.

She'd seen the CEO on newscasts, a large and affable man who spoke smoothly about nothing to reporters. The DIE people she'd met were just a series of nondescript middle-management types who handled specific projects, then disappeared.

As far as she knew, they didn't even have a main office, preferring to let their people work out of their own homes or offices. It was a neatly conceived idea, distracting to the eye, making it difficult to track who was actually doing what. But Jaguar had heard that their interests included research into the empathic arts for military use. Like the Pentagon, they experimented in ways she didn't approve of. Unlike the Pentagon, they were efficient, and therefore, she felt, more dangerous. She wasn't sure if they ordered hits, or if they liked to keep their hands clean for the research they did.

"I wonder," Jaguar mused. "Maybe NICA called the hit and screwed up. DIE might be here to remedy the failure."

"That'd be ugly, because they're about the only group I know that might actually get away with it. At any rate, Clare's not talking. She's not afraid or anything, either. She was offered immunity and protective relocation—the works—if she'd talk. She said confidentiality was a professional courtesy she offered to her clients, and she couldn't possibly betray it."

"Jesus—and was she using the proper fork when she said it?"

"Probably. She's a cool one."

"I guess. Did you give me—"

"The works," Rachel interrupted. "Any and all info on Clare's connection with corporate entities, with government agencies, their people and processes. And personal history, medical history, psychological—the usual. Religious background, food preferences, what she likes to drive, favorite music, favorite clothes. There's some great gaping holes in her life from right after the Serials. I'm not sure what you can do about that."

"Wait and see," Jaguar said. "I'll be back to you after I've met her, see what I need next. By the way, did Adrian hook up with the medical-team members I set him up with?"

"All is well. He met, he spent, he will soon be conquered. I'm in the middle of the list, and when he calls me I'm going to offer to sell him lingerie when he tries to sell me drugs I don't need."

"That," Jaguar said, "sounds like fun. Wish I could listen in."

"Don't," Rachel said. "You always have to comment in the middle, and it makes me laugh."

"Okay. I'll be good. What about the Ascension Project people?"

"Terence Manning is putting in some overtime in the leader role," Rachel said. "They're all set up, too."

When Jaguar saluted her as if she was readying to leave, Rachel stopped her. "There's one more thing," she said, and from the tone of her voice the one more thing was something she knew Jaguar wouldn't like.

"Go ahead," Jaguar said, "I won't bite. Not you, anyway."

"Alex asked if you'd be willing to do this one on tap."

"You mean, with a recording implant?"

"That's right."

"No. I wouldn't."

"Okay."

"That's all? Just okay?"

"He said not to push it if you didn't want to."

"Well—why did he bother asking when he knew I'd say no?"

Rachel shrugged. "You're asking the wrong person."

"I am. But since he asked you to deliver messages, tell him I said no, and tell him I won't play Board games with him. I'd rather go back to the home planet and take a job teaching college students the difference between Zen and failure to get homework in on time."

"Ouch."

"Ditto."

"Give him a break, Jaguar. He's not like you think he is."

"He's a Supervisor," Jaguar said, and this, to her, summed up the matter.

"He's a good man," Rachel said, then clucked her tongue against her cheeks. "Forget it. It's not my job to tell you who he is. You need anything else from me?"

"Just—Rachel, did you meet Clare?"

"Briefly," Rachel said. "Why?"

"I want to know what you think. I was surprised Alex gave the assignment to me, and I'm trying to figure out what he's up to."

Rachel pressed a finger thoughtfully against her lips, and considered for a moment before she spoke. "She's an assassin," Rachel said at last. "Alex probably thought you could figure that out better than anyone else."

Jaguar laughed. "Maybe," she said. "Maybe you're right about that."

The long mirror behind the bar was coated with the ancient smoke of millions of cigarettes, and splashed with amber liquid that had dried to the consistency of a polyurethane coating. Adrian could see his own face, distorted by patches of gray, patches of brown, but still his young, handsome face with its boyish grin and alive eyes that had a tendency to see others peripherally, where vision revealed the edges a person would rather hide.

It was a good face, and people trusted it, thought it was open and lively. People, he thought, were real idiots. He stole a glance around the room, saw that nobody had their eyes on him, and examined himself, lifting his chin and smiling. Good face. He liked it. It would get him places someday. He'd make some money here and get the hell out of this damn city, back to New York, where something was always happening. New Manhattan was even better than the old pre-Serial borough had been. There were opportunities there that no longer existed in L.A. or Chicago since the Killing Times, though there was money to be had in any city, he'd found.

But New Manhattan was where he wanted to be.

He reached down and rubbed at his leg, which twitched just at the thought of going. Going. Getting the hell away from that crazy cop he had to deal with. Not that she couldn't be fun, but she was . . . something. He wasn't sure. Some kind of mind-fuck going on. Flashes of memories from his childhood kept coming up when he thought about her, unbidden memories that were visceral.

The smell of his father's whiskey. The sickly taste left on his lips after he kissed his mother's cheek. Something about her makeup, and her sweat. Sickly sweet. He felt nauseated a lot, and then angry in knifelike jabs that left him even more queasy than before.

He took a long sip from his beer and shook off the feeling. He wondered if she was some kind of—they were called something he couldn't remember. Witches, he called them. People who messed around with telepathy and that sort of thing. Something scientific about it these days, he knew, and once in a while the news would carry a story about another one arrested for fraud or for murder.

Maybe he should have paid more attention to that sort of thing, but he'd always been too busy to deal in any bullshit he didn't think would make him some cash, and he couldn't figure out how to cash in on that sort of thing. Witchcraft and shamanism. Stupid shit.

He swiveled back and forth on his bar stool, scanning the scattered groupings of people at tables having lunch, casting his glance up and down the bar.

He was supposed to meet with the Ascension Project leader, a man who said Adrian would know him by the daisy he wore in his lapel.

"Daisy," Adrian muttered to himself. "Fucking jester shit."

He swallowed the last of his beer and slid the empty toward the bartender, watching his own face in the mirror.

"Another?" the young woman asked.

"Another," he agreed, smiling at her. She was a little younger than he. Certainly younger than Jaguar. When she brought back his full glass, he touched her fingers briefly in taking it from her, then smiled at her in embarrassment.

"Sorry," he said.

"Not a problem," she replied, grinning.

"Yeah—well, I know how hard it is tending bar. You

deal with assholes a lot. I don't want to make your work any worse.''

"I appreciate that. It's unusual, but I appreciate it.''

He wished he could ask her where she lived, to find out if it was in range of the damn implant in his leg. He could do with a little interaction that didn't include Jaguar. Something pleasant and not demanding. Something like this young woman. He smiled at her again, and was about to continue the conversation when the mirror showed him the aspect of a man standing behind him.

The man smiled and nodded, either at Adrian or the bartender. "One of those would be nice," he said, and sat next to Adrian.

Daisy, Adrian noticed. This is the guy.

He patted Adrian on the back and said, from behind his teeth, "Pretend like you've known me for a while. Like, how's it going, Adrian?"

"Sure. Fine, except that I don't know your name."

"Call me Terry."

"Is that your name?"

"Could be. It's something to call me, anyway. When I grab my beer, we could go over there and throw some darts."

"Fine by me." He stood and stretched in a leisurely way, picking up his beer and waiting for Terry to follow suit. They walked to the holodart board, and Terry fed it tokens, pressing the release for the darts.

Adrian grabbed his dozen, the lightness of them confusing him for a moment. He fumbled them, dropped half, and bent over to pick them up.

"Lemme help with that, buddy," Terry said, and patted him on the back.

"Sure—hey, shit—" He slapped at the back of his neck. "Watch it, will you?"

Terry backed away quickly, looked down at the darts he had in his hands, and smiled sheepishly. "Sorry," he said. "I thought they were off."

"Yeah, well, that's okay. Only be careful. Those things sting like a bitch. Is it bleeding?"

"A little. Lemme get a napkin." He got one at the bar before Adrian could think to say he'd ask the bartendress to help him.

When he returned, he pressed it hard against the spot, making it hurt worse. When Adrian yelped, he apologized again, and backed off.

"It's fine," Adrian said, gathering the rest of the darts from the floor, careful not to press any switches. He preferred the old-fashioned kind of dart, where you could see the point before it hit the board, but they were hard to find anymore. The laser darts, though painful, couldn't kill anyone in a bar fight, and insurance carriers liked that.

"Don't worry," Terry said as he made his first throws. "I'll make it up to you. I understand you want to do a little business. You want access to the Ascension Project membership."

"That's right," Adrian said. "A little interaction with some people who might buy my wares."

"You got up-front money?"

"Some," Adrian said. He wouldn't use all that Jaguar gave him if he didn't have to. "I like to work percent of profit better, though."

"Don't we all. But," Terry said, his hand swinging back and forward as he released a dart, "what we like and what we can get are two different things."

"That's for sure," Adrian mumbled. A hard sell. But he had the money, which was all that mattered. He'd talk the guy into splitting the difference. After all, why should he take 100 percent of the risk in this. If he couldn't go fifty-fifty, they'd have no deal, and he'd walk away.

Adrian gazed wistfully over at the bar, where the young woman moved easily between beer tap and customer. Maybe before he walked away, he'd get her address and phone number, just to remind himself that there was some fun left in the world.

4

COOL SILVER AND WHITE.

Everything in the House of Mirrors was cool silver and white, giving the illusion of space that opened to infinity. Mirror echoed mirror beyond the visual capacity of any human to see an end. Everywhere you turned, you met a new image of yourself, reflected now tall and thin, now short and round, and then, unexpectedly, what you imagined you might possibly look like if you could really view yourself whole, without emotional prejudice.

The halls were not complex enough to get lost in, but the visual echoes could be confusing. The narrow halls at the entrance led, in a series of turns and shifting perspectives, to a central open room where mirrors had been placed flat against one wall, curved across the ceiling, and at odd angles everywhere else. Wherever you looked you saw an image of an image, refracted into part of another image, which was only part of yet another reflection.

Jaguar had worked one other case here, and she'd developed the habit of walking up to her reflection and pressing her hand against it as a means of reminding herself that she existed, was solid, her hands attached to her arms, her physical self contained in her skin rather than these flat impressions that sank into each other endlessly. She still hadn't decided if the images were depth in an illusion of surface, or surface in an illusion of depth.

Depth and surface were the same in the House of Mirrors, a place designed specifically for those prisoners whose fear had something to do with distorted self-image. Usually self-aggrandizers, those with messiah complexes or satanic worshipers were sent here.

The testers on Planetoid One had decided that Clare's fear was based on an almost total ego depletion, which she projected onto others, seeing those she killed as without soul, without any existence. This, they decided, was merely a reflection of her own inner state, which she contradicted by creating a self that was the ultimate killer, larger than life, more capable and smarter and without vulnerability because of it.

Jaguar wasn't sure yet if she thought that was a load of bull or not. She'd have to spend time with the woman and reach her own conclusions.

She trailed a hand across the smooth glasslike surface of reflective wall, walking toward the innermost chamber. At the entrance to it, she paused, and for the first time saw Clare Rilasco, painted endless in an infinity of perspectives, as she sat in a white chair in the middle of the room, dressed in a formal, stark white cotton suit, staring at her own reflection and smiling.

Cool silver and white.

The Ice Queen, admiring the beauty of her own reflection, her own reflectiveness.

Jaguar admired her coolness, sitting there in the midst of her inescapable image, split and reshaped and rephrased, sitting there and smiling at herself as if she had just purchased a new dress that she particularly liked and was going out to meet someone she particularly wanted to see her in it.

Or out of it.

She was beautiful, and she was a killer, credited with taking the lives of over a hundred men, some of them important in business or politics. Although she'd been investigated in a number of cases, not a thing could be traced to her, and she kept her white suit and white hands clean. Jaguar had to admire her for her competence in her chosen field, and her ability to be what she was.

She was a predator animal, and as such would feel no guilt about what she did. Her relationship with fear, if she felt any, would be strictly pragmatic. She would let it tell her when there was danger, and then proceed along the line of greatest likelihood to save her own ass. These were both qualities that Jaguar found admirable, but they would make her job more difficult.

"Start at the start," she told herself, and she walked across the smooth white floor, toward the smooth white woman who sat in the center.

Clare heard her, and her eyes refocused as she saw her in the mirror. Jaguar came up behind her and stood, one hand on the back of her chair.

"Hello." Clare smiled. "You must be my . . . teacher?"

"That's what I'm called. Your teacher. My name is Jaguar Addams."

Clare let her gaze run up the length of the reflection in the mirror, stopping briefly at Jaguar's amber face and sea-washed eyes, taking in the dark silk of her hair, the long, lean health of her body, with approval.

"We look well together, don't we?" she said, smiling at their reflections. "It's the contrast between dark and light, as if we were the completeness of a day, or the two sides of a horizon meeting at dawn and the end of the night."

Jaguar looked at the two pairs of eyes, the two alive faces, and nodded. "We look well. How do you know my title?"

"That lovely man told me. Alex Dzarny. Mm, but I wouldn't mind a little bit of time alone with him."

Clare laughed into the mirror, and Jaguar frowned. She had never considered how other women would see Alex. He was a constant part of her life, but she'd preserved very strict personal boundaries with him. Of course, she thought ruefully, leave it to him to arouse desire in a she-demon like Clare.

Clare, who continued to gaze at her own reflection, hadn't once turned to face her, hadn't, as far as Jaguar could tell, moved a muscle except her lips in speaking.

"I hope you won't take offense," she said, "but I was rather hoping Alex would be my teacher, for the obvious reasons. Still, you're just as much a treat on the eyes as he is, in your own way. Have you ever slept with him?"

"No," Jaguar said. "I haven't."

She let the sentence stay flat and unelaborated in the room, waiting to see what this woman would come up with next. Remarkable serenity, Jaguar thought. In her profession, probably a prerequisite for staying alive.

"That's a shame. If you had, you could tell me all about it."

"That would take time away from the work we have to do," Jaguar commented.

"That," Clare said, waving a graceful hand toward the mirror image of herself and smiling. "Must we?"

"I'm afraid so. Have you been told anything about what we'll be doing?"

Clare shook her head. "Not a lot, though my understanding is that my job isn't much different from yours."

Jaguar tilted her head inquisitively. "How so?"

"It's about fear. I find fears to use as a point of weakness and they help me accomplish my assignments. You do the same thing."

Jaguar grinned wryly. It was as good a job description as she'd heard. "I thought you concentrated more on desire than fear," she commented.

Clare's face brightened and she smiled into the mirror, running a finger across her teeth as she did so. "How very astute of you," she said. "I'm glad I'll be working with someone who's intelligent and observant as well as beautiful."

"Thank you," Jaguar said. "Am I also correct?"

"Yes, to a certain extent. Of course people's desires are so often the same as their fears. They fear not getting what they desire."

"Such as?"

"Oh—money. Power. Me."

Jaguar laughed. "And what do you imagine my fears are?"

"I wouldn't want to guess yet. I'd have to study you further. I imagine they'd be minimal, and not along the usual lines. But your desires—now those might be worth exploring."

Jaguar ran her tongue over her teeth and smiled. "And what would you do if you knew them?"

"Why, I'd offer them to you, of course. Pull you closer and closer to me with them, until—well, we'll draw a pretty veil over the rest."

She was good, Jaguar thought, painting just enough of a picture to get the energies of the imagination working, then stepping out of the way. She dealt in generalities to deflect giving any real information, and whoever listened to her heard the specifics they wanted within her words. If she allowed it, she imagined they'd talk the philosophy of murder all day in cool and self-reflective tones. Jaguar thought she'd get back to specifics.

"And what was the recently deceased Gregory Patricks afraid of?" she asked.

Clare gave a small laugh, her fine teeth flashing at them both in the mirrors. "Oh, that would be telling."

Time, Jaguar thought, to shift the perspective a little. She found it dizzying to speak to reflections, seeing herself as she spoke to someone whose reflection stood in front of hers. She walked around to the front of Clare's seat, standing directly between her and the image projected onto the wall. Clare didn't startle, or move. She merely stared at Jaguar as if she were still a reflection in a mirror.

"I would imagine," Jaguar said; "that he was the kind

of man who never swam in dark water." She watched
Clare's face closely, looking for any kind of reaction to
this. Maybe a slight shift in focus, a little more alertness.
The barest minimum necessary. She was reserving her energy for something else. Perhaps expecting things to get
much worse. But her voice remained exactly the same.

"What makes you say that?" she inquired politely.

"He would be afraid of what would reach up from the
bottom to grab him. He was afraid of depths, in general.
Am I right?"

"Very good," Clare said, a certain respect in her tone.
"And you never even met him, did you?"

"No, but I knew his policies. They weren't that different
from the pre-Serials federal policy. Cut education. Cut the
arts. Focus on material gain for already-established companies and let the money piss down to the little people. It
was stupid then, and it's stupid now. You would think the
Serials would have taught us something."

"Perhaps," Clare noted, "people have forgotten already.
We do forget quickly. And some of us didn't have any
trouble with the Serials at all."

"Very few people can say that. Are you one of the
few?"

"Oh yes. I've always been lucky. Wealthy parents, a
good home, the best schools. And we lived so far outside
the city, we were perfectly safe. I never even saw a news-
cast about them."

"Nice for you," Jaguar said, trying to keep the edge out
of her voice. She checked in with herself and found—what?
Resentment. Stupid, but there it was. She felt the same knot
in her stomach when she thought about Alex's luck. It was
resentment and more than a little jealousy for those who
had come out unscathed. And what did Clare do with her
luck but turn assassin.

"How did you manage your luck?" she asked.

"I managed it . . . carefully," Clare said, and a smile
twitched around the edge of her mouth.

Back to specifics again. "As carefully as you manage desire?" Jaguar asked.

"Pardon me?"

"Patricks's desire was—money, power, and you, wasn't it? I understand he sold off some preservation land. He wanted to make Colorado rich with casinos, strip mining, and strip joints, right?"

"I believe so. To be honest, I was very bored by all the government strategy. But I believe you're correct. Some state park or other he wanted to convert to casinos."

"Yes. Casinos. He claimed money from the casinos would help preserve the remainder of the lands, but I gathered that was bullshit to appease the protesting masses. No, I was not an admirer of your late lover."

"Nor was I," Clare admitted. "But the job takes one into some interesting beds, doesn't it?"

"It can. And are your jobs often your lovers? You take them as lovers before you kill them?"

Clare laughed lightly, and lifted a hand to touch Jaguar's hair. "Such a beautiful woman," she crooned, "and how many of your lovers have *you* killed?"

"I didn't kill them," Jaguar replied, placing her own hand over Clare's to stop its motion. "They died in the course of the assignment."

"At the end of your gun, or—you look more like the sort to carry a knife, actually. So on the blade of your knife? Is that how they died?"

"Sometimes." She shrugged. "But that's a little different than your lovers."

"How so?"

Jaguar held out a hand, palm up and empty. "They were prisoners," she said.

And Clare let loose a peal of laughter clear as ice melted into rivers of rushing water. "My dear," she said, when the waters ceased to roll, "they're *all* prisoners. Every last one of them."

Jaguar felt her body stop as if a wall had been placed in

her path. Everything just stopped, and she felt the resonance of an inner truth at the words this woman said.

They're all prisoners, except for Nick. Except for Nick.

She stared down at Clare and her forehead creased, light lines she could almost see reflected in this woman's eyes.

But Clare had already taken her attention away from Jaguar, and was smiling, nodding wisely, at her own reflection in the mirror.

"Why did you let yourself get caught, Clare?" she asked softly. "So many hits without a hint of trouble, and on this one you fall all the way down on your face. Why, Clare?"

"Perhaps," she said politely, "so that I could have the pleasure of meeting you."

Was that it? Did her employers, whoever they were, want her on the Planetoids for some reason? Or was that more obfuscation? Mirrors in mirrors in a House of Mirrors. Clare could be giving her what she wanted to see, and nothing more. Reflecting the familiar back to her. Jaguar shook her head. Try something else.

"But you're not an empath," she said lightly. "You didn't know I existed before you got here."

"Is that what you think?" Clare asked. "Then I'll let you think that."

Slippery as wet glass. An absolute absence of friction making for an absolute absence of foothold. She thought of watching Hecate stalk the grounds of the breeding complex, her motion a frictionless glide over the earth. They were similar, Hecate and Clare, except that they were attempting to breed the killer back into the cat, and out of the woman. And how did one establish communication with a creature that was a killer by nature?

Carefully, with a slow hand that offered safety for both parties.

On an impulse, Jaguar put a hand on Clare's shoulder and caught her gaze reflected in the mirrors. "You have beautiful hair," she said. "Would you like me to brush it for you?"

Clare blinked in surprise. "Brush my hair?"

"Yes. Your hair. Would you like that?"

"That would be lovely."

"Then that's exactly what we'll do."

"What I want," Jaguar said to Rachel's face as it appeared in her telecom, "is a cross-check of the corporation Patricks was selling the land to. The Golden Corporation. Who they dealt with, what they dealt in aside from Patricks. All other business connections. It may take some doing."

"I understand," Rachel said. "Anything else?"

"The CEOs. I want to know who they've been fucking around with in their spare time. Same thing for the CEOs of associated corporations. And find out if any have past dealings with either Clare, or with NICA, the Pentagon, DIE."

Rachel leaned back in her chair. "You mean, organizationally?"

"Or personally. In terms of government contracts—could be NICA covering for DIE, too, so look out for that. Or, if any of the CEOs have a lot of personal long-distance calls to anyone at these organizations, but they happen to be home calls. That sort of thing. Like I said, it'll take some doing. Oh—and I'd like to know what specific research DIE has going lately, if you can think of a way to get at that."

"DIE's research? Jaguar," Rachel said, "I'm not sure that's such a hot idea. I mean, you know the people at DIE—they're like the original rat babies. They only come out at night, or when they sniff fresh kill. If you start poking around at their business, you'd be drawing them to you like—like—"

"Like I was anything that smells, right? Don't worry, Rache. I know what I'm doing."

"You think so," Rachel said. "You want me to look into Pentagon research, too? And NICA?"

"No. Just DIE. They do the bulk of the new stuff for

the others. And I already know what the Pentagon's up to."

Rachel saw a certain look of distraction that told her Jaguar's thoughts were already elsewhere. Whatever she was working on, she'd play this one close to her chest. In a minute, Rachel thought, she'd ask her to do the same.

"Rachel," she said, "keep this quiet, okay? You have my access to private files, and you can delete your time when you're done."

"Right," Rachel replied. "I'll have to get around Terence, though. He likes clearance on everything."

"And he is such a long way around," Jaguar noted wryly. "If you delete, I think he'll miss it. Lemme know what you come up with."

Rachel's telecom went blank, and she sat staring at it for a moment, thinking through her next moves.

After a few minutes she pushed her chair back and stood, turned, and found herself face-to-face with Alex. She drew in a startled breath and held a hand up to her mouth.

Alex grinned at her. "Sorry," he said. "I have a very soft walk." He backed up a few paces and motioned with his arm for her to pass freely.

She stood and crossed her arms, frowning at him. "That's not fair at all," she said.

"What's not fair?"

"Eavesdropping."

Alex laughed. "I'm an empath, Rachel. I do it all the time. So does Jaguar. You know that."

"Yeah, but this is like the normal way. Did you find out what you wanted to know?"

"She wants to track the corporation to one of the intelligence organizations. She'll have you check them all before she's through. I thought she would."

"Any idea why?"

"A few bubbles floating around. Nothing definite. I'll talk to her about it when I have the chance. And I want you to pass me anything and everything you give her. Got it?"

Interesting, the way her thoughts were running. He knew that she'd already gathered information on specifics of the land deal in Leadville, on Patricks's tax status and other finances, and the same for the Lieutenant Governor. Nothing on either, so she was moving further afield. Good for her, he thought. He'd handed her a tough one, and she was going to crack it, just to prove she could.

But her interest in DIE and NICA, the Pentagon—that could be trouble. It made sense, since the hit was political, that it might have backing from a governmental agency, or an affiliate. The Pentagon had taken heat for that sort of thing in the past, but Alex couldn't imagine Clare working for them, somehow. She had too much finesse to be associated with such a corpulent body. However, both NICA and DIE were known for a silent efficiency, for learning everything and giving away nothing. Nobody knew for sure that they hired assassins. But he couldn't think of anyone who wanted to test the theory with their own lives. Except possibly Jaguar.

"Okay," Rachel said, and then, echoing his thoughts, "but it's not particularly safe. And the corporate mind-set isn't something Jaguar has a very good handle on. When you talk to her, remind her to be careful."

"Rachel," Alex said, "I only wish it would do any good."

The bar was crowded, and the crowd was lively. Jaguar, her hair sleek and her black boots shined, was singing a clipped and acerbic song about unrequited lust. She could see Adrian sitting at a table, listening, his eyes glued to her.

This was her favorite part of the Planetoid. She had started singing on a dare from one of her former prisoners who played guitar and said Jaguar was just too scared to get up and perform. She'd surprised him. He didn't know that her grandparents taught her to sing for ceremony, encouraging her to use her voice the way athletes use their muscles—with precision, with the freedom of unrestrained passion, with something like joy, if anything as direct and cutting as her voice could be called joyful. She sang in college, too, to earn extra money. The stage was familiar turf.

The audience, like the general population, was made up of many ex-prisoners who were waiting out their prerelease year, and many who had chosen to stay and become team members for Teachers, helping them set up programs, working their assigned parts in those programs. They all liked a night out, and they weren't the kind of people who took anything for granted. Responsive didn't begin to name their attitude.

It was also the one place where she allowed people to call her Jag. Most of them, she figured, were only up to one syllable at a time.

The band she was working with was all ex-prisoners, some of them past assignments of hers. Players changed on a regular basis to accommodate arrivals and departures from the Planetoid, but this group had been together almost a year, and they were getting quite good. Their timing was tight, and their improv was loose. They knew each other's rhythms and riffs, and weren't afraid to take chances with each other or the music.

The Governors' Board would probably have disapproved, but Alex had put this activity in her report file as community-service volunteer time. She was, after all, encouraging new skills in the prisoners.

She sang out the song, then announced the break. She was sweating, feeling buzzed from the sound, as she turned to her keyboard man, Gerry.

"Jesus, Gerry." She laughed. "What the hell were you on about tonight? The size of your nipples?"

"I don't know, Jag," he said, wiping his face with a towel they kept on stage. "It's a new piece. I was letting it fly."

"You sure were." She reached for the towel. "Sounded great, though. I think they liked it."

"They *are* big nipples," he said. "Wanna see?"

"I think," she said, "I'll defer the pleasure."

She walked off the stage and over to where Adrian sat, beaming at her. She picked up his beer and took a long pull from it, then sat down. "Enjoying yourself?"

"Man," he said, "you're great. You ought to forget about being a cop and go on the road."

"Sure," she said. "You ever deal with the music industry? More criminals there than on the Planetoids."

He laughed, but he wouldn't let it drop. "Really. You should just do it."

"Whatever for?"

"Fame and fortune."

She reached over and ran a finger across his smooth face. "I have you to get me the fortune. The fame is something I can do without."

He held her fingers, and kissed them. "You always smell of mint. Why?"

"Because I always carry it with me."

"Mm. It's nice," he murmured into her hand. "Didn't you ever want to be somebody?"

She blinked at him, surprised.

"I *am* somebody," she said. "Aren't you?"

He nuzzled the palm of her hand. "Right," he said, speaking into it. "I'll be somebody after I make a little more money. Nobody's anybody unless other people say you are. You know that."

"No," she said, "I don't. I don't know that." It was soon to be approaching the fear, but she'd take the opportunity to work it. Something soft, she thought. A little gentling of the spirit.

She pulled his face toward hers and began the process of making contact. An odd moment for it, but Teachers were always flying by the seat of their pants in terms of timing. As she was about to respond to the sorrow she saw lingering in him, she felt a hand on her shoulder. She startled, and turned.

"Slumming again, Jaguar?" Nick said.

She grimaced, then smiled tightly. "Nick, dear," she said. "I'd invite you to pull up a chair, but there aren't any. So maybe," she suggested, "you ought to just fuck off."

He chuckled. "Always do what you're best at, right? But I don't think so. I'm at my best watching you work someone over."

She pushed herself away from Adrian and the table and made as if to stand, but Nick put his hand back on her shoulder and pushed her down, holding her with the pressure of his weight.

Jaguar surveyed him, going cold and still between a sense of loss and imminent danger. There was loss here. He'd taught her so much. It was Nick who told her to avoid all the fancy techno-tools the Board tried to foist off on Teachers. Stick to the basics, he told her. They wouldn't let you down.

"Use your head and forget the rest," he had said. "Like the sensors. They scan for everything except glass. You know how much damage a glass knife can do to a gut?"

She felt the cool edge of the glass knife she carried resting against her wrist. It was a gift. From Nick.

There was loss and danger. She had to get him away from Adrian before he blew the assignment. She pushed his hand off her shoulder and he laughed.

"Jag," he said, "what have you been saying about me, and who have you been saying it to?"

"Besides that you're a lousy fuck, which I tell every woman I know?" she said coldly. "Not much. I don't like to waste breath."

Adrian narrowed his eyes. "What the hell is this?" he asked, pointing at Nick as if he were a specimen in a laboratory.

"Nothing much," Jaguar replied. "Every party needs an asshole to keep things lively." She leaned across the table and stroked Adrian's cheek briefly. "Could you be a gentleman and go get me a tequila? Double shot, something gold and expensive.''

Adrian made a sound of protest, but she shook her head at him, held his eyes briefly with hers, and stroked his face once more. "Salt and lemon with it," she said. "And no ice. Got it?"

He pulled back from her hand, eyed her suspiciously, then rose and made his way toward the bar.

"You're a rotten Teacher, you know that? Letting this happen in the middle of a case. With your subject right here, too." He tossed a nod toward Adrian's receding figure.

"And you're determined to fuck it up on me, aren't you, Nick?"

"That little boy? You could take him overnight. What're you waiting for?"

She leaned back in her chair, stretching her long legs out in front of her. He lifted his leg and placed a large foot on her chair, next to her thigh, leaning his elbow on his knee and resting his chin in his hand.

"I'm trying to do it right, Nick. You can't just walk into someone as if they're your living room."

He reached over and ran his thumb along the line of her jaw. "*I* can, baby."

She kept her body still, her eyes steady on his face, as she felt the pulse of need to push into her, to have her, to be in her. But she'd been practicing the arts all her life, and knew the gestures of resistance. He was potentially strong, but he had no deftness, and no technique. She blocked him, and held him just outside of where he wanted to be.

"You couldn't last time, Nick."

He chuckled, pushed her face away. "Well, well. Our Lady of the Empathic Arts speaks. If you're jealous because I'm working your turf, why don't you just say so?"

At this, Jaguar had to let go and laugh. "Jealous? That's your realm, Nick. You're the man who got crazy over the amount of time I was spending with my supervisor."

"Your supervisor and I had a little talk the other day," he cut in.

"I know all about it," she said. "Alex told me."

"Alex told you," he mimicked her, "*Alex* told you. What did he tell you? That he'll look out for you as long as you give him a piece now and then? Protect you from the Board? Get rid of old Nick when you're sick of him?"

She said nothing as he turned his face down to hers, narrowed his eyes, then slid his gaze away.

It was enough. She could see the shadow sickness in him. It hadn't been that apparent last time she saw him. It was moving fast, but he could still return from it.

"Nick," she whispered, "you need help. Why don't you let someone help you?"

"You can help me," he whispered back, leaning close to her again, pressing his tension through his hand, into her shoulder. "You know how to make me feel good, Jaguar. You always have."

There. This was the hard part. Right here, where he claimed her by his need, by their long association, by past friendship. She felt the pull of it, that longing for an old warmth, long dead.

Your darkness. Where you walk with the dead.

But there were so many connections between them, and none of them dead yet.

About five years after the dust settled from the Killing Times, a group of volunteers started sorting through the warehouses of items that had been collected from the dead. Houses full of furniture, closets full of clothes—the stuff of life was given away to charities. Personal items such as photo albums and letters were sorted, and any remaining family members were contacted to come back to their cities and collect their past.

Jaguar had been called back to Manhattan for her grandparents' pictures, ceremonial clothing, and jewelry. When she walked into the noise and chaos of the warehouse with its long tables and long lines of clamoring people, she found herself looking into Nick's face once again after six years.

"Nick?" she said. "Are you still alive?"

He laughed, then eyed her good. "You grew up nice," he said.

He told her he was just here for a few days, volunteering on this assignment. That he'd started working on the Planetoids. Couldn't seem to stand Manhattan anymore.

He pointed up, toward the sky outside the window of the room they were in, and she followed his finger with her gaze, looking out and up. Out and up and away.

"Can I get a job there?" she asked.

"You?" he had said. "You could probably get a job just about anywhere you want." And he'd arranged for her to visit with another Teacher who was returning that afternoon. She'd met Alex, spoken with him, ended up back in school, and was now a Teacher herself.

She owed Nick. She owed him a lot. Maybe that was the problem she had with him.

"Why are you filing a complaint against me, Nick?" she asked now. "You know what I did for you on that last one."

"I know," he admitted. "But you won't back me up with the Board, and I'm not ready to retire. Jesus, Jaguar, you can take this one for me. All you'll get is a little slap on the wrist. Naughty, naughty Jag. But you're used to that."

He was right. She'd get off easy, but he might be forced into early retirement. The Board was careful to watch for any signs of burnout, and Nick would probably look like a classic case to them. She'd be helping him out, maybe evening the debt between them.

"Back me up," he continued, "and then . . . I'll let you help me with the other. The empathic stuff. We can try again, together. C'mon, Jaguar. You know we just fight because we're two of a kind. We've both been through it.

I know what you need, who you are, what you've seen.
Let's give it another try."

Another try. They were two survivors. Two people who
understood what it meant to survive hell.

"Jaguar," he crooned at her, "aren't you sick of sleeping with prisoners? Wouldn't you like something better
than that?"

She searched his face, asking his eyes to be still and
connect with hers, but they wouldn't. Shadowed. Cold and
distant and dark, chasing some monster inside himself that
even he couldn't name. Did her face look like that, evading
contact?

Where is your darkness?

Words came out of her mouth, surprising to her in their
harshness, their anger.

"I won't back your lies, and I won't sleep with you,
Nick. Sleeping with prisoners is better than sleeping with
a dead man."

She saw his face grow white, blood leaving the surface
of his skin as his rage at her grew. He leaned closer and
lifted a long strand of her hair, feeling the silk of it between
thumb and index finger, then winding it slowly around,
down to his hand.

"Watch it, Jaguar," he said. "I put up with a lot of shit
from you because we got history, but I'm not as easygoing
as I used to be."

He twisted, then jerked hard, snapping her neck back. He
held her there, and with his free hand he caressed her throat,
feeling the place where the carotid beat like thunder in her
neck.

Out of the corner of her eye, at an odd angle, she saw
Adrian weaving through the crowd with her tequila. She
had to get Nick out of here. Had to get him away before
Adrian saw this and smelled the setup she'd created for
him.

She reached up and wrapped her hand around Nick's

wrist, pressing her fingers between the joints of bones. "Let go," she said.

"You let go," he responded.

She could see Adrian drawing closer. Damn. Damn and hell. Someone had to let go first.

She dropped her hand.

"Subject coming back?" he asked without looking. Then he laughed. "I'm not as dead as you'd like to think, Jag. Just remember that."

He slowly unwound his hand from her hair and released her. He waited with his foot still on her chair until Adrian returned, then pushed her chair roughly back and turned toward him, punching him playfully on the chest and causing him to slosh tequila over himself.

"Watch out for her, buddy," he said. "Ask her sometime what happened to her last assignment. And Jaguar," he added in parting, "say hello to Clare for me."

When he left, Adrian eyed her suspiciously. "What was that?"

"Another cop. Don't worry. Just some shit about his propensity to screw up cases and find someone else to blame. I had to testify at one point. He wasn't happy about it. He still thinks my word carries weight. That's how crazy he is."

"Jaguar," Adrian started, but she stopped him. She was distracted by Nick's mention of Clare. What was that to him, and how did he know she had the assignment if it was classified?

"I want to know what's going on," Adrian insisted, and she turned her attention back to him.

"Leave it alone," she said. "I gotta get back to work." She stood and leaned over him, nipped at his earlobe. "Did you like that last one? Lust takes a nap at the back of your head," she sang. "Waiting for you, waiting for you, waiting for you."

"Sure," he said. But he pulled away from her.

Shit, she thought. Just when they were doing so well.

5

''I DON'T CARE WHAT HE WANTS TO CHARGE ME with, you tell him to leave me the hell alone. He's not to touch me, he's not to talk to me, he's not to even *think* about me.''

Alex looked from Jaguar, to Terence Manning, who had been going over recent statistics with Alex when she flung open the door and began telling him, with the precise and pointed asperity of white-hot anger, about Nick's recent visit to her.

''Will you,'' Alex said, ''calm down. Say hello to Terence. Be sociable.''

''Hello, Terence,'' she said, then returned her attention to Alex. ''I am *perfectly* calm. I'm also justifiably angry. That asshole's about to blow my whole assignment for me. He's not fit for this work anymore, Alex. You should pull him. Now.''

Alex swiveled his chair back and forth, considering her. She could be right, but she was also holding something back. What, though? Something Nick had on her? Something she knew about him? He focused on her, grabbing hold and pulling in just a little. Those sea eyes, green and gold and soft and deep. She was—wait—what the hell was that?

This wasn't the way it worked. She was pulling him in.

He felt the tension of it, a wire strung between them. Then the inrush of feeling, here where she occupied him. So quickly. She could act so quickly and she was so smooth, like the edge of her glass knife, slicing air, slicing through to a place she had no right to be.

He felt something like her laughter, and then saw himself young and walking down a city street strewn with bodies, smelled fetid death. A young man in the army, trying to be a hero and save people from their own idiocy.

Her eyes showed him to himself as he bent over the groaning form of a young woman, her gold-skinned face and dark hair perfect under the perfect brilliance of sun and clear sky.

Can I help you? he asked her, *a polite young man from a safer world, trying to exercise courtesy in the face of unimpeded death like trying to be respectful to a rabid dog.*

Can I help you? What do you need?

And the young woman's beautiful arm raised, an automatic weapon in it. Her perfectly beautiful grin as she fired. His dodge, just in time, so that he caught the bullets in his arm and not his face. His rage in kicking the weapon from her hand, then kicking her over and over and over again. His rage, and the betrayal. The betrayal of such a perfectly beautiful kind.

Perfect beauty. Perfectly beautiful killer.

Then, just as swiftly, the image dissolved, the feel of it gone as Jaguar pulled back, her laughter riding the wake of his memory.

He sat in his chair again, with Jaguar staring at him, her eyes smooth as a glassy sea.

Perfectly beautiful.

She tilted her head to one side and said, very low in her throat like a purr or a growl, "Care to go for a swim?" And as she spoke he could see, gleaming red at her wrist, the tip of the retractable glass knife he knew she carried there.

He leaned forward, placed the palms of his hands on his desk, and pushed himself to standing. No, he wasn't shaking. He was very calm. Quiet. All quiet now.

"You're way out of line, Dr. Addams," he said coldly. "Whatever Nick's doing, I'll handle. You better keep track of yourself."

"Oh, I can track myself. Don't you worry." She leaned toward him, resting her hands on his desk and putting her face level with his. "I can track a cat under a new moon, or the smallest scent of death in open air. I can track last week's eagle in a cloudy sky. I can even track you, Alex. Even you. And if you don't get this asshole away from me, I'll take care of him myself. *My* way."

Terence whistled low as she turned on her heel and left.

"Things gone that bad between them?" he asked. "Or—maybe I don't want to know?"

"You don't," Alex replied. Quiet, he told himself. Just stay quiet.

"I didn't think so. That Jag," Terence prattled on, "she's a tough cookie. I wouldn't want to mess with her. Nick's an idiot if he thinks he can get her back this way." He shook his head. "Mm-mm, but she's a looker, too. Can't really blame him for trying. Did you ever try to—you know—with her?"

Alex pulled his attention back into the room. What was Terence saying? Something outrageous, it seemed.

"I'll bet it'd be like trying to do Teflon," he continued without waiting for Alex's answer. He slid a hand smoothly and swiftly down his arm, curving the line of motion up at the end. "Like Teflon. She's got no place you can stick to, and no soft spot at all. Always smells of mint. There's some story about that, isn't there? Jag and her mint?"

"Don't call her that," Alex said automatically. "She hates it."

"Huh? You think she uses that—you know, mind stuff? She's got that look in her eyes."

Alex tried to keep his attention on Terence, but found

the conversation was boring him. He needed to focus on what to do about Nick. Needed to think about what she had just done to him. Needed some clear space. Had to deal with Terence, first.

"The empathic arts," he said, "aren't approved for use. Not officially, anyway."

"Right. Like that makes a difference. Like it ought to. Don't get me wrong, though. I wouldn't go near it. Not me. Gives me the shivers just thinking about walking around in some of the minds we see."

"That's why we advise against it."

"Yeah. I think you gotta be cold. Cold as death to use that stuff. And Jag—I mean, Jaguar. Well, I don't even have to say it, do I?"

"It would be better," Alex agreed, "if you didn't."

Terence winked knowingly. He was glad he'd caught this little interlude. It gave him an idea. Something he could discuss with the Looker tonight.

Jaguar left Alex's office to meet Rachel at a diner and get the results of her most recent research. Usually, they would pass this sort of information over the computer lines, but Jaguar didn't want any record of what she was looking for. If she could avoid trouble, she would, though it would be a new experience for her. But too many eyes were on her, and she didn't like that. It wasn't safe.

She went over the new information while Adrian was out, looking up prospects from the Ascension Project.

Rachel brought her nothing on Clare's life during the Serials or immediately after, and this was disappointing, but not surprising. The three years that covered the Killing Times and the year following had been lost to many people, and a quarter of a century later the ripples of it could still be felt in a number of ways. Although the cities had rebuilt themselves, and the social structure had rewoven itself into a whole again, nothing would ever be the same.

Jaguar wondered if it would have been easier to live

through a war. In the Serials, there was no enemy to point at and say, "See. There he is. There's the problem." No enemy to identify and remove.

Instead, the killing had arisen from within the chronic sickness of a culture steeped in denial and underground despair, covered by the hope of technological salvation and material wealth. A pile of physically homeless and spiritually starved people, tottering on the crumbling foundation of a culture that could only consume. In this catastrophe, everyone was the enemy, from the woman who sold groceries to you, to the cabdriver, to the man in the blue suit with a briefcase who went to work every day on Wall Street until the day he took out a knife and started playing Jack the Ripper in the night.

You had to defend yourself against an enemy who could be anyone. An enemy who was the person you saw when you looked in the mirror.

In the end, even the army simply waited until enough people killed each other that there was a manageable number left. Only a few groups had the courage to go right into the cities and help in the heat of the riots and killing sprees. Nick was in one such group, working with a few other cops and a priest and a New Age guru to stalk the city, combing it for survivors and getting them out, out, out of the hell.

How many children had he rescued? Picking them up as he picked her up, by the backs of their shirts. Keeping them from stepping on the live wires—electric devices that the safety squads ran around their homes to keep the killing out. Yelling at them and checking them for weapons all the while.

How could he have gone from that to what he'd become? It was a betrayal. It felt like a betrayal that he could do so. How could he lose himself so completely, and why hadn't she?

She felt her anger at him rise, then soften in the question she asked herself.

How could he lose himself so completely, and why hadn't she?

Your darkness, Jaguar. Where is your fear?

Survivor guilt. Survivor fear. Survivor resentment. She looked at Clare, and resented her luck. Looked at Alex and mistrusted his. Nick probably looked at her and did the same.

"Stop it," she told herself. "Just—cut it out. You have work to do, and plenty of it."

She turned her mind away from Nick, away from herself, and continued reading. Most of the report was old news, held up in as many lights as possible. She read, keeping a running file in her head of what might and might not connect to create something like a coherent whole out of so many various and apparently unrelated bits of information. It took an uncomfortable attentiveness, a hyperawareness that was tiring, and she knew she'd have to go through it all again—and again—seeking the bits of information that would stop her, make her think, cause that little click of apprehension in her mind.

The first item she noted was that Clare had already known a Planetoid worker, years ago, on the home planet.

As a teenager, she'd been picked up for possession of cocaine, and the officer who brought her in was Nick Lyola.

"Great Hecate's cloak," she said. "Can't I get away from the bastard?"

It could mean nothing—a blip in the scheme. The random at its meaningless best. It could correlate with what Clare said about wanting to meet her. It could all be more smoke in mirrors. In a universe of infinite possibilities, the odds were anyone's guess. It was pre-Serials, and Clare was young, so she was probably just experimenting. The amount she had wasn't enough for sale, since the charge was possession. Nick had recommended probation and regular sessions with a counselor. The courts had assigned her to a probation officer for counseling rather than a social worker. In all likelihood, she'd had no further interaction with Nick at all.

The next item of note was about the Golden Corporation, and it was negative. There was absolutely no connection between the Golden Corporation and any of the government offices Jaguar was interested in. The Golden Corporation had two primary sources of income—casino management and the exploitation of mining rights of various kinds. They'd begun their existence copper mining in Brazil, and had gone on to explore the potential of renewable resources—such as the Cut Thread plant found in the rain forests, which was increasingly employed in the manufacture of the conductive lines that surgeons used in replacing damaged neurons. They continued to mine for garnets in upstate New York, and were slated to have first crack at mining on the moon, the nights for which they had optioned, if the Global Union of Peace ever let the legislation through for them to begin.

They purchased a chunk of the preservation land to mine for pyrite, and another for Casino development, contracting out the building to construction companies that also had no connection to NICA or DIE. In other words, all news was negative, except for one interesting item.

"Pyrite," Jaguar mused. "How very odd." What, she wondered, did they do with the mineral commonly known as fool's gold?

She filed this item, and continued reading.

Rachel had gone on to explore the possibility of a connection between the Lieutenant Governor and corporations opposed to the development deal. There was nothing to indicate any such connection. The only interesting items about the Lieutenant Governor were that he hoped to run for president someday, which made Jaguar groan in disgust, and that he had recently attended his wife at the birth of their first child, a daughter named Golda.

"Fool's gold," she muttered again, and flipped back to

the Golden Corporation, reading through the annual report, which was a public document.

She stopped only briefly, to note that the corporation anticipated the amount of money garnered from the sale of pyrite in the next fiscal year to make up about a quarter of its profits.

"Fool's gold?" she asked herself.

She read the report again thoroughly, to see who the buyers would be. From what she could make of the business jargon, a variety of purchasers would be making use of the metal. All of them were in the business of distribution of goods. The middlemen who bought, held, and sold, but did nothing beyond that. All were small, low-profile groups.

"Thank you, Rachel," Jaguar said. "Very much indeed."

She wasn't sure what she had learned yet, but something in her visceral region told her it was important. She closed the file and went to her room to pick out something in a warm color. Perhaps her red silk, although that crossed the border from warmth into heat.

Still, it would do the job she had in mind, which was to add something that might melt the ice in the House of Mirrors.

The lakeside wharves were dark and deserted, except for one man in a dark blue suit who stood at a dock, staring pensively out across the ruffled waters toward an unseen shore. As he stood he periodically lifted his wrist close to his face and make clucking noises at it.

The Looker was an exceptionally punctual man, and found tardiness disturbing, no excuses allowed.

When he finally heard, from some distance, the sound of footsteps coming toward him, he was even more disapproving. His contact should not have allowed himself to be heard. What kind of man were they hiring for this job, anyway? Late, and noisy, apparently.

The Looker tensed, and turned on his heel to face his appointment as he walked the long dock toward him.

The two men stood sizing each other up for a minute. The Looker spoke first.

"You're late," he said.

"Stuck in traffic," the other man said. Then he stuck out his hand, stiff and formal. "I'm Nick Lyola."

The Looker jutted out a pointy nose even farther and pointed a finger with long nails at Nick. "Don't tell me that," he hissed. "This is strictly no-name."

"Hey," Nick said, raising his hands, in the position of surrender. "Nobody told me."

"When we spoke earlier in the week, I said as much," he said triumphantly. Catching the incompetent in error brought its own joy.

"Okay," Nick said, scratching at his ear. "Okay. So I forgot. Anyway, you must know who I am, otherwise how'd you find me?"

The Looker said nothing, and Nick held up his thumb and index finger in the shape of a gun, cocking an imaginary hammer and pulling at an invisible trigger. "Gotcha," he said, grinning.

The Looker said more nothing. Nick shrugged, backed off a step, and shifted from one foot to the other.

"So," he said at last, "what's the game? You said you had a job for me. Something to do with Jag."

The Looker pursed his thin lips and breathed in half the air of the wharf through his thin nose, then expelled it with flaring nostrils. "I have an assignment for you. Classified. It involves the Addams woman merely by chance, and you were chosen because of your relationship with her."

"Yeah," Nick said, "that's cute—my relationship with her is more like a boxing match these days. What am I supposed to do?"

The man blinked three times, then continued. Nick wondered if he was receiving instructions from an invisible telecom even as he spoke. There seemed to be some delay between the questions that entered his ears and the resultant answers. Some kind of delayed processing time, or something.

He continued to say nothing, but raised his hand toward Nick, palm out. Nick stared at him, then at his hand, then more closely at his hand.

In the center of his palm was a small flat chip that gave off a lightly gold metallic sheen. Nick pointed at it.

"For me?" he asked.

"You have," he said, "some empathic ability?"

Nick shrugged. "I thought I wasn't supposed to tell you nothing."

The Looker nodded in approval.

"This," he said, "is a projection chip. It allows an empath to both receive at higher-than-real emotional amplifications, and to project scenes toward a subject with increased intensity."

Nick felt the chip between his fingers, brought it to his nose, and sniffed it, held it up to the light, and examined it with one eye closed.

"You don't have to bite it," the man said through clenched teeth. "It's not a fake coin."

"I'm just trying to figure out what I do with it to get it to work," Nick said. "Eat it? Stick it in my ear? Stick it up—"

"Don't be juvenile. You implant it subcutaneously in the region of the medulla oblongata."

"Like I said, stick it up my—"

"At the back of your head," he said, his lips growing tighter by the second.

Nick laughed, flipped the device with his fingers, and caught it in his other hand. "Okay. Don't get so bent. I know how to insert an implant, and I got what I need at home. What do I do once I got it in, and how's it gonna help with Jag?"

"She's an empath," the man said coldly. "Practiced. Very practiced. Use it to . . . influence her. To disturb her."

"What for? I mean, I know why I'd like to, but what am I doing for you?"

"Maintaining security."

"Yeah. Right. How?"

"Get her off the Rilasco case."

Nick lifted his head from staring at the disk, and whistled at the man. "Rilasco, is it? Jag getting a little too close to the bone with her? A few things you don't want known, maybe?"

The Looker said nothing.

"Okay. I can take a hint. Suits me fine, anyway. Do you mind if I try a trick or two of my own while I'm in there?"

"We assumed it would be to your advantage to do so. As long as you get her off the case, we don't care what else you do."

"Great. Am I supposed to contact you when I've got her taken care of?"

"No," he said. "We'll know."

And with that, he turned back toward the water, staring again at the unseen shore. Nick, taking this as dismissal, clattered his way back down the dock, whistling as he went.

The Looker stood at the end of the dock, waiting.

His next visitor of the evening was both punctual and a silent walker. He turned and greeted him with approval.

"Hello, Terence," he said. "Did you hear?"

"I got it," he said, then shifted his weight, looking around. "I hope Nick can manage it. He's looking a little frayed at the edges these days."

The Looker shook his head. "You recommended him for the assignment. If you're thinking better of it—"

"No. I think it's the best move. They already have a connection. From what I heard in Dzarny's office today, it's a pretty hot one right now, so if anything goes too wrong, it'll just get blamed on that. Minimizes the risk some."

"Good. Because most important is to get that Addams woman off the case. Any other Teacher would be no problem. But with her—Terence, I don't need to explicate, do I?''

"No. You don't need to explain, either. And if Nick blows this one—''

"If he does, we'll dispose of him.''

"No,'' Terence said. "I know you want to play with your Supertoys—''

"E-wave amplification devices,'' the Looker corrected.

"Right,'' he said. He knew what the devices did, and how powerful they were, but he preferred to think of them by their common name. Toys. Supertoys, but toys. Just boys and their toys, on a more lucrative scale than grade school. If he thought of them that way he didn't have to keep remembering what the Looker was using them for at his research center.

"If Nick can't handle the technology, there's something else we can do with him. I thought of it this morning, because of the fuss Jag's making,'' he explained, and waited while the Looker ran the information through his personal process of decision making, which was to take a deck of cards from his suit pocket and shuffle.

"No,'' he said. "We've started with this. We'll stick with it unless it proves futile. When you choose to move your cards a certain way, Terence, it's important to stay with what you have until you see it no longer works.''

"Yeah,'' Terence said. "Sure. And if it doesn't work, then what?''

For the first time in the years of their association, Terence saw the Looker's mouth twist into what might have been, on any other person, a smile.

"Then,'' he said, "you cheat.''

The Looker turned back to the water, and Terence watched his own back on the way home.

Alex's apartment overlooked one of the nicer shores of the Lake Ontario built for this replica city of Toronto. He would often sit at the front window staring out at the shadings and shiftings of the lake while he brooded his way through a difficult assignment or a Teacher's problem.

The designers had done a good job—almost too good, because the one complaint made about all the replica cities was that they were better than the originals. Of course, that was due in part to their newness, and in part to the absence of heavy industry on the Planetoids. They imported most of their manufactured goods from the home planet, and as a result, the years of pollution that left scars on the home planet never happened here.

Alex also thought the population of the replica cities had a better attitude. They were all misfits on the home planet in one way or another, but here they were involved in something real. A real, if flawed, attempt to treat the problems of crime and violence instead of stuffing the criminals into a hole and trying to forget they existed.

Every night he could look out his window at the play of water and light and remind himself of that. Then he could clear his mind, and perform his final ritual before he went to sleep.

Every night, right before he fell asleep, he made sure to check on Jaguar.

His empathic touch always remained light, and cloaked. Just a brush of his consciousness against hers. Enough to know she was alive and well, and enough to see whatever protocol she happened to be breaking with her current assignment. This gesture bordered on the intrusive—a sort of Peeping Tom discourtesy—and he wasn't sure if she could feel his contact. If so, she'd never said anything in objection. Of course, he could justify his actions on the grounds that she had a propensity for trouble, and he had to be able to back her up when she went out on one of her shaky limbs. Or, he could say that she was such a strong empath, he wanted to make sure she wasn't playing with the darker sides of the arts. Both justifications held some of the truth. Neither one told the whole truth.

He'd gotten into the habit when she first came to work

for him. As all Teachers had to, she'd gone through the
testers' hands when she was hired, and they'd reported a
high level of e-wave activity, indicating more than one psi
capacity, along with aberrant neurophysiological response
in the autonomic system, primarily in reflex arc synaptic
time. Then the report had broken from its officialese to
comment that the subject had a pronounced capacity to
block incoming waves, and if other capacities were present,
they could not at this time be fully defined.

Their equipment had gone flooey.

Alex had her tested again when she was transferred to
his zone, with the same results.

Jaguar's only comment to him, when he questioned her
on it, was that the damn machines never worked in the first
place.

She was right. They were notorious for missing specific
psi capacities and psychological or emotional subtleties.
Alex agreed with Jaguar that it was a mistake to try to fit
an art within the framework of a linear science. But on the
other hand, he saw her trying to hide a grin, and knew she'd
had a hand in the equipment's breakdown. Apparently
among her empathic gifts was a talent for screwing up technology.

He'd asked permission to make empathic contact with
her, in lieu of further testing, and she'd said no. Absolutely
not. When he asked for her reasons, she said simply that
she didn't want to, and it wasn't a job requirement. Alex
let it ride, though he wanted to know more of her specific
capacities, and more of her experience in the Serials. All
Teachers were required to share that information with their
supervisors, because the traumas they carried might affect
their ability to deal with prisoners, make them more suited
for certain kinds of criminals, less suited for others. Jaguar
had given the bare facts—she'd been living in Manhattan,
being raised by her grandparents because her mother had
died in childbirth and her father was unknown. Her grand-

parents had been killed. She had escaped and gone to live with friends of the family in New Mexico.

She'd never allowed more than the surface contact that a private conversation required, never told him more than that. Yet she could walk into his center as if she'd been doing it all her life, and find his central point of fear from the Killing Times without breaking her stride.

A perfectly beautiful woman. A perfectly beautiful betrayal.

She'd found that memory as if it was her own, and used it to throw him off balance, which indicated to Alex how threatened she felt. Two cases at once might be too many for her after all. Two cases, and Nick all over her.

Alex was worried about that. Nick wasn't responding to the messages on his belt sensor telling him that the charges against Jaguar had been dropped for lack of evidence. He would know that meant Alex was backing her. He'd be able to read between those lines. He was on rest leave and not required to report in right now, but surely he would want to know what was going on with his charges.

Maybe he did know. Maybe he knew more than Alex did.

He wondered how much empathic contact there had been between Nick and Jaguar during their work together. How much did she teach him, and how much did he know on his own?

Most of the empath Teachers chose not to use their talents on a regular basis. Some were still nervous about being found out, because although the existence of psi capacities was now admitted as scientific fact, actually using them was still a touchy political issue. Less so here than on, for instance, Planetoid One. And certainly less so here than on the home planet, but empaths didn't like having too many people know who and what they were.

Beyond that, it was difficult to bear the experience of getting that close to someone else's shadow side, which is what Teachers were usually looking for in the interchange.

It took some learning, some ritual training, and that was difficult to come by. Not many ritual elders survived the Serials long enough to pass on what they knew. After the first year of violence, vigilante groups had formed, calling themselves Safety Squads. They'd run through cities with nerve gas, homemade biobombs, whatever they could get. And they targeted one specific group of people.

They decided since so much of the killing was ritual, ritual leaders must be at fault. Priests and nuns, those who wore the side curls of the Hasid, those who wore crystals or feathers, were marked. At one point they decided that sage-green clothing was the color of the empath, and went after anyone wearing a dress or shirt in that shade. And in fact they targeted well. Although the idea that psi capacities were a scientifically provable fact was new then, those who were beginning to explore them tended either to be part of a traditional religious community or part of the new wave of philosophies that included relearning Native American ways, or Eastern philosophies, or both. And those who supported what they called Earth-Based Ritual wore sage-green clothing, to identify themselves. They were easy targets.

The Safety Squads ended by killing themselves with their own inexpertness in handling the weapons they chose. But while they were at their work many empaths died, and many more were left with genetic damage that would plague them and their children and their children's children. The ritual leaders responded by putting their lives on the line, going out into the streets to care for the injured, bury the dead, do whatever needed to be done. It was a time that contained as much courage and grace as it did horror.

Alex had avoided the worst of it. His family bred and trained racehorses, and lived well outside the range of the city terror. They would listen to the news without being able to really comprehend what was happening in the cities, except when they felt the ripples of chaos affecting them personally. Shipment of the feed they needed was late more often than usual. Races were canceled. Jockeys were killed.

He was nineteen by the time the new President—some-one who provided real leadership instead of making speeches from his safe house in D.C.—called for a draft, and began utilizing the army for domestic service. He'd enlisted, and ended up in Manhattan, cleaning up the mess after the Safety Squads. It was here that he first found someone to help him learn to name and use his empathic abilities.

Sophia, an old Russian woman. He'd extricated her cat from the hands of an angry teenage boy, out to kill anything he could because he'd seen too many of his friends die. The boy called her a witch. She said he was right. She showed Alex a gap-toothed smile, and said he was a witch, too.

Alex got her out of the city, transporting her, along with a truckload of other older people who had managed to sur-vive thus far, to one of the churches that had opened its doors as sanctuary to the homeless, the frightened. He vis-ited with her as often as he could, and she taught him a lot. Then he began teaching himself.

He read Jung and Estes, learned the theories Jonathan Post propounded in *Unparticular Magic,* a mixture of the pragmatic and the mystic, predicting the onset of the Serials based on the author's belief that society had lost all sense of the spiritual and the ritual as a positive containing space for shadow and for light. When that happened, Post said, ritual behavior would play itself out in dangerous ways—murderous ways. He predicted that serial and ritual killing would precede a social breakdown, and that increases in acts of domestic terrorism and pointless random killings would follow.

And at some point the violence would reach critical mass, invading the population like a metastasized cancer. But by then any attempts at warding off the blow would be too late.

He had been right, but nobody listened.

The killing spree burned itself out in more than ten million dead just in the United States, and the survivors bearing the mark of that time in too many ways to count.

Clare had survived. Nick had survived. Both were scarred, perhaps beyond repair.

Jaguar had survived, but what did she have to do to stay alive?

Alex assumed that Jaguar had learned the empathic arts from her grandparents and their people, and was already practicing in a childlike way when the Serials began. That would make her even more susceptible to a lingering, chronic shadowing, similar to the kind of shadow sickness found in those who didn't observe the proper ways of making empathic contact. She would be permeable to the evil of the Serials in a different way than someone who wasn't an empath, or so young.

How had she survived, and what had she done to protect herself? Perhaps her grandfather taught her ways before he died. He had been a powerful leader of his people, both he and his wife of the rapidly dwindling Mertec tribe, spiritual and ethnic cousins of the Maya. They'd assimilated into a number of Pueblo tribes, and into mainstream culture so thoroughly that most of them didn't know where their blood ran from. But Jaguar's grandfather held one of the first UN seats for Native Americans. He had a reputation as a man of vision, and a man of peace. Alex knew he carried the arts of his people, and that his granddaughter still used them.

He hoped she was using them wisely. He hoped that whatever was bothering her about Nick had nothing to do with that.

Tonight, he found her and established a light sensory contact. Enough to see and listen in as she worked her case in the House of Mirrors.

Jaguar was laughing through her eyes, Alex could see Clare laughing as well. Then she was—what was she doing? A tingling interrupted the flow of consciousness, almost tossed him out of the empathic space, and he focused.

She was establishing empathic contact with Clare. For a moment he was tempted to jump in and see what she saw. Then he pulled back. He couldn't join her in that. She'd notice immediately, and it would probably destroy any chance she had of getting somewhere. He could only guess from watching her and Clare's face shift expression where it was they walked together.

Jaguar's face smoothed out, and—a tear? A tear? Was she crying?

"Now what?" he murmured into the quiet of the night.

"So I thought, if you know how to make a French braid, we could—" Clare stopped speaking and watched Jaguar watching herself stretch in the image-lengthening mirrors of the central room. "You're not with me tonight," she noted. "What is it?"

Jaguar turned to her and smiled. "What?"

"I said," Clare repeated, "you're distracted. Why?"

Jaguar let her arms reach out as high as they would toward the ceiling, then drop to her side. She hadn't been listening. Not paying attention. That was dangerous, and it was Nick's fault, damn him.

"I've got a few other cases on my mind," she said. "Did you want to do something with your hair? Is that what you said?" She had been spending quiet time with Clare, trying to build a relationship that established trust and boundaries. Like all dangerous animals, Clare had to be made to feel safe, and to know who was in charge.

Clare nodded and walked over to her, put a hand on her shoulder. "You work too hard. You should relax more." With her other hand, she indicated the thick white rug that covered the floor. "It's soft and clean, and if you lie down, I'll give you a back rub."

"I think," Jaguar said, "I'll pass."

"You're not afraid of me, are you?"

"No. But I'm not stupid either. You're an assassin by profession. Granted, the odds are very slim that you've been able to get any weapons in, but you still have your hands, which are beautiful and I would imagine very strong.'' This was a good opportunity to try for the alpha-female role. She'd use it.

She put her hand on the hand that held her shoulder and gripped it tightly, feeling the automatic tightening of Clare's grip in response. She squeezed further, watching Clare's face in the mirror as it concentrated.

Nothing too heavy registered yet. Just an increase in focus. An attentiveness beyond what was necessary. With a swift, imperceptible movement, Jaguar slipped her free hand around and ringed Clare's neck with it. With another flick of her wrist, she released the red glass knife she kept at her wrist, and pressed it against the carotid.

''You see?'' she said. ''It would be too easy.'' She released her hold, and Clare pushed herself away with a gasp.

Good, Jaguar thought. There is a crack in the veneer. Or else she was a consummate actress. She waited for Clare to speak.

''You're very good,'' Clare said. ''I could have used you a few times on assignments.''

Jaguar acknowledged the compliment with a slight bow. ''I have you at a disadvantage. You're my prisoner and you don't know what I mean to do with you. For all you know, my job is actually to kill you.''

She could see that Clare was paying close attention, her instincts heightened to respond to whatever might come next.

''Nobody ever talked about what went on here,'' she said. ''Not even the two men I knew who came back from here.''

''They didn't tell you?''

''They wouldn't. But they came back, so I assume some people do survive your programs.''

''Most do. Even most of mine do,'' Jaguar added. ''Even most of Nick's do. But I almost forgot, you know Nick.''

Clare blinked at her, and walked toward a mirror, where

she stopped and touched her reflection at the throat, where a red splotch was forming. "Nick?" she asked.

"Nick Lyola. You knew him as a police officer in New York. He arrested you long ago, for possession of cocaine. It was before the Serials, so you were . . . just sixteen?"

"About. Juvenile offender. Stupid kid stuff. But Nick— oh yes," she said, caressing the red spot in the mirror, as if she were trying to rub it out, or soothe it, Jaguar couldn't tell. "I remember him now. He was a lousy fuck."

Jaguar laughed. "Something else we agree on," she said. But strange, that Clare should have been sleeping with someone like Nick when she was that young. If she was sleeping with him. If it wasn't all just smoke in mirrors. She could pursue that later, when they were braiding hair or manicuring their nails. Right now she had other lines to try.

"Clare, what did Patricks want with pyrite?"

Clare turned and tilted her head. "I don't think I've ever been injured before," she said. "All these years, and not a scratch. I've prided myself on that."

"I know," Jaguar said softly. "Tell me what Patricks wanted with pyrite."

"Odd, that the first injury should be from someone I like so much. Do you think it's by way of initiation? The bite of the jaguar, or some such rite?"

Jaguar decided to try one more time. "What did Patricks want with pyrite?"

"I've only killed two women," she said, "and I didn't really enjoy the jobs. They whimpered, at the end. I don't imagine you'd whimper, would you?"

"Only if it suited my purposes," Jaguar said, giving up.

"That's what I thought." She stood with her hand on the image of her throat in the mirror, stroking it. Soothing it. Jaguar walked up behind her and turned her away from the mirror. Clare smiled, and touched Jaguar's face.

Jaguar felt the opening of opportunity here. It was too soon to go in deeply, but a good place to make the initial contact. She pressed two fingers against Clare's forehead, waiting for the hum that indicated a flow of energy between them, allowing her access beyond the wall of ice, the slick mirror surface presented here.

Clare closed her eyes, tilted her head back. Jaguar had the impression she was waiting to be kissed, or killed. She couldn't quite tell which. It didn't matter.

"Have you ever met an empath?" she asked softly, whispering into her ear.

"Yes," Clare said. "Wait. Are you—?"

"See who you are," Jaguar said. "Be what you see."

6

THEY WALKED TOGETHER DOWN THE CITY STREET, arm in arm, on a day when the air was filled with heat and the smell of urine, of sweat, of exhaust from cars.

"This isn't yours," Jaguar said, turning to Clare and touching her on the forehead.

"No," Clare said, "of course not. It's yours."

"But that's not supposed to—" she began to say, and gunfire cracked to her right. She threw Clare down to the sidewalk, flinging herself over her, bracing them both against the side of a building.

Jesus. Get down. Stay down. Keep your head covered. Christ, what's a kid like you—

Beneath her, she could hear Clare laugh. "You know where we are, then? You know *when* we are?"

Jaguar lifted her head slowly. Looked up and down the street. Saw a man raising a meat cleaver over a small yellow dog that cringed and whimpered. A common kitchen cleaver. A common dog. Manhattan. During the Serials. The Killing Times.

"No," she said. "I don't want to be here."

He brought the knife down, and his laughter howled down the street to them.

"We have to—to leave here. We have to leave." Jaguar

saw that the man with the knife was locked in struggle with
a policeman who was trying to stop him, small-yellow-dog
body lying mutilated on the street. One leg gone. Back split.
Blood. More blood.

The men struggled for the knife. Raised and lowered it.
Raised and lowered it. More blood. Always more blood.
This time, the policeman won. Then he turned toward Jag-
uar. Turned toward Jaguar and Clare, cleaver raised.

"There's no way out, Jaguar," Clare said, matter-of-fact.
Calm and cool as silver and ice. "You know that."

"I got out," Jaguar said. "I escaped."

Clare laughed. "Did you?"

Jaguar stood, and raised Clare to her feet. "I went that
way," she said, pointing west. Due west. She knew nothing
else, except that she once lived in the west with her grandparents, when she was very young, before her grandfather
started working for the UN.

They had lived in the west, and she headed west, directly
into a live wire. Directly into Nick.

"We have to leave," she said.

The man with the cleaver walked toward them slowly,
eyes filled with dog blood, with his own blood, with the
blood of a longing for murder.

A woman in white—nurse? nun? just a woman in
white?—called out to him.

Hey. Hey—what're you—

"No," Jaguar yelled, hand out in gesture of protest as if
she could stop this as if she could do anything about it as
if her rage her fear her hope her anything mattered here.
"Stop—he'll—"

The cleaver went up and came down in an arc that caught
the sun at the edge of it, splitting light and flesh and bone
and the woman, head shattered, stood for a moment, held
up by gravity, a meaningless grin on her face. She looked
at Jaguar before she fell.

Before she fell, over and over as she fell in Jaguar's
dreams sometimes. As she fell, again and again.

"That's the way it was, right?" Clare said, observing the scene with equanimity.

That's the way it was. You started by killing to save a life, and ended by becoming the killer you'd saved someone from. Someone finding the bodies would kill four more. There was a wild contagion about it, and people tried to outdo each other in terms of what horrific act they could employ next. So many cops were killed after a while that they wouldn't work the beats anymore, wouldn't respond to calls. The National Guard was called out, but they just made more bodies in the streets, mostly the wrong ones. The killers and the vigilantes, now one and the same, knew how to slip through the dark sides of the buildings and get away.

"That's the way it was," Jaguar repeated.

A crack to her right. Jesus. Again. What—down. Get down. Stay down.

You gotta get inside, kid. Can't you call someone to get you? Cover your goddamn head, will you?

A man's voice. An older man. Fat and with a scruffy growth of gray stubble on his face. He saw her walking home from school on the last day she went to school. She blinked up at him, and heard the sound of gunfire. His eyes grew wide, arms flung out, torso convulsing, and his chest exploded. Blood spattered her face and the front of her shirt as she backed away slowly, then turned and ran.

"Clare," Jaguar gasped. "Why are we here?"

"We're here because *you're* here. Some part of you is still here."

"But I don't understand. We should be where you were during the Serials."

"I?" Clare said, surprised. "I was . . . home. Studying art."

A brief image of Clare, younger and even more beautiful, animated, with pastels smeared all over her hand, standing in front of a wide sheet of paper where flowers blossomed into skyscrapers and water fell from a hand, pouring over steel encased in vines.

It wavered and disappeared, leaving them crouched against the side of the building, gunfire cracking on the streets.

What had happened? She'd established normal empathic contact, expecting any number of scenes. Expecting nothing. Expecting anything but this, her own life reflected in a killer's mind.

"Wait," she said. "Wait—*why* is this?"

"Because," Clare said. "That's my gift."

Clare. Pure light. Her eyes, suddenly silver and only refracting, giving back what they saw. Who she was. Her gift. The gift of reflection.

"I don't let anyone do this," Jaguar said. "I don't let anyone see this."

"But you let yourself see it," Clare noted. "And that's all that matters here."

Jaguar raised herself up and saw that she was staring into the doorway of the apartment building she'd lived in as a child.

"No," Jaguar said. "Not this. I won't—"

"Do you know what day it is?" Clare asked.

No.

Not here. Not this. She would not allow it. She turned and rocked on her heels in front of Clare, raised her hands, and pressed them hard against her head.

Focus. Focus. Pour yourself out. Empty yourself and find her.

She felt a twisting, as if she was being turned inside out. Her vision distorted, faces breaking into component parts and limbs and torsos bent impossibly around angles and corners of a familiar house. Familiar home.

A home. The home she lived in with her grandparents in Manhattan. Cool, clean apartment, four stories up.

Parts reassembled, and she was in the apartment. Her mouth open to ask Clare where, when they were now, but no words emerged. The windows were open, and curtains blew in and out in silence. Clare left her side, strolling toward the round mirror that hung over the back of the couch.

In the mirror, Clare mouthed words at her, gesturing.

Silence. No sound here. Just vision.

Jaguar followed where her arm pointed as men walked in.

They're dead.

No sound. No words. Just her mouth moving.

All dead men. Men she knew. Men she'd seen killed in the streets. A young boy she'd stayed with during part of her year on the streets. Aaron. A boy. Just a boy. Then, dead men from the streets, prisoners who had died, more little boys, more men. All dead men.

Clare, mouthing words.

No sound.

Jaguar watching the dead, the silent dead, the dead who would not die, who walked into the living room, into her home, into her. Into her.

No sound.

They didn't speak. Dead eyes, staring into her as if they lived there, silent and walking, circling her like buzzards, but they were the dead ones and she was alive. She was alive.

She turned to Clare, tried to tell her.

I'm alive. I don't belong here. I'm alive.

Clare outside, staring at the mirror, at her own face, her lips moving in reflection.

What? What are you saying? I can't see.

Clare, turning her around, turning her toward the center of the room, pointing.

There. Her grandfather, body riddled with decaying bullet holes.

There, in back of him, Alex, gaping wound at the side of his head.

Alex?

No. No. No.

She shouted, but only silence emerged, reverberating and final.

The dead men spiraled in toward her, circling tighter and tighter, hands stretched out in gestures of pleading or violence.

Clare laughed into the mirror. Jaguar took off her shoe and flung it at the mirror, saw it shatter in a space emptied of sound. The mirror shattering and dead men falling all around, like glass flying out, here and there, catching the sun at their edges.

The mirror shattering, and Clare, laughing silently, spinning away from the flying bits of glass and spinning toward her like an endless centrifugal center, spinning madly in silence, and Jaguar, arms out, waiting for her, to catch her or be caught by the silent motion of her dance.

"Cool beans, baby," Nick said as he stretched himself languorously on his couch, arms resting behind his head.

This was so much easier than any other kind of empathic contact he'd made, it was ridiculous. All he'd had to do was find her signals, and he was there with her, and she was there with Clare. He'd been able to see the whole thing, and even add a few touches of his own at the end.

There was none of the effort to find and occupy the space, none of the frightening feel of pouring yourself out into an endless hole. He just had to turn his thoughts, and he was part of the action.

Alex being there. That was good. A nice touch, and one that he'd have to try again. Maybe it'd show her that even the exalted Alex was expendable. Though why she exalted him was something Nick never understood. It wasn't like he'd ever done anything for her except stay out of her way. Wasn't like he knew what it meant to survive what Jaguar had survived. What Nick had survived.

That was where Jaguar had it all wrong. She didn't understand that she belonged with Nick, or with someone like him at least. Another survivor. They were both survivors, and they understood what it took to stay alive in a world that hated you, would eat you if it could. She knew that, but she kept trying to walk away from knowing it. The only reason she tried to walk away from him was so she could forget the shit the world was made of.

And she'd been like that from the first day he found her, scratching at his face and eyes when he was just trying to save her, point out the danger. She'd be dead if he hadn't done that, and she'd be dead if he didn't teach her how to take care of herself for the rest of the time she stayed in the old schoolhouse the rescue crew had converted into a temporary shelter.

She was no more than thirteen then, thin as a split end, her eyes looking bigger in her face because of her thinness. She only spoke to answer questions.

"How long you been wandering, kid?"

A quick glance up at the sky. Counting suns. Counting moons. "About a year."

"Your people dead?"

"Yes."

"How'd they die?"

"They were killed."

Nothing more. That was all. But in her eyes was something sharp and bright. Something that burned hot as dry ice.

She kept herself to herself, and he saw how attentive she was to her surroundings, how closely she observed the people around her. She had a sharp instinct for self-preservation, or else she wouldn't have survived this long.

Then, for no reason, she'd get stupid. One day he was handing out the food for the day—not much, because getting anyone to transport food this far inside the city lines was difficult—and he saw her look up from her plate of bread and processed-cheese food, over to the corner where an old man sat rocking and singing to himself.

Some people saw too much, and just went away, Nick

knew. Best to let them be. Eventually, they died, and it was one less mouth to feed.

Jaguar stared at the old man, and Nick watched her, saw how little her eyes gave away. Then she stood up, walked over to the man, put her plate down, and started picking off pieces of cheese, putting them into his mouth.

"Hey—what the hell're you doing?"

Wide eyes. Saying nothing. Seeing everything. "I'm feeding him." As if that was normal.

"Listen, I can't give you more food until tomorrow."

No words. Her eyes, saying so what?

He tried something else, leaning down to her, whispering into her ear. "He's dying. He's not gonna make it. Can't you see that?"

Her eyes, saying so what?

Then, he got angry, grabbed her plate, grabbed her, and dragged her away from him. He plunked her down on her cot and held her by the shoulders, held her eyes with his own, and saw . . . something.

Something bright and burning in a sea of green. Like fire inside green ice. Like the sun, stuck inside an iceberg. Like nothing he'd ever seen before.

He let go of her shoulders, then stood up and shook his head at her. "Christ, kid. You're not strong enough to be giving your food away. Look at you—another wind'd take you away. Besides, it gives the others ideas. They'll start taking from you. I mean, who the hell do you think you are—Mother Teresa?"

"Who's that?" she asked.

Then he laughed. She was too young to remember that name. It meant nothing to her. He walked away, laughing and shaking his head. About an hour later he saw that she was back with the old man, feeding him bits of cheese, her green-ice eyes burning into him.

She didn't get it then, and she didn't get it now. But maybe he had one more lesson to teach her, after all.

He yawned, and stretched his arms out, feeling his stomach turn over as he did so.

The only problem he'd found so far was that the implant made him queasy. Either that or his dinner packet had spoiled in the microfreeze. He never did understand how to work those things, and when chicken went bad, it went really bad.

Even if it wasn't the chicken, queasiness was a small price to pay for what he could do now. He could find her anywhere. Anytime. And she couldn't escape. That'd be the lesson he'd teach her, and she deserved it, too. Refusing to back him up. After everything he did for her, everything he taught her. She owed him her life, and he was cashing in his chips.

She thought she could get away from anything, and with anything. She'd see this time. There wasn't any escape. Never had been. Never would be.

"I got plans for us, Jag." He chuckled. "You and me, meeting in ways you simply cannot imagine, or avoid."

Life, Nick decided, was good.

"Shit," Adrian said with heartfelt sincerity as he slammed the door shut behind him, tripping over the edge of the rug and stumbling into the living room. He caught himself, pressed hard against the wall, and looked up to see Jaguar staring at him from the middle of the room, arms crossed on her chest.

She'd heard him come in, and had gathered herself together as much as she could before meeting him. Having gathered herself, she only hoped she would hold. When she left Clare, she felt rough at all her edges, and it wasn't getting better fast. Two at once. Too many, and this last one maybe too many all by itself.

"Hard day at the con game, dear?" she asked, flashing a mocking smile at him.

"S'all crap," he said, coming toward her, still stumbling. Drunk, Jaguar thought. He'd taken whatever money he

had left after trying to buy off the doctors she'd sent him
to, and tied one on. Like father, like son. At least she was
making progress with this one.

She waited until he was almost on top of her, then side-
stepped, sending him off balance toward the round table in
the alcove, where he caught himself and propped himself
upright.

"Goddammit," he said, "stand still."

"I am standing still," she insisted as he lunged for her
again. This time she leaned back, then caught him as he
overbalanced toward her.

He let his weight fall heavily against her, his face pressed
into her shoulder, his hands running up and down her back.
"Nice," he crooned, now amorous.

"Where'd you learn to drink?" she said into his available ear. "From your father?"

He pulled himself up and brought his face close to hers.
She thought he would do this, and she caught his eyes with
hers, pressing into the place where he remembered who he
was, how he saw himself, how he hated that self he saw.

But this time, he raised his hand and pushed her face
away.

"Stop that shit," he spit out. "Get the fuck out of my
mind."

Jaguar released him and took two steps back, expecting
him to fall. But he didn't. He straightened himself, rage
creating a semblance of sobriety.

"I went to everyone on that list," he said, walking toward her, backing her toward the wall, "and they were all
dead, or didn't exist, or didn't know what I was talking
about. One woman tried to turn a trick with me, dammit.
Then you—pushing into me, fucking with my mind."

"What do you mean by that, Adrian?" she asked, calm
now. Something was wrong here. He had no empathic ability, and shouldn't be able to name the feeling of contact at
this point. She knew his history, and it was strictly middle
of the road. Strictly from people who thought the empathic

arts were the realm of freaks and circus performers. How could he name what she was doing? When did he learn to do that?

"I mean," he said, "you're trying to get *in* me. I can feel you, with your fingers and your eyes. I can feel it, like some goddamn electric circuit zapping me. You're— you've got some kind of drug you're giving me, or one of those probes the testers use."

He waved a hand in her face, pressing close to her. "You're not a crazy cop," he said. "You're just crazy. You do this for fun."

She relaxed, now. He thought she was using technology to get to him, torture him. That was good. Raise his tension level. Bring out all the fears at once. She stopped to see if she was up to it, then realized it didn't matter if she was or not. Frayed and rough and she had better be ready, because here it was.

She laughed at him, and pushed him back, away from her. "Gee, Adrian," she said. "Maybe I'm not a crazy cop. Maybe I'm one of those—you know—empaths. Shh. Don't tell. Does that scare you? They say that empaths, when they blow, blow big. Messing inside all those sick minds. Some people think empaths caused the Serials, you know. Maybe your father was dipping his stick in one, and that's why he killed your mother. What do you think, Adrian? Did you ever see that when you were a little boy? Hmm?"

"Jesus, you're sick," he said, disgusted.

"Not as sick as you," she reminded him, and pulled him close. "Because you still want me, don't you? Even now, when you think I'm using probes on your brain. You can't stay away from me."

She pressed herself against his groin, feeling the rising heat there, in spite of whatever alcohol he'd consumed.

Then Clare's face made an appearance in her consciousness, laughing without sound.

That silence, and the smell of dead men all through her, invading her again.

They're all prisoners. Every last one of them.

Goddammit, what if they are? What of it? What should I do—go back to Nick?

She pressed closer to Adrian, anger rising in her like a wave to meet and crash against his own impotent rage.

"You eat my sickness like the people you con eat the death you feed them," she said, her own voice seething. "Or like they would, if you could find any. If you could do anything right. You're just like your father, aren't you, little boy?"

Adrian backed away from her, his face a study in revulsion. He wasn't angry anymore. Just repulsed.

"Jesus," he said, "who knocked you around too much? You poke at me about the Serials, but what the hell are you sitting on?"

She reached to him and grabbed his face hard, shook it.

How dare he. Con man selling snake oil to dying people. How dare he? She felt as if any coolness of character she possessed had been pulled into the vortex of Clare's ice ego, and all that remained was her fire, burning over the boiling point for reasons she couldn't discern.

"What the fuck do you want, anyway?" Adrian growled at her.

What did she want?

They're all prisoners. All of them.

"Nothing," she said, "I want nothing from you, or anybody."

And in anger, she pulled him close and kissed him hard.

The Looker sat at the desk in his hotel room, considering the solitaire layout in front of him.

"Much too much in the way of red," he muttered. There was nothing he could move here. Nothing he could shift. Nothing he could do.

He leaned back and riffled the cards in his hand with his thumb.

Diamonds and hearts. Hearts and diamonds. No aces, unless he had one in his hand that was still hidden.

He began pulling from the deck.

More hearts. More diamonds.

Too much red.

His eye was briefly distracted by the blip of a small light on his comlink, a closed-line circuit that ran directly from the Research Center to his files.

He frowned at it, shifted his glasses on his nose, and reached over to flip it open.

He'd told the center not to attempt contact with him except under emergency situations. Though his line was the most secure on the home planet or the planetoids, he didn't want to take any chances. There was too much at stake. And too much had gone wrong already.

He was disturbed at the failed attempts to have Clare disposed of properly, not sure if it was bad luck or bad strategy that caused the trouble. It seemed like the bad end to a series of bad moves that had started with the decision to buy Governor Patricks. Of course, it made sense at the time to do that, and seemed a simple enough business deal to negotiate. They would use their influence to push the sale of the preservation land through so he could have his casinos and, through a complex series of intermediaries, see that he received a generous campaign contribution. He would ensure mining rights and a good price for the pyrite on the land in question. It took a good deal of the raw ore to make one transmission chip, due to the particular chemical process involved in activating its potential for e-wave transmission, and they wanted all they could get, as cheaply as they could get it.

His group had been pleased at the mutually beneficial agreement, but the Governor reneged on his part of it and began talking about taxing the ore, partly to reassure his constituency that the destruction of the preservation land would generate enough money to justify its loss, but partly to remind the Division who was in charge.

There was no point in continuing a business relationship

with such a man. He obviously had no honor. Fortunately, the Lieutenant Governor who now held the office was much more trustworthy in these matters.

But Clare had gotten caught. Of all people, Clare—the best they had, on the most simple assignment. She'd done so many hypodermic bubble deaths without leaving a mark, and to leave her—her panties. The Looker had been particularly offended by the tears of the outraged, betrayed Governor's wife. Such scandal it created. Such noise, and visibility. His group had never allowed one of their assignments to become so public, and so messy.

Clare had talked openly on the witness stand when she didn't have to, but at least she mentioned no names. Her motives were always mysterious, elusive, as she was. Although the absolute mastery she could gain over a man or woman looked like telepathic work, she had no empathic ability, no psi capacities, and all attempts at empathic intervention with her failed. The Looker often itched to get his hands inside her brain and do the surgery necessary for a thorough examination. When they got her back to the center and debriefed her, he would try to avoid any cortical damage. At least then he could obtain a postmortem read of her. Of course that would render her useless as a subject in his primary research, but one had to make difficult choices sometimes.

He glanced at his solitaire layout and pulled a card. A black jack, which would go on the red queen. But then, he had two red tens. He had to decide which one to move, and he knew that this decision could determine the outcome of the whole game. One wrong move was all it took.

The wrong choice at the wrong time and you were lost. Then all you could do was . . . cheat. If even that failed, you could only hope to fold and walk away. Walk away quietly, and preferably while you were still breathing.

The Division was set up to ensure, as much as possible, that this happened. More than any other intelligence group, they had created a working order that provided a shield of invisibility for their people. They had no central headquarters. Reports on research and on completed assignments were made via computer line only, to coded compuboxes that served as the first in a series of relays. Where they ended up was a matter for speculation. He assumed it was NICA, when he bothered to think about it at all. To him, it didn't really matter.

All he knew was that he'd been approached by a nondescript man in a blue suit whom he'd never seen again, when he was working for the Pentagon, on psi research. The man offered him an opportunity to make progress in the field of his interest beyond his wildest dreams. Any support he wanted would be his. He'd have access to the materials he needed, a contingent of lab workers, a quiet house that they'd find and equip for him, but which he would own as his personal home.

All he had to do in return was work with a specified number of outside assignments each year, acting as liaison, transferring messages and collecting information from the liaisons they had specified as his contacts.

It was perfect.

They'd found him a caretaker's house in an unused cemetery, just outside a park where children played. He was close enough to the major research centers to utilize their resources if he needed to, and obscure enough that no one would pay any attention to the nature of the work he did. The Division was big on obscurity, and he was glad. Some people, he knew, were squeamish, and found his line of research unnerving.

Of course, he wasn't exactly comfortable with his interactions with Clare, though she was a fine source of material for his work. Like Terence, he'd resisted the notion of working with an assassin. He had hoped to obtain his research material from hospitals and morgues, or from donor programs. But when it had been explained to him—over the coded line through an unnamed source—that this would increase the Division's visibility and decrease their control, he'd agreed to let Clare be his supplier. He firmly believed that the absence of governmental control had created the onslaught of the Serials. He'd go far to see that control protected and maintained.

The sort of power they were exploring in their research needed to be guarded, kept in the hands of those who knew how to use it, as he did. As the Division did. Psi capacities needed monitoring and technological control. Monitoring and control were the keys to safety in all things.

That was how he'd survived the Serials.

He holed up in a basement in Denver while devastation raged in the streets. He had stocked in food for a year, and every day ate exactly what he needed. No more. No less. He disciplined his body through exercise, and kept his sanity by reading the classics and writing about them. He kept a scientific journal of possible experiments, formulas, ideas, so that he wouldn't forget who he was, what his job should be.

He had a new solar-fed system for his viewer, and so he could watch the news, monitor the progress of the killing, gauge how much longer it might last. He wasn't sure, at one point, which would run out first—his food, or the violence—but in the end, he'd calculated almost perfectly when to come back out.

After eleven months in hiding, he deemed it safe enough to leave his basement in search of food.

By then, the killing in Denver had subsided, though the East Coast was still rioting. He remembered the glare of sunlight—how foreign it seemed. The feel of its warmth, and his realization that his skin must be bleached white by now.

When his eyes adjusted, he looked around and saw that the street was strewn with bodies, rotting and covered with maggots and flies. He particularly remembered a cat, scrawny and almost hairless from mange, licking at the blue and putrefying hand of a young girl.

At least, he thought, she won't go to waste.

Because what horrified him most was the waste. All those bodies. All those dead bodies, and he knew that Denver's death rate was lower than other cities'. Bodies that just ceased functioning, just stopped acting in the world. A small hole in the chest and it was all over. Death was such a waste of manpower, of womanpower, of the machinery of the body.

That was when he conceived of the idea he continued researching to this day, and would continue to research until he died, at which point he would donate his body to the ongoing work. Many years passed between that moment and the day when a man in a blue suit approached him with the opportunity to carry out the work, but here he was today, actually doing it. Pseudogenics. Instilling kinesis into dead bodies through e-wave amplifiers. Letting someone else's mind become the central control for the dead. Within a week, he expected to see his research become a reality capable of application.

Now he waited while a series of pictoglyphs scrolled across his computer screen. The people at the research center wouldn't do this unless the news was important. When the green light on the screen ceased its blip, indicating the end of communication, he read through the code, deciphered it, and then smiled.

"Good news for a change," he murmured at the screen. "Project developments."

Subjects had responded to the simple set of instructions issued through the central amplifier. The amplifier was not breaking up its wave frequency, and the transmitters were stable. Researchers were now increasing the complexity level of instructions according to the Looker's protocol.

That was very good. *Very* good. So much invested. So much risked. And now, it would pay off. Pseudogenics would change the world, and he would be in control of that change. He would be the one who had the foresight to see it through.

And once research established ways of creating a central

amplification of telepathic commands, they could try again with live subjects, which had proved difficult up until now. Working with the dead cut down on the variables and simplified the human subject to its basic neurological necessities. It was the best place to start, but from there, the Division could go anywhere.

He would be pleased when he could get off this Planetoid and get back to the center. Of course, if this crisis wasn't averted, there might not be a center to get back to. He was aware that Clare had to be dealt with first. And this Addams woman. He wished the range of the central amplifier was long enough to reach her here, but it wasn't yet. Still, it would be interesting to see how the transmitters worked between two empaths vying for control. Every problem contained its own opportunities for learning as well.

The screen ceased its blip, and he reached over with his left hand, typing in a simple code.

"Continue," was the translation of his response. Just continue.

Then he went back to his game, reshuffling the cards and starting again.

7

WHEN SHE LEFT THE HOUSE FOR HER GIG, SHE WAS feeling even worse. Adrian had been unable to perform, which was good for the case, but bad for her. She was surprised at the level of anger she felt at him, and unsure what its source was. Perhaps the contact with Clare—that ice against her fire, melting and cooling her and then causing her to charge up to high in order to compensate.

She'd almost blown it, out of an inability to gather her seams in and stay cool. Now the postempathic feeling, which was generally euphoric, made her feel shocky instead. As if she'd been hit hard in the jaw. Something was wrong. Something was not working the way it was supposed to.

Was this how shadow sickness started, and had she picked it up from Nick somehow? She'd been very careful, blocking him hard and sure.

Something was wrong.

The streets were dark and not much traffic interrupted the flow of her thoughts, which were all also dark. She walked fast, the heels of her thigh-high boots clicking hard against the pavement. Something was wrong. All her instincts told her something was wrong. What?

She slowed her pace, walking toe to heel to quiet her own steps. Was that someone following her? She stopped to gaze into a store window, waiting for the sound of footsteps that slowed and then stopped. She ought to know how to recognize a tail by now, even if it was someone as good as Nick.

Though it might not be Nick. It could be someone Clare's people sent. Someone who didn't want Clare to talk. Wanted to—

In her peripheral vision, she saw the movement of shadow against building. Someone following her. She would stand a minute and think what to do next. The store window reflected her face dimly, in translucent echo of herself, eyes wide and alert.

Jesus, she told herself, calm down. A tail is nothing to get that excited about.

Then why were all her neurons firing at once? What was it she felt getting closer and—

"Shit," she said, "too late."

Reflected in the window, Nick walked up and put a hand on her shoulder.

"Ready or not," he said, "here I am."

She brought her leg out for a roundhouse kick, but he was gone.

Gone?

"Nick?" she said. He was there.

Wasn't he?

She stood and listened to her own breathing, letting air flow into her. Something—was it what happened with Clare? What the hell was it with this case, anyway?

She felt the hand on her shoulder again. Behind her. She whirled.

"Nick, what is this shit?" she demanded of his image as it stood, seemingly encased in the window she stared at.

"Maybe you're losing it, baby," he suggested. "Maybe it's not me that's got troubles. Maybe it's you."

She raised her chin up, her jaw growing tight and firm. "I doubt it," she said.

Then laughter, and an explosion.

Explosion.

No. A hand hitting. No.

Implosion. She felt herself sucked into a whirlpool of darkness. Her own face disappearing from the window. There. Not there. Where? Nick, laughing triumphantly, and she carried away in his laughter, drowning in shadows and a tumbling darkness.

Falling. She was falling, hit hard or dragged down into whirlpools and eddies. Voices whispered her name as she fell, tumbling through something infinite and dark and where would she land would she break into a thousand pieces or fall into water and drown she didn't know.

What makes you think you can escape? You better than everyone else?

Fool, she cursed herself as she fell. Time to think. Enough time of falling and then . . . a hand. A voice. Nick. Hand on her shoulder.

She, still in that darkness, dizzy and swaying, something hurt. What—her shoulder? Her head? Hard to breathe here. She twisted toward him with great effort and heard his voice, slowed like a broken tape, laughing at her, Nick pointing at something.

Pointing at.

Pointing at . . . there.

A gun firing. A gun firing. A gun firing and she flinched with the sound of each bullet. Blood everywhere. Not again. Yes, again.

Her grandfather, falling. Blood and he was falling, like a great tree. Falling over and over again. Nick pushing her into the blood. An ocean of blood and she was screaming, falling again into the ocean of blood drowning her drowning her. Couldn't breathe here in the blood in all this blood.

Nick, you asshole. What the hell is this?

There was his laughter, slowed and dropped in pitch.

Who do you think you are, Our Lady of the Empathic Arts?

Empathic contact. It was empathic contact. Some part of her was standing on a street, looking in a store window. She hoped it was most of her. And she wouldn't let him do this. He wasn't practiced enough, hadn't the skill or the strength to work this powerfully inside of her. *Inside* of her. Or was she inside of him?

She could pull herself out of it. She knew enough. She'd been taught by the best.

Her grandfather, his hand pressed against her forehead.

Her grandmother, handing her mint. The fresh scent of mint, covering the rotting smell of death.

Where is your darkness, Jaguar?

Her darkness. If she swam up, looked for the light. The streetlight. Some light. Her eyes were somewhere and could turn toward it. Push, she told herself. Focus. There's a light out there somewhere.

There was a streetlight. She focused, reached up and out, hand touching something cold. It was her hand, slapping out at something cold. She reached for it, felt nothing, but kept reaching, kept slapping until her mouth found air and she gasped in breath.

Nick, cursing her, grabbing for her, feeling her slip away.

"No," she gasped, sucking in air, swaying hard, her hand touching something cold.

She slapped her hand against it, whatever it was, cold and hard and real. Now punched out as hard as she could, heard a shattering and the alarms going off everywhere.

The alarms?

She blinked hard, gazed down at her hand, and saw it was bleeding. Looked around and saw that she was standing in front of the shop window, which she'd broken, setting off the burglar alarms.

"Dammit," she said, watching the blood drip, "now what?"

Wings zoomed in low and flanked her as she stood. A

man and a woman in uniform pulled stun guns and pointed them at her. A third woman emerged from the back of the wings and approached her, talking as she came.

"Hands in front. You're under arrest," she said, and Jaguar felt the slap and sting of the electrode cuffs around her wrists.

"Why'd they put me in the museum?" Jaguar stared at Alex, who stood on the other side of the freestanding iron jail cell, hands behind his back, rocking back and forth on his heels and pointedly not smiling.

Behind him, models of prisoners dressed in gray, ill-fitting jumpsuits occupied other such cells. A view screen showed old footage of prison riots from pre-Serial days. Jaguar stretched languorously across a thinly padded steel-frame cot, her narrow face framed by the lines of steel bars.

She supposed Alex had been dragged away from a date to get her out, and that he wasn't happy about it. She figured Gerry wouldn't be too happy about her failure to appear at the gig, either.

The Planetoid police were required to hold whomever they picked up until they were cleared by a Supervisor. They didn't always know if they were part of a Teachers' program, or if the person they arrested was a prisoner, or a Teacher. They had a series of holding cells in the basements of their offices, but Jaguar had been brought here, to the prison history exhibit at the city's museum.

"You have a reputation for breaking the computerized locks on the other holding cells, Jaguar," he said, and he raised his hand in the gesture of the empath. She was, he had to admit, very good with a lock. But iron was beyond even her will to bend.

"Nice to know I'm good at something." She leaned back on the cot, bringing her legs up under her, her bandaged hand cradled in the curve of her arm. Alex half expected her to start licking it.

"What happened?" he asked.

"I was followed," she said.

"By whom?"

"Nick."

"I had him checked. Hasn't left his house all night."

"He followed me."

Alex tapped his foot, and she turned a Cheshire-cat grin on him.

"Is something wrong?" she said.

"Of course there is."

"I'm alive," she mentioned, by way of good news.

"And I doubt that you deserve to be."

"Well, if that's the question, let me know when you figure out who has the answer. How've you been?" she asked amiably.

"Fine. Bored, without any reports from you," he said. It had been a week since she sent anything through to him. "How's it going with Adrian?"

"Right on target, as usual. He's about prime for intervention."

"And you?"

"Me?"

"Are you about prime for intervention?"

She rolled over on her back and lay staring at the ceiling, saying nothing. The sound of footsteps could be heard coming down the hall, and Alex waited until they stopped in front of the cell.

"Have her right outta there for you, Supervisor," the guard said, turning a massive key in the lock. "You'll need to sign some papers."

"Send them to me. I'm in a hurry."

"I was told—"

"Send them to me."

The guard shrugged and left, and Alex swung the door wide open. Jaguar slowly lifted herself from the cot and stood, stretched, walked over to him, past him, and out the door.

She would have continued down the hall, but he stopped

her by putting a hand on her shoulder and turning her toward him.

They stood and stared at each other, still saying nothing. His hand, unconscious of his intent, began massaging her shoulders lightly. Then he picked up her bandaged hand and let it rest in his, examining it.

"Does it hurt?" he asked quietly.

She blinked in surprise. She had prepared her defenses, but not for this. His kindness and her own fatigue made her more vulnerable than anger ever could. She wished she had more of Clare's coolness right now. That absence of passion—of any emotion at all—would seem like such a blessed relief.

"Nice of you to ask," she said at last, keeping her tone light. "After putting me on two cases at once and ignoring the maniac who wants to hang my hide as a personal trophy on his wall."

He let go of her hand and frowned at his own instead. "Jaguar, Nick didn't leave his house tonight."

"He followed me, Alex. Either you believe that, or you can go ahead and call me a liar."

"I could call you tired, Jaguar. And I could pull you from the Rilasco case."

"What does that mean?"

"It means, I'm concerned about your capacity to handle two at once, especially with one of them as difficult as Clare."

"No," she said sharply. "You will not pull me from Clare."

"Why not?"

"Because there's not another Teacher on this Planetoid who could get as far as I have, and you know it. She's not—as she was described by the testers."

"How do you describe her, then?"

"Reflexively," she said cryptically, and flashed him a brief smile.

"How helpful," he said. "So explain the discrepancy

between Nick being at home and your contention that he followed you.''

"I can't. Not yet. I'm speculating that something's affected—'' She glanced up and down the hall, then continued, quietly. "Alex, could Adrian's implant have an effect on empathic space or capacity? It's never happened before, but I know there's a new kind in use. What's in those things anyway?''

He narrowed his eyes at her, suspicious that this was an attempt to deflect his attention from the issues at hand. She looked entirely serious, and he considered the possibility.

"I'm not sure how it could be, Jaguar," he said. "They're just a combination of conductive metals and a chemical coating sensitive to changes in the transmitter. They operate on the same amplification system that the testing equipment for psi capacity operates on.''

"Superluminary transfer of information," Jaguar said. "I know that. Transferring information across either space or time separations at a speed equal to or greater than light. That's why the psi testing is so crappy. You can't conduct along something as complex as the cerebral cortex with transmitters designed for three-line variables. They just can't account for the webbing of energy involved.''

"Jaguar—you've been reading.''

"I learned how as a child, Alex, and have been practicing regularly ever since. And the superluminary stuff interests me. It's related to the empathic arts. An attempt to explain them in a way that satisfies the requirements of quantum physics. Like the human energy field.''

"No offense meant. I'm just never sure what goes on inside the complexity of your own cerebral cortex. At any rate, implants work because they're only utilizing one or two neurological pathways. With psi testing, they're overreaching the limits of technology.''

"And what about taps—like the one you wanted to put in me.''

"They're a little different. Not much. There's an amplification requirement that you don't need for implants, and since it's supposed to pick up verbal interactions, they have to be sited differently, pick up on a three-line rather than the one line of the implants.''

''Do they work?''

''For the most part. Of course, with your tendency to blow things up, I'm not sure how long it would have lasted in you, but that's a different matter.''

''Stupid,'' she said. ''Trying to do with technology what the human mind can do all on its own, thank you very much. Superluminary transfer of information—technobabble for telepathy, though they won't admit it. But what're they *made* of? Plastic? Crystal?''

''Actually, mostly pyrite, I think. The new ones, anyway. And the taps. The old ones were transistors, but they broke down so frequently that—''

''Pyrite?'' she asked.

''Yes. A naturally occurring ore found in—''

''Fool's gold?'' she asked.

''Of course, they have to distill out any of the complementary ores. And it has to be the right kind of pyrite.''

''The kind found in abundance near Leadville, Colorado?'' she asked.

Alex stopped speaking, and narrowed his eyes at her. ''What?'' he asked.

And she shut up like a clam.

He saw her close down swiftly, surely, and what appeared to be permanently.

''Jaguar,'' he said, ''what?''

The eyes she turned to him were veiled, and under the veil was a brightness that could have been triumph. The certainty that at last you understand. The fierce pleasure of the hunt, which she tasted in her wild soul like no one else he knew. But she wasn't one to share her prey, once caught. He wasn't sure if that was just distrust, or if it was an animal instinct in her, guarding the meat until she could chew it at her leisure, and alone.

"You're going to tell me, aren't you?"

She lowered her eyes, and raised them, catlike in their neutrality. "Tell you what?" she asked.

"I've gotten nothing from you all week, and I want to know what's going on. I want the works, and I want it fast. Don't," he said. "Just don't argue with me."

He raised two fingers and pressed them to her forehead.

She didn't pull away from him, but he could feel everything in her close. All of it, closed down, shut tight, marked clearly DO NOT ENTER.

Her eyes flashed anger at him, and he pulled away, held his hands at his sides in tight fists.

"If you want a report," she said coldly, "I'll give you one."

He felt cold himself. Her secrecy and hiddenness, her capacity for silence, were becoming a real problem. How could you get anything done if the people who worked for you engaged in them as much as the people who were working against you.

He stepped back from her and pointed a finger in her face. "Jaguar, this is bullshit, and it's got to stop. I know you've made empathic contact with Clare, and I know Rachel's doing research for you that I'd call questionable at best. You think your silence creates safety, but it doesn't. It just makes the work more difficult."

"And do you tell me everything you're up to?" she shot back at him. "How about the way you watch me when you think I can't tell? The contact you make every night. You don't tell me that. You just go ahead and cover your ass. And who's left to cover mine?"

So she'd felt his contact. Score a point for her. But he had a play of his own to try.

"Is that your fear, Jaguar? Is that what's left for you from the Serials?"

"What business is it of yours?"

He could feel the hiss and spark of her anger. She never spoke about that to him, or to anyone. Never let anyone see or know what had happened to her, beyond the fact that her family had been killed. She reached into her pocket, and when her hand emerged, he could see it held a dried leaf of mint. She consulted it, shook her head, then raised grim eyes to his.

"You want to know what I did in the Serials?" she asked, dangerously quiet, smiling her perfectly beautiful smile. "I'll tell you if it means so much to you. After my grandparents were killed, I lived in the streets. I took up with a boy I met at the curb. A boy named Aaron. We found an alley with a vent that we'd crawl into and sleep in all day. At night, we hunted."

Alex kept himself quiet. He'd asked for this, now he'd have to take it. But he had a feel in his mouth like he was holding a very bitter pill at the back of his tongue.

"We hunted," Jaguar continued, "for food. Any food we could get. Aaron got really good at catching rats. He'd catch them, and wring their necks very fast, like this." She made a twisting motion with her hands, stepping closer to him as she did so. "He had these gold monogrammed napkins—I don't know if they were leftovers from his family or what, but he'd wrap the rats in them and bring them back to me, so we could skin them, eat them."

"Jaguar," Alex interrupted, "I saw this. I saw children doing this when I was in Manhattan."

"Good," she said, "then it doesn't shock you to hear it, right? Right? And I can tell you the rest—that one week we had no luck catching anything, finding anything. Then Aaron came back to our vent and unfolded his little napkin for me, but this time it wasn't a rat inside. It was a hand. A small hand. Young. Cut clean away at the wrist. I didn't ask him where he got it from. I was . . . hungry."

She paused, searching his face for a response and finding none. He could find none in himself, either. Nothing to say to this. Too much to feel.

"But when we crawled back into our vent hole and went to sleep, I felt sick. Sick to my stomach. I woke up, and I saw Aaron, looking down at me in a new way. A way he'd never looked at me before.''

Alex swallowed hard, closed his eyes. Hungry. The children left on the streets were hungry.

"I left the next night," Jaguar said. "Pointed myself west and walked. I was walking so fast I almost put my foot on a live wire, but some cop from a rescue crew was there, and he picked me up before I fried myself.''

She stopped speaking and waited for him to say something. Anything at all. He watched his emotions swirling wordless inside him, breathed deeply, reminding himself that he'd asked for it. He'd asked for it.

"I was—I guess I was thirteen by then. Living on the streets for over a year, and surviving it. I'm telling you this because the cop who picked me up was someone you know.''

She paused, then spit the words out at him. "Nick," she said. "Nick Lyola.''

Nick. Nick had rescued her?

A tight knot formed in his belly. Nick rescued her, and now he was filing charges against her. She was enraged at him. A tight and twisted knot, almost impossible to untangle.

He looked around, thinking fast, thinking in circles that went nowhere. More knots, inside him. They were surrounded by the ancient machinery of entrapment and torture. Manacles, balls and chains, prison cells. Knots of history and hate and longing and fear.

"If he saved you, why are you so angry at him?" he asked. "Or are you angry at him *because* he saved you?''

"What do you mean?" she asked.

"You're not the type to let anyone see where you're vulnerable. But Nick knows. Is that why you hate him?''

She drew her chin up, searing eyes piercing his. She heard the unasked question under this one. She knew he was asking if that's the kind of person she was, if he could trust her, if he could ever imagine he knew who she was at all.

She said nothing. She wasn't about to help him out of these ropes, these chains.

"Are you still sleeping with Nick?" he asked, unexpectedly, surprised at what he said even as he said it.

She tilted her head, and a slow smile spread across her face. "No, Alex," she said, "I'm not."

She did not say why do you ask? She didn't need to say it.

She already knew why, even better than he did.

"He couldn't do it, could he?"

"Well," Terence said, "he never was a very good empath. I've got the alternative set up, though. We can go ahead with that."

"Perhaps we should use someone else for that."

"No. He's the most likely candidate, given their history."

The Looker sat at a picnic table in a park near the lake, his pale eyes protected by thick sunglasses that wouldn't stay up his thin nose. He shuffled his cards and sniffed.

"You're right. Go through it with me again," he commanded.

Terence did so, and the Looker laid out his cards, with four aces up.

He smiled at them, and turned dim eyes to Terence. "No," he said when Terence was finished. "Remove her."

"From the case? That's what I'm doing—"

"Not from the case. From the Planetoid. From this life cycle."

Terence ran his tongue along his upper lip. "It's not necessary, and I don't think you—"

"How much are we paying you for this?" he asked coldly.

"A lot," Terence said.

"And how much do we know about you? Don't bother—

the answer is the same.'' He held a hand out to Terence in a conciliatory gesture. ''We'll add a ten percent bonus for successful completion of the assignment.''

Terence breathed in as much of the air as he could find in the room, then let it out, ran a hand through his hair. He wanted to avoid this. He was a numbers man. A records man. The Looker observed his gestures and spoke reassuringly.

''I understand your reluctance. I felt the same way once, when I first worked with Clare. But you must know that this is a matter of national security, and one life is . . . nothing. You must also know that a failure to cooperate on your part could result in termination of your employment. Do you know what I mean when I say 'termination of your employment'?''

Terence swallowed through a dry mouth. He'd seen the experiments at the house in Denver. He knew where terminated employees ended up, what happened to them next. The Looker told him all the bodies there were from medical experiments, but that begged the question of who conducted the experiments that created the bodies in the first place.

''I see that you do,'' the Looker said. ''So, you see, it's really a matter of self-defense, isn't it? You don't have a choice at all. It's not as if you're doing anything other than defending your own life, which is a perfectly valid reason for taking preemptive action in a situation such as this.''

Terence frowned. Self-defense. The Looker was forcing him into it. When you put it that way, everything looked different. He felt his shoulders unknot some, his heart slow a little, and he tried to ignore the vague sense that he was about to cross some line. Once he did, there would be no return trips. But there was still the question of how to complete the assignment. On that, he didn't have a clue.

''I'm not sure . . . how . . .'' Terence fumbled for words. ''She's got a pretty fine instinct for self-preservation.''

''I'm aware of that. You'll have to think of something. I have another consultant here on the Planetoid who can provide any assistance you require so that you don't have to be personally involved. All we expect is that you'll protect our interests, and that no harm will come to the subject we wish to recover. Can you do it?''

He turned over the options in his mind. No choice, he told himself. Strictly self-defense. Besides, getting rid of Jaguar would be doing more than one person a favor, when it came down to it. And there were a few ways he could think of, if he had a little help.

''I got a few ideas. I'll need your other consultant, though. I want him to get hold of her—''

''No need to tell me about it. You just take care of this, and we'll take care of you.''

8

HER DAY WITH CLARE WAS QUIET, AND SHE WAS grateful for that. They had lain on the floor in Clare's bedroom, sprawled across a white carpet, looking over dresses in a catalog that Clare had requested. Jaguar chose to keep today's interactions in this room, which had only three walls of mirrors and none of them set at odd angles. The simplicity of vision in here, in comparison to the central hall, was soothing.

"The long blue silk would be marvelous on you," Clare said.

"Actually, I think it's better for your coloring."

"Perhaps you're right. Then what about that green-and-gold number?" She pointed out a long dress, slit up the front, heavily beaded in emerald green with random bits of gold.

"Oh yes," Jaguar said. "That'd do it. Just fine."

Clare was such a pleasant companion, she had to remind herself repeatedly that this woman was about as cold-blooded a killer as she was ever likely to meet. That something was missing from her. Something stolen. Something that left her with an intact ego, and no connection to the pain of other people. Jaguar knew all this, and she knew it would take something more than she could give to fix it, but she still believed Clare was right about the green dress, and enjoyed the day.

She remembered spending similar days with Rachel, when she'd first arrived, crazy with anger at the way her Orthodox Jewish sect had treated her, treated all women, and in need of a gentle process to make her realize first the source of her anger, then the source of her fear. Jaguar had spent hours reading to her from children's books, watching her rant and rave, then, as she tired, stroking her hair, soothing her, singing to her.

But Rachel was different. Rachel's fear was of losing her soul, which was human and passionate and real. She had two feet firmly on the ground, and was one of the most balanced people Jaguar had ever met. It was her balance and her warmth of spirit that made it easy to like her. She elicited warmth from others, just by nature of her being.

If Clare had any warmth, either of rage or love, Jaguar hadn't found it. Ghandi-like, she had cleansed herself of all desire, all passion, almost every fear. Even the Jaguar Hecate had emotions, which she expressed, but Clare had refined the simplest animal passion to the pure point of the job at hand. And she was an almost perfect killing machine, remaining invisible because she would only reflect the desires of others. She would be anthropomorphized into many shapes by those desires, the way animals were, and still remain free of the passions humans projected onto her. Jaguar felt a twinge of jealousy at her capacity to be like this. But what was she to do with a woman who was this pure, this free of normal human emotion?

Sit and look at catalogs, she supposed, until she figured something else out. She was tempted to try empathic contact again, just to see what would happen this time.

Not today. She wasn't up to it.

"Clare," she said, "what did you do after the Serials?"

Clare turned and looked at her, in the mirror. "What?"

"I mean, you got through the Serials, and then what?"

She smiled softly. "I left home."

"Why?"

"My father wanted me to have sex with him again."

Jaguar felt the pause in her own heartbeat. A major trauma, and it wasn't in any of the reports. Not there. Very absent. Was she making it up now—another mirror game, reflecting what she thought Jaguar wanted to hear? Or was it real events remembered, emotion frozen and buried?

"Again?" she asked.

"Well," Clare said, "of course he'd been having sex with me since I was a little girl. My mother," she added, as if this explained anything, "wasn't as blessed in her looks. But then I didn't want to anymore."

"You didn't want to anymore?" Jaguar repeated.

"No," Clare said, sounding sad. Then she leaned over and whispered confidentially in Jaguar's ear. "I never really *enjoyed* him, you know. But I knew how to *please* him."

Jaguar nodded sagely. "I understand. Was he . . . angry?"

"Oh yes. Quite. He wanted to disown me. He—he beat me. I had to leave, and make my own way in the world after that."

"How did you manage?"

"I looked for work as an artist. You know. Advertising, graphics, computer production. I would have taken anything, but nobody wanted someone as inexperienced as me. I even tried work as a secretary, but I wasn't very good at it, and I was fired. I got a few jobs dancing instead."

"Dancing."

"Yes. In bars. For men who needed something to masturbate to. Then I started having sex with some of the customers. Just for fun, but they paid me handsomely before I even asked, so I kept doing it. Then I realized that was no good. If I was going into business for myself, I'd better do it right. So I set up as a call girl."

"Highly paid, I would imagine," Jaguar commented.

"Yes. I was quite good at it, too. Only, then a customer

got rough with me. He was going to cut my face. I had to kill him.''

"Of course. How did you?"

"It was easy. I just—chopped his windpipe—and he choked to death. Then another customer helped me get rid of the body, and made some career-shift suggestions to me."

"Who was that, Clare?" Jaguar asked.

"Nobody you know," she answered. "But I found it much easier than the work I had been doing. Much cleaner, too. And then, if I wanted to, I could have sex. But I didn't have to if I didn't want to. You see?"

"I see," Jaguar said. "So . . . that was the first time," she commented.

"Oh no," Clare said. "Not at all."

Jaguar waited for further information, unsure if it would arrive or if Clare would simply change the subject.

"I killed my father before I left," she commented, then added, "Mother, too. I had to, because she walked in on us."

Jaguar continued to wait. Clare turned the page of the catalog and brought her finger down to rest on a deep maroon dress with a slit up the side.

"That would be marvelous on either of us," she said. "Don't you think?"

She left the House of Mirrors and stood for a moment outside, flipped her dark glasses down, and made a visual scan of the area around her. No sign of trouble that she could see or hear. She tilted her head back and let the sun pour down on it. It was another warm day. The heat against her skin felt good. She decided to take her time before going back to Adrian. She could walk down the path that led to the jaguar cage, stop and visit with them for a while. No contact. No searching for any space other than the day she was in. No grappling for elusive answers. Just a little time to admire the big cats. It would be good to do something that simple. She'd made enormous progress with Clare today, and deserved to reward herself.

About halfway down the path, a rustling movement in the nearby trees made her aware that she wasn't alone. She stopped and peered through the rows of pines that lined her way, into the sprawling wild honeysuckle and buckthorn beyond.

Could be Maria, out on her daily rounds. She shrugged, and moved on. If it was someone else looking for her, they'd find her here or at home. If it was someone she didn't want to talk to, like Nick, she had better keep moving anyway.

Or, she thought, if it's Nick, I'll twist his bits until he screams.

She resented the constant interruption to her thoughts, her concentration, which was hard enough to maintain while dealing with two prisoners at once. She wanted not to think about any of it for a while. Later she could review her day with Clare and decide what course to take next. For now she needed to clear herself, and she needed to be alone to do it.

She turned sharp past the falcon house and pressed herself into the wall, waiting. Nothing happened. She went around to the back of the building, and walked around again to the front.

Nothing. Maybe she was imagining things. She waited and listened, but heard no sound of footsteps, and the ground was dry, with plenty of leaf cover. Surely a rustle or a crunch would let her know that whoever watched her was still there.

Then, as she stood at the side of the building deciding what to do next, she caught sight of motion in her peripheral vision.

Someone was walking, but walking ahead.

"Nick?" she asked herself, since he was the only person she could think of who would follow ahead of her. If it was he, she knew where he would go, because she knew where she had been headed.

She took a direct path toward the Jaguar cages, now keeping her steps silent and her breath slow.

She saw no one standing there. The big cats were resting, strewn across each other like luxuriant living rugs. The male lifted his head at her approach, but made no sound.

A hand clamped down hard on her shoulder, but she was ready. She whirled, her hands locked, ready to smash into Nick's face.

"Hey," Gerry said, catching both her hands in one of his. "New kind of handshake?"

The jaguars growled low and jumped to attention.

Jaguar grinned at him. "Hello," she said. "Come here often?" She pulled her hands out of his and rubbed the backs of them.

"Actually," Gerry said seriously, "I don't. I needed to talk to you fast, and Rachel told me to try here."

"How'd you get in?"

"The old lady knows me," he said. "I help her out with the bears. Cleaning their habitat, y'know?" He pinched his nose between his fingers and made a face.

So much for tight security, she thought. "I know, Gerry. So what's the trouble?"

"I'm setting up for tonight, and I can't find your guitar. The bass. You left it, didn't you?"

"Is that the emergency?"

"Yeah—I mean, that bass makes just the sound for 'Dumpster Blues.' The synth isn't even close." His face dropped into a pout, and Jaguar hoped he wasn't going to throw a fit of artistic temperament for her. Gerry maintained a very even keel, except where his music was concerned, and there he was about as reasonable as a two-year-old.

"It should be there," she said reasonably.

"It's not," he insisted, kicking at the dirt with his toe.

"Well, what would you like me to do? Rematerialize it?

Make a new one? Stamp my feet and howl?''

Gerry scratched at his head and thought about this, decided he just didn't know the answer, and gave it up.

"I just want it," he said. "Now."

"Look," she said, "keep poking around. Either it'll be there, or we can dump the 'Dumpster' tune for tonight and use . . . how about 'Bears in the Kitchen'?''

Gerry brightened. ''Bears in the Kitchen'' was one of his favorite pieces—one he'd written that the other band members consistently avoided playing because the changes were beyond human speed, and the lyrics were indecipherable. He'd jump on the chance to do that one. "Hey—that's a great idea," he said.

"That's what we'll do, then. But keep looking. I'm sure I left it there, and it's bound to turn up. Who'd want that old thing, anyway?''

9

"I'M JUST SAYING MAYBE YOU OVERSTEPPED yourself in assigning her, Alex. That's all."

This, from Paul Dinardo, who had gotten a full report on Jaguar's recent trouble, and who had called to let Alex know he was concerned.

But he was always concerned about something, and frequently it was something to do with Jaguar. It was his job to be concerned. He was on the Planetoid Governors' Board, and his assignment was Alex's zone.

Alex rubbed his hand over his face, temporarily obscuring himself from Paul's view on the telecom. Paul might be right for once in his life, but he wasn't about to admit that right now. Dealing with the Board's nervousness and needs was a bit more than he had scheduled for the day.

"It's a risk, Paul. I'll grant you that. But it's in place, so let's just go ahead with it. I think she might be getting somewhere."

"You don't want to pull her?" Paul asked.

"Not yet. I need to know a few things, though."

"Such as?"

"First, is there anything new to fill in the holes in Clare's life during the Serials? We've got stuff from before, but big gaps during and immediately after."

Paul snorted. "Records have disappeared. You know how it is for those years, anyway, Alex. And obviously whoever hired her has a damn good eraser."

Alex nodded. He knew this, but he wanted it confirmed, and he wanted to see Paul's reaction when they spoke of it. From the look on his face, he thought about it the same way Alex did: whoever Clare worked for was careful, and thorough.

"As I thought," he said. "Then my next question. Do you have any information on NICA's research interests, or DIE's most recent psi projects?"

He saw Paul startle. "DIE? What've they got to do with it?"

"Maybe nothing. I'm looking into all the agencies who've shown interest in the case. DIE's just top of the list in alphabetical order, and they do psi work. NICA's next. They've been asking questions, too."

"Alex, they always ask questions. NICA, DIE—all of them. Christ, if you spit they come around and ask questions. Every other week they're calling me about something. It's just routine."

Paul was right. Monitoring. Always monitoring. The Pentagon was that way, and NICA, but DIE had a reputation for a great deal more efficiency than any federally run organization. He'd had one consultant visit him in the past, asking for lists of their Teachers for their files, and he'd refused. Since they weren't federal, he didn't have to give it to them. A week later NICA had come in to audit the lists, and Alex was sure all the information had been passed on. The most they could do was create delays in the system so that information got to them late, and in as unhelpful a form as possible.

But whereas NICA moved through the weight of their federal backing and collective power, DIE moved by stealth. No one knew for sure how many people the group employed, and since their computer lines used the most sophisticated closing device available, no one was likely to

find out in the near future. They had no obligation to report
to anyone except their CEO and their stockholders, which
was easy since their CEO was their principal stockholder.
And all interactions were conducted on an individual basis
with a series of men and women marked by the mediocrity
of their appearance. They monitored faithfully, but they
didn't waste time or their people's energy on unrelated
agendas. Their interest in Clare was more than an esoteric
exercise in ways an assassin can fail.

"I know," he said, "but I'm interested. What're they up
to these days?"

"The usual, Alex. Stuff they won't tell. And since
they're private, you can't run back at them with the tax-
payer's-dollar routine."

"Right. Someday they'll be a regulated office. Serve
them right."

"You want to sign up to be on the Board that regulates
them?"

"No, Paul. I was thinking of nominating you, though.
How about Patricks's interest in pyrite?"

"What's that?" Paul asked. "Some kind of drug?"

"No. Not a drug. Never mind. Are you sure," he added,
"that you're giving me everything I need to run this assignment?"

Paul paused briefly, then leaned in closer to his telecom.
Alex grinned, watching him. People acted as if leaning in
and whispering over the wires that carried their image and
voice would somehow protect their privacy. Animal instincts, still at work. Good for them.

"You've got everything I know, Alex. I only wish I did
know more because there's something screwy about this
whole thing."

"You think?"

"I think. Listen, you keep me posted, will you? And
consider taking that Addams woman off. I've heard enough
bad reports about her to last my lifetime."

When he buzzed off, Alex sat back and considered. Paul

obviously knew nothing. Just as obviously, Jaguar did.

Pyrite, he thought. Fool's gold. That's where Jaguar's interest ran.

Pyrite, and experimentation with creating a technologically controlled base for superluminary transfer of information. DIE would be in on that, of course. They were always in front of the other agencies in terms of research. But how did it all connect with having a Governor killed? Paul wouldn't know. Jaguar wouldn't tell. Rereading Rachel's reports a sixth time probably wouldn't help either.

But he had a friend in Colorado who might have something valuable to share. Neri Gaston. They'd been in the National Guard together, long ago, and had gone very different ways after the Serials, but for very similar reasons. Both looking for a way to explain what had happened. Both looking to be part of the process that ensured it didn't happen again. Neri was at the Think Tank, researching what was euphemistically called psychological intents and control possibilities. Psi work. His facility was located just south of Denver.

He reached for the telecom, then pulled back his hand. With so many intelligence contingencies around, it might not be such a good idea to talk to him about this over the lines. Safer, he thought, to arrange to meet him in person, find a quiet place to talk.

Perhaps he could get Neri to meet him in Leadville, or near it. He wouldn't mind getting away for a few days. Maybe some space between him and the place where Jaguar put her feet down would help him untangle his own emotional knots about her. And he might be able to scout around for some dirt on the casinos, the mining facilities. It could prove to be a very productive trip.

There was a direct shuttle going to the home planet this afternoon. The direct service booked up heavy, but they kept a few spaces for Governors and Supervisors who hadn't planned ahead. He could wait two days for the next one, or he could just go. Today.

He tapped a finger on his desk. Then he picked up his telecom and reserved a seat.

It felt good to be singing. The crowd was hot, and the music was good.

Jaguar was winding her way through a long scat line, backed up from the sound receptor. Her guitar, all ready to go, was next to the amp, and she knew she'd have to reach for it in a few moments so she kept her eye on the edge of it. Gerry had found it right on stage, hooked to the receiver and ready to go, when he came back from the Sanctuary. He supposed someone had found it and put it there, he told her, calling himself an idiot in the happiest of tones and asking her if she'd mind doing the "Dumpster Blues" and "Bears in the Kitchen" all in one set.

"How about," she suggested, "we combine them and call it 'Dumpster Bears'?" Gerry had seriously considered this, until he saw her grinning mischievously at him.

Still, she was glad the guitar had been found. It was old, and it had no capacity for any of the tricks that the new Martins or Fenders had. Couldn't hook it up to a harmonic sympathizer without blowing its circuits. It wouldn't even take an old midi line. But her fingers knew the strings like old friends, and Gerry was right when he said it had a voice you couldn't reproduce with synth.

She scatted along, enjoying the feel and the sound of the music as it bounced through the echo box. Waited for her moment.

When she was ready, she nodded at Gerry, who looked at her, then at her guitar. She turned and reached for it. Out of the corner of her eye she saw Gerry hold out a hand, heard him shout, but for some reason she didn't immediately connect this with what happened next.

Just before she had it in her hands, she had the sensation of being run over by an elephant. Something bulky and soft thumped her good, knocked her down. At first she thought it was a repeat of whatever had happened to her the other night in the streets. Then she realized it was Gerry, his amorphous form spread across her, on top of her, the two of them supine across the stage.

"What's wrong, Gerry?" she grunted, breathing with difficulty. "Did I drop the pitch?"

"No, Jag," he said. "Take a look." He removed himself from her, pointing toward her guitar.

Then she saw it.

The lead wires were exposed at just the place where she put her hands.

"With the whole system revved up—toast, Jag. Crispy critters. That's what you'd be if you grabbed it."

She stood and dusted herself off.

Gerry was facing the audience. "Sorry, folks," he said to them. "Technical difficulties. We're gonna take a break and see if we can clear them up."

"I don't know where Alex is," she insisted again to Gerry, and to Oji, as the two band members continued to pummel her with questions.

"Look," Oji said. "Someone came in here and fucked with your stuff. This isn't no accident shit. Someone wants you dead. You get that?"

"I'm so sorry, Jag," Gerry said, for the fiftieth time. "I should've seen it before. I should've."

Jaguar ignored him.

"I get it," she said to Oji, "but I still don't know where Alex is. We're not bound at the hip, you know."

"Not for want of trying on his part," Oji whispered. Jaguar glared at him, then chose to let it pass.

"Ask Rachel," she said. "Maybe she knows."

The green room door opened, and the third band member, Pinkie Curtis, stuck her head in. "I got hold of Rachel," she said. "Thought she might know something, and she did. Alex is on the home planet."

"What?" Jaguar said.

"You know. Earth. Personal leave. Not sure where, or how long he'll be away."

"Right," Jaguar said. "There it is. Do you mind if I go home now?"

"No way," Pinkie said. "Rachel said we're supposed to keep you here even if we have to sit on you. She's on her way. Wants to talk to you about something."

When Rachel arrived, the others disappeared and left them alone.

She had, Rachel-like, brought along two steaming cups of coffee, and she handed one to Jaguar, let her take a sip and savor it for a moment before she spoke.

"Okay," she said, sitting on the couch next to Jaguar and curling her legs under her. "I'm gonna break a lot of promises, so you'd better listen, because I don't want to have to repeat myself and break them more than once."

"This," Jaguar said, "sounds serious." She breathed in her coffee, cradling the mug in her hands and letting the warmth seep into her. It was late, and she was tired. Rachel looked tired, too.

"It's serious. If it wasn't, I'd be home sleeping. You know where Alex is?"

"Home planet. Personal leave." She made a face, and rolled her eyes. "Probably some woman."

"No," Rachel said definitively. "Not a woman. He's in Leadville."

Jaguar took a sip of her coffee, frowned down into it.

"Did you hear me?"

"I heard. Are you saying he's interfering with my assignment, or is he—Rachel, are you trying to tell me he's got some kind of scheme going with the Governor's people?"

Rachel looked at her hard, her face going blank and then crinkling into laughter. "Alex? A scheme? Jaguar, you've got him all wrong."

"Look, Rachel, if he's playing some kind of game with

my case, since it's my hide that almost got skinned tonight, I would think that you'd want me to—"

"Shut the hell up, Jaguar," Rachel said.

Jaguar took a sip of coffee too fast, and choked. Rachel leaned over and pounded her on the back, hard.

"Stop," Jaguar said, pushing her away. "Cut it out. Rachel—what's wrong with you?"

"Just," Rachel repeated, "shut up and listen. You've got this thing stuck in your head about Supervisors, and you can't even see the person you're working with behind the title. It's stupid, if you don't mind my saying so. Or even if you do."

Jaguar sat and let herself absorb the phenomenon of Rachel being offensive and angry. It was rare, and it was fascinating. And she knew that it meant Rachel was stating a profound truth. She listened.

Rachel watched her until she was sure she was listening, then she continued. "Alex is in Leadville because he's terrified you've got yourself caught up in something bigger than you. Something you won't be able to get out of. He took his own personal time to go do this, just to make sure *your* ass is covered."

"Rachel," Jaguar insisted, "how could I know he'd do that?"

"You of all people could know. You just didn't want to. And he didn't want you to. He also didn't want you to know that when you got booted off of Planetoid One, he made sure you were transferred to his office instead of being fired."

Rachel waited a moment for this to sink in, then went on. "And, he didn't want you to know that he paid half your tuition when you were in college. The part that wasn't covered by scholarship."

Jaguar waited to see if there was more. Rachel said nothing.

"Is that the lot, then?" she asked.

"I'd think it was enough," Rachel replied.

Jaguar swirled her coffee in the cup, watching the whirlpool of motion until it settled down. Alex paid for her tuition. Alex in Leadville. Someone trying to kill her. A whirlpool of motion in her cup.

"Why are you telling me this?" she asked at last.

"Because I wanted you to understand how much danger you're in, and he's in, and we're all in at this point. And because I wanted you to know what kind of man you're working with."

Jaguar nodded. "He . . . paid for my tuition?"

"That's right."

"Did he tell you that or ask you to tell me?"

"Are you crazy? Of course not. I found out."

"How?"

Rachel relaxed now, the tension in her shoulders leaving her. She leaned back on the couch. "When I first started as a team member, I clerked for him. Remember? He wanted an inventory of his files before he reorganized them, and I stumbled into his personal files. He had a ledger from when you were in college. And there were some memos about Planetoid One. I told him I found them, and he didn't say anything except don't tell you, and delete them immediately. It wasn't information he needed anymore."

Jaguar found herself smiling. She could see him saying that.

"Look," Rachel said. "I kept it in confidence, just like he asked me to, but I think you should know what kind of person he is so you can stop treating him like an enemy. It's dangerous. It's up to you if you let him know that you know, but remember that he doesn't want you to know. Okay?"

She raised an eyebrow at Rachel. "If I could figure out your sentence, I might be able to agree to it or not. As it is, maybe it'd be better if we just went home."

Rachel grinned. "Okay," she said. "You're right. Let's call it done, and get some sleep."

• • •

In Leadville, the local news was all about the signing of the ordinance that would start the building of casinos in this poor region. It would occur in a few days, and any number of parties and ceremonies were being planned around it. The main street of town, which was composed of a diner, a church, a few stores and bars, was being set up with platforms and signs welcoming the builders. On his arrival, Alex spent an hour in one of the bars, listening to the locals talk about it, watching the news, getting his bearings.

Then he walked around, looking at the mountains beyond the empty lots, the abandoned buildings.

He knelt down and picked up a handful of deep brown earth, letting it sift through his fingers with chunks of rock, pieces of dried pine needles.

The air was thin and sharp at this elevation, and mountains stood at his back, at his shoulders, in his face. Looking around at the sheer ridges, the crests of snow, and the empty houses and lots, he realized that the casinos the Governor had planned would bring income to this area, income that hadn't ever been anticipated. Of course, that would be impossible without the increasing use of wings and air runners to get people up this high. Across a flat lot, he saw the building equipment necessary to begin construction on landing sites for these vehicles.

Alex smiled, almost hearing Jaguar groan at the thought of it. Casinos.

What had she said to him—that now every woman in the area could get a job as an exotic dancer or a prostitute. Take your pick. Full employment for all.

He wasn't sure which side he fell on in terms of the question of gambling. He knew that this town had been built as a mining town, and that its fortunes rose and fell with the rise and collapse of silver mines, copper mines, and later, uranium mines. He knew that even before the Serials, a hundred miles' worth of land had been dedicated to preservation, and now this small town, like many others around it, eked out its living from the tourists who came through.

It wasn't as popular as the other National Preservation Lands, though. There was something too wild, too lonely and sad about the region for it to be attractive on a grand scale. Maybe there were too many ghosts lingering in the edges of the trees, or not sleeping in the mines.

And he knew that in spite of the excitement, many people were still against the casino and were planning protests to coincide with the celebrations.

Opponents were raising an outcry about the devastation of this wild land, the animals that would be displaced or killed, the trees that would never grow back as more and more developments were built to accommodate the casino and tourist needs. The land had been set aside for preservation. A place for the cougars and bears to play without human intervention. A place for the trees to continue growing. Some people wanted it to stay that way.

And while the casino development was being simultaneously celebrated and protested, Alex noticed that nobody was talking about the mining at all.

Pyrite.

This land was still a primary source of the metal called fool's gold, and it was going to be mined and refined as construction occurred. There was every reason to expect the ore to be plentiful. Geologists knew what a rich source existed here. But nobody was talking about it. All discussion centered around the casino.

The silence had the smell of a DIE operation.

Alex stood, stretched his legs, turned his back to the wooded lands, and made his way back to the main street, to the run-down, gray-sided diner. He went in and found a booth, ordering a cup of coffee and a piece of apple pie from a waitress whose waistline looked stretched from childbirths, from years of slouching, from apathy. Then he waited.

After he'd chewed his way through half the pie, he saw

a man enter the diner and ask at the counter for him. The waitress pointed, and Alex waved.

"Hello, Alex," the man said, adjusting the collar of his white shirt and taking a seat next to him.

"Neri," Alex said. "It's been a while."

"A while, and a ways," Neri replied. "And I don't have a lot of time, so you better tell me what your justification is for pulling me up this mountain."

"Just a chat," Alex said. "I missed you."

Neri rolled his eyes and brought his broad hands up to slap them on the tabletop. "Dzarny, you haven't got an ounce of bullshit in you that works, and never did. You call me, and tell me we have to talk, so I think—what's up with Dzarny now, after all these years off the home planet?"

"And what did you answer yourself?"

"Not much," Neri said. "I didn't have time. Because the next thing I know, Dzarny's saying he wants to meet me way up next to heaven, which is about four hours away from where I'm supposed to be at a meeting right at this minute, so I begin asking myself another question."

"Which is?"

"How close to the line is his ass anyway? Then I decide I better just go and see for myself. So now I see you're alive, and that's okay, but I still have no time for a chat."

"Neri," Alex said, "haven't you figured out a way around time yet? I hear the taxpayers give you a load of money to just sit and think about that shit all day long."

"They do," Neri agreed cheerfully. "Boatloads full of cash and jewels and whatnots. The whatnots are especially fun," he noted. "But I haven't solved the problem of ubiquity yet."

He waved the waitress over and ordered coffee, then, after a long discussion with her on the relative merits of their chocolate cake versus their cobbler, asked for one of each. The waitress left them, and Alex shook his head.

"How hard are they working you that you eat this way and stay so thin?"

"It's not the work," Neri said. "It's the whatnots."

"As I thought. What problems are you solving these days, Neri?"

"Oh," he said, "the usual."

"Superluminary transfer of information," Alex said.

"That's right. I wish you'd sign on with us," Neri said. "We need subjects like you desperately, not only to work with but for the . . . whatnots."

Alex grinned. "Sorry on both counts. I'll work with you guys when you get a clue that the arts are more than science." Then he added, over Neri's snort of derision, "And I'm just not a whatnot, Neri. Wasn't made that way."

"A waste," Neri said. "But there it is. You're hetero-sexually challenged. Well, I hope you make some fine woman happy."

"I hope I make many fine women happy for now," Alex said. "Tell me what you're doing with pyrite these days," he concluded.

Neri startled, dropped a spoon, and retrieved it.

"Goodness," he said. "You are good. Have you been listening in?"

"Not at all. Word gets around, though."

"Well, it's not supposed to. Highly highly classified stuff."

"I know that, too. So tell me about it."

Neri leaned in close. "It's a wave amplifier, specific for theta and omega."

Alex nodded. Those were the brain waves associated with states of consciousness observed during use of the empathic arts. "I thought so. Is it chemical composition?"

"Crystallization factors. You want the speed lecture on it?"

"Don't need it. What I really want to know is who's funding it."

"Oh, DIE, of course," he said. "Contracts up the wazoo.

All under some other name, as usual. Probably like last time—they're using Seagram's or something as a cover company. You know, I shouldn't be telling you any of this.''

Alex felt the tingle of comprehension, of completion, as Neri said this. DIE. Jaguar suspected as much. They both knew, and had known for some time. But now they really knew.

''I know,'' Alex replied, keeping it casual, as if it were just more dish. ''And I expect to pay dearly for the information.''

''You will? Then let me tell you more. Ask questions.''

''How do you know it's DIE?''

''All the earmarks. More money than God to throw around, a series of sponsors that don't make any sense, and strange little nondescript consultants coming through now and then to gather data. I mean, they're good, but they can't be totally invisible and get the work done, too. Besides, it's all on the up-and-up. No criminal activities involved. However, our contract does swear us to secrecy about what we're doing.''

''What do they do with the data you give them?''

''I haven't got a clue on that. They wouldn't let an outsider near it. We're corollary research, passing stuff to them.''

''Okay. So extrapolate from the research they have you do, and tell me what you think they're working on in their own dens.''

''Two things. A technologically based telepathy—something to pass information between agents. They want machinery that they can monitor better than an empath. The usual control issues. I swear, all these gals and guys ought to be in therapy. Do them good.''

''And? What else?''

''Well''—Neri leaned in close and stage-whispered behind his hand—''there's rumors of pseudogenic experiments.''

"What?"

"You know. The postmortem polka? Dead people. Keep the mainspring wound with a Supertoy and make them dance."

"I know what the term means, but Neri—are they seriously attempting it?"

"Seem crazy? So was brain surgery before we figured it out. Besides, what's it cost to research? Dead people are so available, and so much easier to work with. They don't form unions or ask for personal leave or take coffee breaks. And *quiet*. You can imagine how nice it'd be to work with them."

"But is it . . . possible?"

"Sure. If you want a sort of jumping dummy, you can play around with chemical levels, diddle with electrons, at least to a point. You know bodies continue to move postmortem. Hair grows. Nails grow. Dead guys sit up and scare the shit out of new doctors. I know," Neri said, holding a hand out to silence Alex's protest, "human life is more than motion. There's the individual mind and soul and so on. But that's where all the trouble starts. Better to just skip it. Hook up the bodies to a Supertoy and let 'er rip. You want more pie?"

"I don't think so," Alex said. "Not right now. But I thought there's been a lot of trouble with the Supertoy concept."

"Between *live* subjects, yes. It's probably easier to work them postmortem, actually, because—well, death is the great simplifier. As you know, the human factor's been a big problem for all psi research."

"That's because—"

"I know. It's an art, not a science. But science pays, and artists starve."

"Truer words were never spoken. What's their goal, and how far have they gotten?"

"I'd imagine they want brute force. Army of the dead would be high on the list for long-term goals, and DIE thinks long-term. That's the best thing about them, actually."

"Can they do it, Neri?"

"Dearest one," Neri replied, shaking his head, "I'm telling you they *are* doing it. Now. I swear they're just waiting for their uniform requisitions to move the boys out."

Alex poked at the remainder of his pie and stayed quiet while the waitress brought Neri's order to him. Psi work, genetic tinkering and pseudogenics had always been seen as fringe work, but the pentagon and NICA maintained a solid if secret interest in all three. They didn't make their findings public, because they knew how twitchy the general public was even about the empathic arts. The public should be twitchy, Alex thought. He was. And Neri, for all his casual tone, kept glancing over his shoulder, out the window.

"Are your people doing any of the research?" he asked, when Neri was served.

"Do you have any idea what pseudogenics entails? Us theoreticians are far too squeamish. We just hear whispers in the wind. Can't confirm a damn thing, so don't quote me on any of it."

"Neri," Alex said, "look at me."

Neri lifted his attention from his plate and Alex stared at him hard. Neri kept the surface light. That was his way. But when Alex listened to his eyes, he heard fear. Neri had driven four hours at a moment's notice to see Alex. He needed to talk about this before Alex asked. He wanted the madness stopped. He was very frightened.

Alex lifted his coffee cup and moved the conversation into less threatening zones.

"So how's everyone surviving their grief?"

"Grief?"

"The dear departed Patricks."

Neri rolled his eyes. "At the Think Tank we got out our party dresses. Didn't you know the dear deceased governor was talking about taxing the pyrite, and the Think Tank folks were sputtering like old ladies, screaming they voted for him because he said no taxation, and so on.''

Alex leaned back and chewed on another bite of pie, which took longer to digest than the news. The Governor hadn't behaved himself, apparently. Perhaps the Lieutenant Governor was more amenable to tax breaks. He wondered if Jaguar knew of this bit of information. He hadn't seen it in Rachel's reports, so he assumed it was local knowledge that hadn't traveled abroad yet.

"Like anything else?" he asked, when Neri had scraped his plates clean with the side of his fork.

"Many things," Neri said. "Whatnots."

Alex laughed, and waved to the waitress. "You don't give up, do you?"

"You said you'd pay dearly." Neri pouted.

"I meant the check," Alex said. "Knowing how you eat, I thought it might cost me dear. Are you up for a walk? You could show me where the mine will be sited."

"What makes you think I or anyone else knows that?" Neri asked.

"Anyone else, I'm not sure about. You seem to make it a point to know just about everything."

"Flattery," he said, "will get you everywhere."

The waitress brought them the check, and Alex handed her his cash card. Then they rose and left together, Neri linking his arm in Alex's and chatting full speed, admiring the earring Alex wore in his left ear, and the thin braid that extended down the back of his hair.

They hit the sunlight, thin and brittle as an old lady's fingers, and Neri pulled away from Alex to draw his arms around himself.

"It gets so cold way up here," Neri said. "I think I'll just duck into my vehicle for a jacket."

Alex watched his lanky figure lope toward the street where his airrunner was parked, in front of the Church of the Most Sacred Heart. He watched him bend over near the door and retrieve a piece of metal, hold it up to the brittle sun, and examine it. He watched the sun glint off of it. He watched him shrug and drop it.

He watched him reach over and open the door, and then the world exploded around him in a bright, inexplicable flash of light.

No sound. Just a flash of light, and Alex was tossed back by heat, his body slammed into the sidewall of the diner, and the diner shook, and as he looked up and all around, bits of light and bits of Neri fell from the sky, spraying down across the Sacred Heart with its circle of discompassionate thorns.

He watched without believing that it was really Neri, without feeling it to be anything real. What he did feel was an instinct to survive this, to get away from it under cover of smoke and flame. While the white heat of it still kept anyone else who might be watching blinded, he walked swiftly away, his head ducked low, watching his back as he went.

He edged around the building and then headed down a side street and aimed toward a thick patch of trees across the lot. Beyond it was a cemetery. Beyond that were the ruins of mines. The Little Johnny, the closed grave of twenty men. The Frances Duffey, named after a little girl who had been passed through the narrow opening of a cave in order to bring food to trapped men, keeping them alive until they could be dug out.

He thought maybe it would be best to spend the night somewhere in there, knee-deep in the dead, than in a place where death walked alive all around. He could walk toward a different town in the morning and rent another air runner.

He wasn't about to open the door on the one he'd arrived in.

10

''CAN'T YOU KILL HER? IT'S A SIMPLE ENOUGH job, and she's mortal after all, subject to the laws of life and death like the rest of us.''

The Looker was nervous.

At his hotel-room desk, he shuffled hard, and he slapped the cards down in front of him even harder. Terence wondered if something was going on besides Clare to make him lose his cool this way.

''I never hired on to kill anyone,'' he reminded him, ''much less trying to get Addams. You don't know what she's like. Some kind of cat with too many lives.''

''She's human,'' he said. ''And you're all nervous old men, afraid to get your hands dirty. Are you aware that her supervisor is in Leadville?''

So that was it. Dzarny was getting too close to home base. Terence felt himself beginning to sweat. ''I knew he was away, but I didn't know where.''

''Now you do. And are you aware that this woman you seem incapable of controlling has been researching the Division in a determined way?''

''No. I didn't know that. She must've covered her research, because nothing's come through the files on it or I would've known.''

"We are paying you to know," the Looker said, emphasizing each word with the slap of a card. "We are paying you to know everything. I shouldn't have to go further than you to learn any of this. And I shouldn't be wasting so much time here, on a job that could be cleared up like that."

He took his hand and swept the cards off the desk, sent them skittering and floating to the floor, across the rug, onto Terence's feet. Terence sucked in a breath, and held it. The Looker turned to him.

"Do you have any idea how easy it is to kill someone?" he asked.

Terence didn't move one molecule.

"You do know," the Looker continued, "because you know how easy it would be for me to kill you. Right here. Right now."

He swallowed hard, asked his lungs to start working again, and spoke. "That's right," he said. "Killing someone's easy. It's the not-getting-caught part that's tough. Especially here."

The Looker narrowed his eye, pulled his glasses down his nose, and peered over them.

"You don't know the Planetoids like I do," Terence said. "They've got their own system. Sometimes it's loose, because you gotta give a lot of leeway to get these jobs done, but people like Dzarny and Addams, they're playing for keeps, and they know it. They can be careful, and they know how to work outside the system to keep a cover. You don't know how good they are."

A clucking noise emerged from the back of the Looker's throat, and he pushed his glasses back up his nose, opened a desk drawer, and pulled out a new pack of cards. Shuffled. Terence waited until his breathing and heart returned to normal, and then he spoke again.

"I—look, I'm sorry, but this case is way out of my league. You may be used to this sort of thing, but I'm just a record keeper, and I didn't sign on for this kind of trouble.''

The Looker wrinkled his nose in distaste. ''Nervous old men. Never mind. We have to act quickly. If you can't dispose of her, who can?''

''I still think Nick's the likeliest candidate.''

''I don't like him, but I can think of only one other alternative, and I don't want to take it yet. Stay close to him, though. If he fails, you take care of him and don't worry about it getting messy. We'll clean up after you. Are you set to begin immediately?''

''I got her files all filled in nice with stuff the Board'll eat like candy,'' Terence said. ''Nick's probably crazy wondering why he's not dead yet, so he'll do anything you ask.''

''Then let's not delay. The sooner we start, the sooner we'll know if it's going to work.''

''Okay. What're you gonna do about Dzarny?''

The Looker peered over the rim of his glasses, examining his cards. Too many low cards. A difficult layout. ''Dzarny,'' he said, ''has dealt himself an interesting hand. I don't think I'll have any trouble playing it.''

In the bright sunlight of the days that followed his final attempt to get at Jaguar, Nick kept himself to himself, kept his gun handy, and waited for whatever would come next.

He often broke into a cold sweat for no reason and he spent a lot of time in his apartment with the shades drawn down tight. He carried an image in his mind of a man in a blue suit with a long, thin nose and a set of very sophisticated ways to kill someone who had failed in an assignment.

As if that wasn't bad enough, the implant was making him feel sick. He was queasy all the time, and the shadows under his eyes kept growing darker and darker. Jaguar would say that was the shadow sickness coming out. Maybe she'd say it was good that it was coming out, instead of festering deep inside him.

And maybe she was full of shit, too.

That didn't matter, though. Even if she was full of shit, he wanted her. He couldn't seem to get rid of that wanting, and he couldn't explain it. She'd explain it. His fear. The shadow sickness. Whatever it was. Bullshit, he thought. Bullshit. He wanted her off the Planetoids, dead, anything but in his face all the time. She owed him, and she wasn't coming through with the payment. In fact, he wondered if she'd been doing some mind bending of her own, probably just for fun.

Shadow sickness wouldn't explain the stabbing pains in his chest. If she was messing around with him, he'd kill her—slowly and with great care, but he'd kill her so she stayed dead. Maybe she'd done something to him during the contact. Empathic contact should be like normal contact. She said it wasn't. She said it reached more directly into your neurons, the messages ingrained along pathways that ran deep within your body and—she'd say—your soul.

He didn't believe in souls. If humans had ever had any such things, they'd lost them during the Serials and they weren't coming back. He thought even Jaguar lost hers then. Her family dead, her childhood shattered. She'd walked the streets and watched the murders growing more frequent. Seen the shift from frequent to commonplace occurrence, lived through the nerve gas and biobombs that followed. She couldn't be any different than the rest of the human race. Than him. Of course it killed her soul.

It had killed his.

And empathic contact was just another kind of telecom as far as he was concerned. A different technology, using the human instrument instead of electronically devised ones. He always thought it would be a good idea, because he trusted himself more than he trusted the tools other people invented. Like that damn implant the Looker gave him.

Shit, if they were gonna shoot him, he might as well get rid of it. Maybe he'd feel better.

He went into his bathroom, avoiding looking at his face, and craned his neck so that he could just see the back of it out of his peripheral vision.

The subcutaneous slit, with its silicone seal, was visible. He scraped at the silicone, knowing he should use the gel to remove it and not his fingers, but not caring. He scraped until the skin around it was rubbed red and raw, and the slit opened. He pried under it with a tweezers, and pulled the implant.

Immediately, he was attacked by a wave of dizziness, queasiness. He leaned over the sink and retched, cursing himself because now he'd have to clean that up, too.

When his stomach had emptied itself of lunch and breakfast, he wiped his face with a towel, looked at the mess, and walked out of the bathroom, closing the door behind him.

He'd deal with it later.

And already, he felt better. Not normal, but a little lighter.

"Lighter." He laughed at himself. "Sure, lighter."

He went to his desk to retrieve a pack of cigarettes he kept there, and the telecom buzzed him.

His hand stopped, hovering over the receive button.

Because he carried the image of a man in a blue suit, with a long thin nose and a variety of weapons. A man he'd failed.

If it was him, it would be better to know what they planned next.

He flipped the telecom to receive, and saw blankness, but heard a disembodied voice.

"I've blanked the screen," the man's voice said, "but you'll easily guess who this is."

"Gotcha," Nick said.

"Your last attempt failed," the voice continued, sounding neutral. As if it was just a slight delay in plans. Nick waited, deciding it was best not to explain or apologize. They wouldn't care, anyway.

"We've decided to try an alternate."

"Okay. What?"

"You've been attempting to bring up charges against her with the Board, correct?"

"Yeah, but Dzarny's got that all locked up. I suppose I could—"

The voice interrupted him. "You are to gain access to her files. The coded files for Supervisors."

"Yeah," Nick said, "and then what?"

"Continue in your charges." A pause. "Use the files. Take the opportunity to complete your assignment."

Nick was about to ask what the hell that all meant when he heard the click and the buzz that indicated the other party had signed off.

A clap of thunder woke her, and she sat bolt upright in her bed to see flashes of lightning through her bedroom window.

"Hecate," she heard herself say, and then realized she was waking from a dream.

Thunder rumbled. She ran a hand over her face, down her neck, her breasts, to her belly, where she pressed her palm into herself.

"Bad dream," she said, wondering if this was all a bad dream.

She'd been on the streets of Manhattan again, the stench of rotting bodies filling her nostrils. She had reached for the mint in her pocket, and a hand stopped her.

Looking up the arm, she saw a watch, ticking time away, hands running fast around the hours.

Looking up from the watch, she'd seen the face of a man who wore glasses, which shifted to Nick's face, which shifted to Alex's face.

He looked at her and said, "Trouble, Jaguar. Get her out of there."

Get her out of there.
Who? Clare?
She pulled herself out of bed and went to stand at the window. She had too much to think about. Too many pieces of her flying everywhere.

Alex had paid her tuition. He'd paid her tuition, and kept her from being fired. He'd done that, and not once had he ever used it against her. Not once had he ever thrown it at her to get her to cooperate, behave, do what he wanted out of obligation or guilt. Not once.

And now he was in Leadville, because she said pyrite. And if DIE tried to kill her, what would they do to him?

He was in Leadville, and he'd paid her tuition, and seen to it that she didn't get fired. She wondered how many times since then he'd done that, without her knowing about it. She wondered why he did it. She wondered why she was having such difficulty fitting the idea into a place that made sense within her worldview. It just hung there, disassociated from the rest of her understanding, a bit of cognitive dissonance to disturb her dreams.

Knowing that someone was trying to kill her made more sense. That was a problem she could grapple with. It had happened before, and would probably happen again. All she had to do was figure out why, or who. Or both. Certainly knowing one would tell her the other.

It could have been Nick, she supposed, but this didn't seem like his way. It was too impersonal. His satisfaction in her death would be watching her go down, feeling his own power grow as hers waned. He'd want to see it happen, want his hands inside her. Know who she was through knowing her pain. Know her darkness, her fear.

She ran her hand across the window, wiping away drops of moisture that had accumulated. It was muggy tonight.

Maybe the rain would clear the air. The mass generator that had given the Planetoid gravity and an atmosphere approximating Earth's also had a tendency toward the middle of the road in weather. This was the first real thunderstorm of the year, and might be the last. Summers and winters were more consistently mild. She was glad of the storm. It matched her mood.

Or maybe she was just getting melodramatic about the whole thing. Something going on with her, and something about this case, pulling her back into a time nobody wanted to remember, but everyone had to. She couldn't quite pin down what it was about these assignments that dragged her into the time of the Serials. Almost every prisoner she dealt with had been through them, and carried scars. More often than not, it was something from that time that led to their crime. None of them had moved her into her own memories before. Why should it be happening with Clare? With Adrian?

She was being pushed, and she didn't know by whom. Nick, maybe?

If it wasn't Nick, the only other logical assumption she could make was that whoever hired Clare wanted her off the case, which meant she was close to being right. Too close. Pyrite, and DIE. This had to be about DIE wanting pyrite for psi work. And Alex was in Leadville.

Dangerous. And she'd put him in that danger.

But it didn't matter if she knew that DIE was involved. It wouldn't have mattered even if she knew for sure that they'd hired Clare. There were too many gaping holes in that thing called proof, and they were so good at hiding that by the time she gathered enough to fill in the holes, she'd be a very knowing corpse, her dust floating with the stars.

She'd either have to back way off and await developments, or she'd have to find a way to push it forward at her own pace, in her own way. If you can't make it better, make it worse.

The question of who hired Clare aside, she wanted to move her program along faster. She understood, at least, why she was such a good killer. Nobody ever really saw her. They would look at her and see only the reflection of their own fears, their own desires. The gift of reflection.

Jaguar wanted to figure out some way to get past the mirror she used and into the place where she really existed, as herself. Sheer force wouldn't work. Trickery might, but it would have to be the right trickery or she could lose all the progress they'd made so far. In spite of her coolness, her strange reflexive soul, Jaguar was moved by her. There was a lostness, and a sorrowing quality that touched some corresponding part in her own psyche, though she wasn't sure why, since Clare was about the most cold-blooded killer she'd ever had the pleasure to work with.

Melodramatic again. Clare had walked with her in a place where she'd let no one else in. Not all the way in, because she kept one day, one set of events locked away safe. But Clare had gone far enough in to find an old wound and open it. Jaguar was grieving her own, and confusing it with her prisoner's, as she was intended to do. Clare, the reflexive killer.

Perhaps. Or perhaps Clare, surviving the Serials without a scratch, had been through a war of the same kind, on different turf. In her own home, and the attacker her own father. At least, Jaguar thought, she felt no more resentment for Clare's apparent good fortune. She'd had no more good fortune than Jaguar.

And it was clear that Clare also intended to be caught on this one, and there could be only one of two reasons for that. Either she was playing out a plot designed by her employers, or she wanted to stop being a killer and find whatever it was she had lost of herself.

Two diametrically opposed options. To act on either one and then find out you were wrong could be deadly.

"And right now," she said out loud, "I haven't got a flying cock's clue which one is right."

The lightning beings danced in the night sky, and she asked them to tell her in the simplest of words what she was to do next. But they only continued to dance, their motion like laughter mocking her own sense of unwilling stillness.

Nick turned with irritation toward the computerized voice coming from the screen he'd opened and put into find sequence.

"What?" he asked. "What is it?"

The computer voice responded. "Improper authorization code."

"It's the only authorization code I have, you box of bolts. Put it through," he snapped back.

The letters re-formed to read: JAGUAR ADDAMS AUTHORIZATION.

"Come to Papa," he said to the screen as words began to move across it.

The screen shifted and a soft voice said, "Failure to input proper authorization code will result in automatic shutdown sequence. To begin in thirty seconds."

"Shit," Nick said. "What's this about? Somebody's got your records locked up tight, and I'll bet it's a Supervisor we share—though not in any interesting kind of way. Now what?"

"You talking to yourself?" a voice asked, causing him to twist sharply in his chair, fist raised.

Terence Manning stood next to him, grinning. "Hey. Hold your fire, all right?"

"Sorry," Nick grumbled, lowering his fist. "I thought you were—never mind."

"You thought I was Dzarny, didn't you? He's off on some home-planet thing. Won't be back for a while, I hear."

Nick narrowed his eyes. Terence always seemed to know everything about everyone. Must be his record-keeper mentality. His computer sounded a high-pitched tone, indicating the automatic shutdown sequence had started.

"Shit," Nick said. "God fucking dammit."

He slammed a fist against his desk and watched his

screen go blank. He'd have to start over again.

"What's wrong?" Terence asked, coming around and peering over his shoulder. "You got shut down?"

"Yeah," Nick said. "Wrong authorization code, I guess. I can never remember those things."

"Pain in the ass, right?" Terence agreed. "Whose file you want?"

Nick looked up at him, realization dawning. He had the record keeper with him. Of course.

"Addams. I want hers. The Board requested it."

"Yeah? You charging her after all? I heard she was pissed as hell at you. In Dzarny's office threatening your life and so on."

Terence knew everything. Nick wondered how much of it was actually true.

"Keep it under your hat, Terence," Nick said. "These things need a little discretion."

Terence beamed at him. "Oh sure. I know." He leaned his elbow on Nick's desk and called up the code for restart, and began the file sequence again.

When the lock appeared on Jaguar's files, Terence rapidly fed it a series of numbers that Nick would never be able to remember. But he didn't have to, because they worked, and her file scrolled across the screen.

"There you go, buddy," Terence said. "All yours."

"Hey," Nick said, "thanks. I owe you one."

"Just remember me to the important people," Terence told him. "When you meet them, that is."

"Right," Nick promised, and turned back to the screen as Terence left, still smiling.

The information that Nick found was enough to make him forget all about his past failures.

It was in Alex's private files, reports on cases that no one had ever heard the real story about. He'd been white-washing them, apparently, but kept a running record of his own on his classified line. Nick wondered why he did that, and if Terence knew that he'd given him Alex's classified code instead of the more general supervisory code.

He put a call in to the Governor he dealt with most frequently and made arrangements to meet with him and another Board member that same day. All he had to do was read two lines from one report, and it was enough to get them going. Especially Paul Dinardo, who set up the meeting with two other Board Governors, but excused himself from signing her warrant.

The other two Board members had signed without a murmur, and kept the reports, which was fine with Nick since he'd made copies for himself just in case.

Even better, he got their permission to bring her in himself, which was code for do whatever you want with her. He suspected it might even be code for don't bother getting her to us at all, just make the whole mess disappear. No wonder Paul excused himself, Nick thought. Dinardo wouldn't be able to face Alex if he'd signed off on Jaguar's death certificate. Certainly nobody would be surprised if Dr. Jaguar Addams was killed resisting arrest. She wouldn't be one to go quietly, after all.

And he assumed that's what the man with the glasses wanted, too. Make the big cat disappear.

He wished he knew a way to get in touch with them and ask. Better not, though. Better just follow his own instincts, and he could have a good time with her—a very good time—fulfill some of his wildest dreams before he fulfilled the dreams of the Board and the Looker.

When he left, the two Board members cast furtive glances at each other. They needed to talk to each other, but not to say what they thought. Tricky.

"This," one of them said, "is something best left to the discretion of the Teacher involved."

The other Board member nodded. He understood. That meant better not mention it to her supervisor. Dzarny's a little weird about Jaguar, and everybody knows it.

"It's so difficult to control workers in this system," the other Governor complained softly.

"True. We don't have nearly enough safeguards against this sort of difficulty. It's like the old institutions for the disabled. Workers used to throw basketballs at clients' heads, and nobody said a word about it."

They shook their heads sadly at this state of affairs, never asking who, in this case, was the client, and who was throwing the ball at the client's head.

11

A FULL TWENTY—FOUR HOURS PASSED DURING WHICH NO
attempts were made on her life, and Jaguar decided to see
if she could get a few more quiet days by avoiding the
House of Mirrors, Nick, even Moon Illusion. If she just
stayed out of the way, Nick might finally see the wisdom
of getting some help, as she had suggested. Whoever tried
to kill her might be lulled into taking a holiday, or at least
taking some time to resettle their feathers at their failure.

And she wouldn't worry about Alex's trip to the home
planet. He was a big boy. She would defer further probing
with Clare until he came back. And she would defer further
probing of what Rachel's talk had meant, too.

Now she would focus on Adrian.

He was nearly ready for a final push, she thought. His
anger at his failure to con anyone out of anything was
building to just the right pitch, and he looked at her more
frequently with loathing than with desire these days. He
was feeling trapped, impotent, used, and rapidly becoming
what he feared most.

She realized that soon she'd have to start turning the rage
into depression, which was a little more difficult to manage.
Depression bored her so quickly. It was . . . depressing.

Maybe it would allow her to catch up on her rest a little
There was that, after all.

She stood in her kitchen, looking over the food he'd
prepared for their dinner. She had asked him to do the
cooking, since any money that went into food was hers
He'd agreed, but not happily.

"Adrian," she called to him. He walked over to where
she stood, pointing down at a bubbling pot. "Does that
have oregano in it?"

"Sure. Sauce always does."

She rolled her eyes. "I'm allergic, Adrian," she said. "I
told you that."

"Christ," he started to say, but was interrupted by the
doorbell.

"Are you expecting company?" she asked. He shook his
head.

She wasn't either. Maybe it was one of the guys from
the band, bringing back the black jacket she had left at the
bar the other night.

She looked out the peephole in the door. It was not someone from the band.

It was Nick.

"I told you," she said calmly through the door intercom,
"to stay away from me. Now go away or I'll call the cops."

She heard nothing. She expected him to snap back that
he *was* the cops. He didn't. Nor, she realized, could she
hear the sound of his footsteps leaving. She stood to the
side of the door and, when Adrian walked into the room,
motioned him to stand back.

Then she heard the high-pitched whine of the jammer as
it shattered the lock and the knob of her door. She saw
Nick's leg, kicking it open, and he was in, sealing it behind
him quickly.

"What," she said brightly, "a surprise." She turned to
Adrian. "Honey, take out an extra plate. Looks like we'll
be having a guest for dinner."

•   •   •

Alex went only far enough into the shaft to be in shadow, but in a place where he could still see light. In the night, throughout a very wakeful night, he'd heard the scrapings and hissings of life moving around him. Bats and mice. Raccoons, maybe. Or spirit life. Trapped men trying to escape. But if that was the case, they would have some sympathy for him. He was in a similar predicament, and they'd understand.

When the sun streamed down over his face in the morning and he determined that he wasn't dead, he began to worry about Jaguar. If they'd killed Neri so quickly just for speaking with him, what were they doing to her? He stood and stretched, crawled out of his hole in the ground, and stood on the ledge that looked over the mist-encased trees and the dew-sparkling grass of the cemetery below him.

The sun was still close to the horizon, so it was early yet. He should get into town and find a telecom. Call her?

That would be dangerous. They could be in her lines by now, if they hadn't been all along. And how long was all along, anyway? They must have someone on the Planetoid, and he assumed it was the strange and rather listless-looking man with the large glasses who said he was assigned as liaison in the case. They must also have someone else on the Planetoid they were working with.

Nick? Perhaps, though he wouldn't want to hire on Nick for anything delicate, and this work seemed to him to be very delicate. The DIE people needed to cover their asses, not expose them further.

At least all the pieces of information were beginning to cohere into something like a whole.

Weaving together the threads of information he'd gathered from Rachel's reports to Jaguar, from his talk with Neri, from his own understanding of how these operations worked, he figured that Clare had worked for DIE for years. Maybe they'd experimented with their Supertoys on her and that was why she was so difficult to find empathically. At any rate, she'd done the hit on Patricks when he started

upping the ante on the pyrite deal. Not that they couldn'
afford his price, but they weren't the sort of organizatior
to let someone else change the rules on them.

Why Clare had gotten herself caught on this assignmen
was a question he couldn't begin to answer. Perhaps it wa'
something personal. Or perhaps she was meant to be on the
Planetoid for some purpose he couldn't fathom yet. The
two attempts made on her life during the course of her tria
made him suspect that she was acting on unconscious motives of her own, but that could have been a setup, too. DIE
was nothing if not thorough.

Either way, they'd want her kept away from someone
like Jaguar, whose skill was probably the only real risl
factor in the situation. And they'd probably been playing
techno-tool games on Jaguar for a while, which might explain her erratic behavior. Of course Jaguar's norma
behavior was nothing if not erratic, but even for Jaguar
she'd been out of bounds lately.

They'd want to keep a lid on their pseudogenics research
on their dealings with Clare, on their Research Center. Ner
said it was nearby. He was tempted, briefly, to try to find
it.

No. He had to get word back to the Planetoid. Jaguar
might be enough to make DIE very nervous, but there were
more of them than there were of her. She had to be warned

He wondered if they had the capacity to get in on othe
kinds of communication. Did their Supertoys allow them tc
listen in if, for instance, he was able to find her and get her
attention empathically? With Jaguar, who was so good at
closing herself off, they might find they'd gotten more thar
they bargained for. He often had. At any rate, he'd have to
try.

He closed his eyes, and as his breathing settled and his
thoughts focused, he found her.

There, in her apartment. She was . . . calling him?

His name. He heard his name. What was going on?

Adrian was there and—shit. Nick was there. Nick was—

"Christ," Alex said, his eyes flying open. "Christ Almighty."

Nick pulled back his free hand and slapped her hard, with the back of it.

"Jesus—Jag—what the hell is this?" Adrian came running to her side, and she held up a hand to stop him. She slowly twisted herself around to face Nick.

"Having a bad day?" she asked, trying to capture his gaze as it darted from one side of the room to the other. If she could get him, she could hold him.

"Baby," he said, "you're under arrest." He waved the papers that she recognized as a warrant in her face.

"That old news? Didn't Alex tell you the charges were dropped for lack of evidence? Nicky, you've got to learn to keep up."

"What the hell are you talking about?" Adrian muttered. She ignored him.

"I don't need my old charges, sweetheart. I've been in your files, and there's some real interesting stuff in them. This warrant's for the rest of your crimes."

Her files? "What files, Nick?"

"The private ones Alex kept on your antics. I got some friends who let me help myself to them."

He moved toward her, and pressed his weapon against her head, pressed his mouth against her ear. "Your precious Alex," he whispered. "Where do you suppose he is about now? I understand he's being taken care of by somebody with more power than even your ego could conjure. And they seem to want you out of the way, too. You should've seen those files."

Jaguar felt the sinking in her stomach that signified danger. Alex. Where was he?

"What are you saying, Nick?" she asked. "Nick, look at me and tell me what you're talking about."

"How stupid do you think I am?" he scoffed. "Look deep into those sea-green eyes. Those witch eyes? Right."

''Who're you working for, Nick?''

''No names, no trouble. All I know is the Board signed the warrant, and sent me out to collect you, personal like.''

''Where's your backup, Nick?'' she asked, knowing what it would mean if he'd come without.

''Don't need any.'' He chuckled as he saw her face express an understanding of what this meant. ''That's right,'' he acknowledged. ''They don't care what shape you're in when I get you to them. Your ass, my sweet, is the perennial, proverbial grass.''

''What'll you do, Nick?''

''What's the worst you can imagine me doing, Jag?''

He backed away from her, keeping his weapon pointed at her face. Always hit between the eyes, he'd told her. Don't give them any time to talk.

Jaguar eyed him coldly, all grief for this loss gone. Now she noted only the necessary instincts of self-preservation that attuned her whole being to what moves he made, what moves she could make in response. She noted that his eyes shifted quickly here and there. That he backed away. That he fumbled when he reached for his weapons scanner. He talked a good game, but he was too nervous or too excited. It made him clumsy.

She raised her arms toward him for the cuffs.

''Not so fast,'' he said. ''I gotta scan you first.'' He ran his sensor up and down her, front and back and sides, keeping his eyes near her face, but not near enough so that she could hold him. He slipped the sensor back in his belt and pulled out the temporary cuffs. She held her arms out, ready for them. She would have a second to act. Maybe two at most.

When he got close enough to put them on, she moved the fourth finger of her left hand to a button on her right cuff and pressed.

The soft snap of the knife into her palm couldn't be heard by anyone except her.

''Nick,'' she said, and in the time it took him to hear

her say his name, she moved. A small motion. Hardly any ground covered or any energy lost.

She thrust her right arm forward and up and pressed into him until she could feel his living heart beat around the edge of her blade.

He gasped once, looked down at his chest, at her blade embedded in it. He lifted a hand to the wound, looked back up at her, then began to drop. She lowered herself with him and did not let go of his gaze.

"You told me about it a long time ago, Nick," she said to the dying light in his eyes. "The sensors don't pick up glass knives."

He was kneeling now, tottering, breath coming only in guttural gasps as his heart struggled against the impediment lodged there. He wanted to say something. Words wanted to emerge from his shocked mouth. She knew what they were.

"The knife in the heart, Nick," she said smoothly. "It was always your deepest fear."

Breath rattled out of his throat as he closed his eyes and slumped at her feet, her knife still in him.

"What the hell," Adrian said, stumbling over to where she knelt next to the still body. "Is he—did you—"

She pulled the knife from Nick's chest and wiped the blade on his pant leg. "He's dead," she noted, putting a finger against his carotid. "Quite dead. Though he still may be able to hear us, you know. Better," she said, "watch what you say."

"You—you killed him."

"Yes. I did." She sighed, held up the hand that curled around the thin, translucent red blade. "Handy thing, this. A present from someone who loved me once, long ago." She pressed a button at her wrist, and it retracted. Pressed again, and it slid silently into her hand. She would still need it. The act was not complete yet, either in practical terms, or in terms of the proper way to deal with the body of a shadowed man. "I guess we'll have to clean up now."

"Clean up?"

"Mm. We can drain him in the tub, then cut him up and take him down to the burn plant. They won't sift for his bones down there."

Adrian gaped at her. She turned a fretful eye up to him as she rose. "Come on, Adrian," she said. "Can't you get anything right? I thought you claimed you knew the score."

"I—I never killed anyone."

Jaguar threw her head back and laughed loud and long.

"What's so funny? That's not funny," Adrian snarled at her.

"Funny? My God, it's a scream." She put her face close to his and grabbed the back of his collar, holding him. "What do you suppose happened to all those ISD patients you sold worthless placebos to, huh? What do you suppose happened to those mothers and fathers who spent their last pennies on your miracle cure, then watched their children die anyway? Granted, you didn't pull the trigger when they blew their own brains out, but you sure gave them something to load the gun with." She shook him roughly, then let go. "Never killed anyone. Of all the willful ignorance. Help me get him into the tub, and *don't* drag him across the carpet—blood's such a bitch to get cleaned."

Alex squatted on his ledge and listened to the tree talk, watched the mist dissolve, observed how ordinary the grass of the cemetery looked with the morning dew dried and gone. Just brown grasses, unkempt and as thirsty as he was.

He ran his tongue over his teeth, wishing for a toothbrush. He'd have to get into town. Do something. But every time he tried to move, he was stopped cold by the image of Nick's face, and Jaguar's glass knife.

Jaguar's glass knife.

Red glass, and retractable into a little holder on her wrist. It was a very practical weapon, and she used it with expedience on Nick. The glass knife was also a ceremonial tool for her, and he could imagine her pulling Nick's still-warm heart from his body, saying the death prayers, feeling only a deep calm.

He hadn't seen that because he stopped looking. Didn't want to see more. He saw a flash of Nick's grin. His shock at the soft motion she made and what it meant. Her knife in his heart. Her words. That was more than enough.

Did she have the sickness, too? The creeping shadow, permanently lodged inside her from the Serial years, just waiting for an invitation to act in the world. Invasion of her psyche by the shadow of that time, corroding her judgment and spirit.

Or had Nick gone over the line? Was he working for DIE, and did she know that? Damn her and her capacity for silence. She'd protect Nick from the Board, and kill him herself. He'd save her life, and then torment her with the salvation. No wonder they'd hooked up. They were two of a kind, morally ambivalent and emotionally closed. He took a minute to blow off steam, kicking hard at a rock, which hurt him a lot more than the rock, he supposed.

Then he focused on what he had to do. What action he needed to take.

It was clear. He had to get to a town, and get in touch with her. Find her, and see if she was all right. If he couldn't reach her, he'd have to find someone who could, because whether she was shadowed or not, she was certainly in danger beyond her own awareness.

He picked his way back down the hill he'd been perched on, saluting the men who rested within it before moving through the trees at the base and across the cemetery. He kept his eyes open for anyone following him as he went, but saw no signs of it.

At the edge of the cemetery, he noticed a caretaker's house, looking forlorn and as ill-kept as the cemetery itself. He considered stopping there to see if anyone was around, or if there was a telecom inside, then decided against it.

He bypassed the town of Leadville itself, keeping it in his vision long enough to get his bearings so he could re-

member where the next town was. It took him another hour
to reach it, and then more time to locate a bar that had use
of a public telecom. Jaguar's line was not working, and he
figured she'd turned it off. She did that when she was working a case in her own apartment. He'd have to try reaching
someone else. Someone from the Board, he thought. Then
at least he'd have a public record of what had happened to
Neri and to him.

The telecom was an older model, and when he pressed
the sequence for Paul's classified line, it took longer than
usual for his face to appear, out of focus and with a tendency to crack at the edges.

"Paul," he said, calm now and sure of what he had to
do, "how are you?"

"Confused, Alex," Paul said, looking at him on the
screen from over a pile of papers. "Where are you?"

"Home planet, getting some work done. Too many assignments, not enough Teachers. You know how it is."

"Sure. I know. Where's Nick?"

So he didn't know. That, at least, boded well.

"Nick? I advised him to take home leave. Thought he
took my advice."

Paul shook his head. "No, Alex. I don't think that'll do.
I sent him with a warrant to that crazy woman's house.
Jaguar Addams. She's to be arrested."

"The charges," Alex said calmly, "were dropped for
lack of evidence."

"We picked them up again. He brought us some of your
private files, and it didn't look good. Doesn't look very
good for you, either, but we can talk about that. You
aren't," he added, "playing favorites here, are you?"

Alex chewed on his lip and thought. Then he moved
forward. "Paul," he said, "did you give Nick carte
blanche?"

"I don't know what you're talking about, Alex."

He nodded. "Sure. I know that Board members never
give signals to Teachers or cops that they should handle a

case as they see fit, without benefit of due process. I know that never happens. But if it ever did happen, would this have been one of the times?''

Paul ran his fingers through his hair and raised tired eyes to Alex. "What's the problem with it, Alex? She's a maverick. A menace. Always has been. Everybody knows that but you.''

"The problem,'' Alex said, "is that, hypothetically, if Teachers ever used the empathic arts, if they ever got the theoretical shadow sickness from that hypothetical use, then Nick would have had, in theory, all the symptoms.''

"What? But the files were—''

"Full of shit, Paul. Faked. I have no private files on any of my people. If I want something kept private, I don't file it. And Nick has the sickness. Or couldn't you tell?''

"Where is he, Alex?''

"I don't know. Aren't you going to ask where Jaguar is?''

"Shit,'' Paul said, with feeling. "If she screws up the Rilasco case—''

"I don't think even Jaguar could make it worse than it already is.''

Paul's face turned a mottled gray, and he pulled back from the screen. Alex could almost smell his fear.

"What's that mean?'' he demanded.

"DIE's in it,'' Alex said. "Up to their filthy red eyes.''

"Shit,'' Paul repeated. "Are you sure?''

"Very. I'll explain when I get back. If I get back,'' he added. "In the meantime I want you to check on Jaguar. Make sure she's aware of what I told you. Tell her to stay away from Clare until I get back, and to be very careful. And Paul—if the warrant's still outstanding, I'd suggest you withdraw it.''

He clicked off the telecom, leaving Paul still babbling, and thanked the bartender for his help.

It wasn't until he stepped outside that he realized how much trouble he was in himself.

Two unmarked wings had landed outside the diner. One to his left and one to his right.

He took a step back, and felt the pressure of someone behind him.

After that he had time only to curse himself once for his stupidity, and be briefly thankful that he'd gotten a warning through, before the world went black.

12

WHEN SHE LEFT HER APARTMENT, INTENDING TO go to the House of Mirrors, she realized she had passed the turn for the street and was headed for Alex's. By the time she reached his building, and parked her car and walked in, she understood why.

She'd learned how to open his lock some time ago, and used this skill when she had to, in emergencies, when she needed a place to hide. Usually she knocked first, but today she didn't bother. If he had returned, he would be expecting her. If he hadn't, it didn't matter.

He wasn't home.

She stood in his apartment, breathing in the pungent aroma of recently burned incense. He'd been thinking hard before he left. Looking for her, she thought. But last night, after she'd taken care of Nick's body, she had tried to make empathic contact to warn him. Tell him what Nick said. Tell him there must be someone else on the Planetoid involved. Someone who had enough access to fake a good file on her.

She couldn't find him.

She should have been able to locate him easily. She knew where he was, when he was, who he was. Knowing just one of those should have been enough. Yet she couldn't locate him anywhere.

A circle of dead men, and Alex caught within it. Alex, walking with the dead.

She wasn't an adept, she reminded herself. That image wasn't a projection into future possibilities. It might have been generated from her contact with Nick. Or from Clare, who read death objectively, without prejudice.

"Shit," she said, "where are you, Alex?"

Then she calmed herself, stilled herself. She had to find him, and she had to be quiet in order to do so.

She let the sweet stillness of the empathic moment envelop her, concentrating on Alex, who he was, the particular molecules of his being. He had to be somewhere. Everyone was somewhere. But she couldn't find him. All she found was an infinite space, cold and emptied of life, filled with loneliness. She removed herself from it, and shook it off.

Dead men, and Alex among them. Dreams of dead men and Clare. Nick, dead at her hand. Pyrite, and the interests of organizations such as DIE.

One thing only was clear.

She had to get to Leadville, and Clare, who knew everything, would have to go with her. She began thinking through the particulars, her thoughts moving fast through sets of options. She looked around the apartment, speaking to the walls and furniture as if they might relay the message. "I'll be there as soon as I can," she said, "if I can find where *there* is."

Then she left his apartment and drove to the House of Mirrors, grateful for light traffic and her car's capacity for speed. She walked into the central room with purpose and stood directly in front of Clare, between her and the mirror.

Clare startled, and refocused on her.

"Come with me," Jaguar said, and led her through the halls, toward the door, to the outside.

When they stood in the bright sunshine, Clare staring at

her as if she was seeing her face for the first time, Jaguar spoke.

"I've killed someone. Another Teacher. I'll need to leave the Planetoid, and I intend to take you with me."

Clare's forehead furrowed as she tried to absorb this, and then her face softened into a smile. "You've killed another Teacher?"

"That's right," Jaguar said. "Nick, in fact. The lousy fuck."

"Well, good job, then," was Clare's rather distracted comment.

"Clare, I have to leave here. I want to work for your people on the home planet. I can get you off the Planetoid, if you'll set me up."

Clare breathed in deeply, a sound of pure pleasure. "You can get me out of here?"

"I can. It'll take a few hours, but I don't think they'll turn up anything on the guy I killed between now and then."

"Where's the body?" she asked.

"Burn plant. I cut him up."

"Mm. I hate that, don't you? But I wish I'd seen you do it."

"Why?"

"Well, for all I know this is a story you're making up. Part of the Planetoid program or a foolish attempt to get me to bring you to my employers."

Jaguar threw her head back and laughed hard. "Your employers? I know who they are, Clare. You work for DIE. Have for years. They took you in after you killed your trick, and you went to work for them. I'm not sure what they're working on now, but I know it has to do with superluminary transfer of information, and pyrite is a necessary ore for their experiments."

Clare's eyes widened. "Who else knows this?"

"Nobody yet. I wanted to make sure of my facts first."

"And have you?"

"Yes."

"How?"

Jaguar grinned. "Just now. By confirming it with you."

Clare turned her face toward Jaguar and stared at her hard through cold eyes. Her expression went through the motions of surprise, anger, and something almost like fear, before returning to its well-instructed neutrality.

"Gotcha," Jaguar said softly.

Clare nodded at her sagely. "You did," she said. "And now what?"

"I'll be back," Jaguar said to their reflections. "Tonight. Be ready for me. Dress in something dark."

She drove back to her own apartment to find Adrian slouched on the couch, either morose or drunk—she couldn't tell which. The depressed phase of the program.

"Adrian," she said, singsong, and he turned glazed eyes up at her. "Sweetheart, I hope you're in a condition to listen, because I have got quite a story for you."

"Fuck off," he muttered.

"Love to, but no time. You know how you said you always wanted to be somebody?"

"Fuck off twice," he muttered louder.

"Right. Well, here's your chance. Because the truth is, you're not in Toronto. You're on the Planetoids. You've been doing your Planetoid sentence with me from the start, and now I need your help in saving a life or two."

He pushed himself out of the chair and shoved a fist in her face. "FUCK OFF," he shouted at her, and then stopped, suspended in mid-action.

"Adrian," she said, "I need your help."

He lowered his fist, and frowned. He might be a lousy con man, and he might be a failure at everything he'd done, but he still knew how to read a face. She was worried about something, and it looked like something important.

"You're in some kind of real trouble, aren't you?" he asked.

"That's right," Jaguar said. "Real trouble. Sit down, and I'll tell you all about it."

First, Alex felt a ringing in his ears that seemed to spread in ripples from the center of his brain, to the space he occupied. It grew in volume and range, encompassing him and then dispersing at the edges of pitch, going out and out. Ripples of sound, sharp at the central point, then harmonics stretching into wavering bands that dissipated around him.

He groaned, felt himself struggling to move, and opened his eyes.

The room he was in was dimly lit, and his eyes took their time adjusting to it. Thought returned before vision, and he knew he was in trouble. When he tried to move and found he was firmly bound to the chair he was sitting in, he knew it all over again.

He blinked, shook his head roughly to get rid of the residual ringing in his ears, and peered through the green darkness.

Green. There were green lights glowing somewhere.

He scanned the room, and saw that he wasn't alone.

There were five men, bound in chairs similar to his, but hooked up to monitors that glowed above their heads.

They all stared at nothing, stared ahead, blinking occasionally.

Alex wrinkled his nose. A funny smell here. Not rotten or offensive, but disturbing. An olfactory sensation more than a scent. It had the feel of electricity burning the surface of skin. The smell of lightly singed hair. Something in between. It made the back of his teeth feel as if he'd been chewing on aluminum.

The monitors blinked and lines wavered across them. Alex watched the men staring ahead at nothing.

"Hey," he said, "where am I?"

They didn't respond. Unconscious, he thought. Some kind of drugged state. He looked at the man across from him and noticed a repetitive, rhythmic twitch in his left eye. Watching, he felt his own eye begin to twitch, and he shivered, shook his head to chase it away.

The smell was disturbing. Elusive. Something familiar about it, but he couldn't place it. He stared at the man across from him, and felt the twitch returning to his own eye. When he moved his gaze down the man's body, the twitching in his eye ceased.

"I'm pulling something in, and I don't like it," he murmured to himself.

He examined the man as much as he could from where he sat, noticing that his skin was gray and mottled. Noticing that there was no color to speak of in the skin of his arms. Noticing that his chest was hollow and sunken and—

"Jesus," he whispered. "He's not breathing."

He wasn't breathing.

They weren't breathing.

None of them was breathing. Chests, sunken and hollow, didn't move.

The man's eyes shifted in his head, turned toward him sightless, and rested full on his face.

His heart pounded as if he'd been caught in an act of absolute desecration. Viewing the dead. Being seen by the dead. Seeing the dead as they saw you. He didn't mean to be here. He didn't want to be here. This was not supposed to happen not these eyes staring at him accusing him what had he done except get caught jesus god what was this like every child's nightmare the sightless eyes staring, twitching and none of them breathing at all.

Waves of despair washed over him and he realized he was caught in an empathic connection with this horror this not breathing not dead not breathing. He blocked it quickly, and found that beads of sweat had formed on his face, and he was cold.

It was cold in here. Cold as . . . death.

Something Terence said. Cold as death. Something Neri said about the dead being easier than the living.

Something Neri said about they *are* doing it. Now.

He rested his head against the back of the chair and tried to let go, set up whatever boundaries he could to keep this not-death from washing over him again. Don't look at their faces. Don't look at their eyes. Don't let their despair get into you. He kept his gaze down, looked at the skin on his own arm, afraid that it, too, would appear that mottled gray, because at this point he wasn't sure what condition he was in either.

Did these men know? Were they aware?

Of course they knew. That was the despair. What he'd felt was what they were experiencing. Consciousness trapped within endless death. The spirit unable to free itself from death. The body powerless to live or to die.

Don't look at their faces. Don't look at their eyes. He knew enough already.

In the wash of green darkness, a door at the far end of the room opened, and a man entered.

He wore a lab coat and carried a small calculator in his hand. As he made his way across the room toward Alex, he stopped occasionally to examine monitors, press a finger against an arm, press some buttons on his calculator. When he reached Alex's chair he stopped and stood in front of him.

"Are you feeling all right?" he asked. "Anything hurt?"

"Just," Alex said, "my pride." He tossed a nod at the occupants of the other chairs. "Are these men dead?" he asked.

"I'm not authorized to answer your questions," was the response.

Alex licked his lips, tasted the salty sweat. "Why haven't you killed me yet?"

"We have no authorization for any actions yet," the man said.

"I see." Alex began to wonder if this man was also dead. Maybe everyone here was dead. Maybe he was, too, and just hadn't recognized the fact yet. He could feel all his neurons pulling into his center, trying to escape the signals that washed in the air around him. He'd have to block it somehow. Too much, this living death, the despair of the body forced into a life it couldn't sustain, the despair of the spirit that couldn't escape.

"Why are you here, talking to me?" he asked, when the man said nothing.

"I'm to check on your physical status, and tell you that if you need anything, you can press the button under your index finger. Someone will come along to help you."

"How hospitable of you. Anything else?"

"Yes. Don't attempt empathic contact. You'll find it painful."

"Why?"

"We've got a blocking device on the area. Electric fence."

So much for finding Jaguar. Or for her finding him.

He looked at the men who sat with him, all in various stages of death withheld. And he knew that here, in this place, he was one of them.

Terence reported the conversation between Jaguar and Adrian as soon as he received it on his recorder. He thought the Looker would be furious, but surprisingly, he was pleased. "She'll do the job for us," he said. "How convenient."

"Yeah, but—"

"Let me think," he said, turning back to his cards. They looked good today. All the aces were up, and he had enough to move around without turning over the rest of the deck yet.

He played through a full hand, and won the lot. Then he sat and smiled for so long that Terence had just decided to clear his throat, get his attention somehow. But he spoke.

"When does the next shuttle go out?"

"The regular service? I think in a few hours."

"You are to get on it, and go directly to the center.

Dzarny's there, and I want you to take charge of him.''

"What'm I supposed to do?''

"Just keep an eye on him. I believe he's sufficiently blocked from any action, but I'd rather have you on hand. I also believe it would be wiser if you were somewhere far away for the next day or two. I'll meet you there as soon as I wrap up this most untidy case.''

Terence felt his heart take a short jaunt inside his chest. He pressed a hand against it hard and massaged. The Looker had a plan. Safer not to know. Safer to be far away. At least, he hoped it was safer.

"Is that it?'' he asked.

"Yes. Except in the event that something untoward occurs. Then you're to kill Dzarny.''

"What do you mean, untoward?''

"It would be difficult to anticipate, ahead of the events, all that might occur. But if I don't return, or if any attempt is made on the part of anyone else to enter the facilities, you're to kill Dzarny. The rest of our people are safe.''

"What're you going to do?''

"That's my business,'' he said. "You just take care of your own.''

13

CLARE WAS READY AND WAITING WHEN JAGUAR AR-
rived.

"I hope you think the black pantsuit is appropriate," was
her only comment. "It's silk, but I find it both comfortable
and serviceable."

Jaguar realized that when she said serviceable, she meant
it didn't show bloodstains readily, and when she said comfortable, she meant you could just as easily kick someone's
face while wearing it as go dancing in it. The perfect outfit.

"Let's go," she said.

They left the House of Mirrors and walked down the path
toward the breeding complex. She'd parked nearby the entrance to the public portion of the Sanctuary, and instructed
Adrian to stay at the gate between the breeding complex
and the Sanctuary. She'd taken a chance and jammed it
open if he needed to get in, and gave him Nick's gun to
use, just in case.

As they walked Jaguar became aware of a rustling in the
bushes nearby. Clare cast a glance in that direction. She'd
heard it, too. Jaguar squeezed her arm, and they walked
faster.

Then she heard a sharp hissing sound, and a man stepped
out of the shadows.

"Hello, Clare," he said politely. "How have you been?"

Jaguar could feel stillness wash through Clare. She turned toward the man, observed the weapon he pointed at them. It wasn't familiar to her. She imagined she wouldn't want it to be.

"I don't believe we've been introduced," she said.

"They call me the Looker," he said, and took a step toward them.

"How nice for you. With DIE by any chance?"

He didn't answer. Jaguar turned to Clare, who smiled at her sweetly, apologetically, and moved toward the man called the Looker. "He calls it the Division," she said.

"I don't blame him," Jaguar said. "Stupid acronym. What were you guys thinking of anyway?"

He blinked at her. "We never imagined that anyone would turn the acronym into a word."

There was one question answered. It was not a scare tactic or bad taste, but pure ego.

"I see," she said. "And, I suppose now you'll kill me."

"Indeed," the Looker said. "We've been trying to dispose of you for some time, but you're very elusive, or very lucky. Tonight has been most helpful. It will appear as if you were helping Clare escape, and she killed you. A very passable way of cleaning up this untidy little episode."

"Nice of me, wasn't it? How did you know I'd be doing this?"

"A colleague had placed a recording implant in your other assignment—Adrian, yes? I met him in the shrubbery on the way over. He's currently incapacitated, I'm afraid to say, and won't be joining us. Your conversation with him was overheard."

"A tap in Adrian. I always hated taps. But why all the fuss?" She jerked her head toward Clare. "Surely she's not that valuable to you."

"No. But our research is at a delicate point, and she knows a good deal about it."

Jaguar frowned and looked closely at his dead eyes. "What research?"

"Pseudogenics," the Looker replied. He waved his weapon ahead of them. "I'd like it if we walked now. Straight ahead, please."

They formed a line, with Clare in front, then Jaguar, then the Looker, and began walking toward the breeding complex. Jaguar took a moment to gather her thoughts. Pseudogenics. Using empathic energy to restore kinesis in the dead. Like the lines of dead men in her visions. Now it made sense. Now she knew the truth. Now all she had to do was live to tell about it. As if a thought had just occurred to her, she stopped and turned to the Looker. "But—what about Alex? He knows about DIE. Probably at this point he knows about the pseudogenics."

"He does. Indeed, you could say his knowledge is personal."

A line of dead men, and Alex at the end of them. Her silent shout into a mirror of fear: *No, No, No.*

"Is Alex—" She couldn't bring herself to say it. There was a hollow darkness growing in the pit of her belly, unexpectedly deep and painful.

"He's been attended to," the Looker said. "Keep walking please."

They moved down the path. Clare, Jaguar, and the Looker.

She had to keep talking. Keep this hollow space in her filled or she would be dead. Last in a line of dead men. Right after Alex. Don't feel it yet, she told herself. Keep talking.

"Clare—are you amenable to all this?" she asked as they walked.

Clare sighed deeply. "I feel a little bad, which is unusual for me, but I think that's because I was looking forward to working with you. Though I'm not sure you'd be a good assassin after all. Too much passion." She wrinkled her nose as if the word was distasteful. "I just do my job."

"Right," Jaguar said. "So when you kill me, I'll try not to take it personally."

"Wise of you." The Looker peered into the darkness. "Let's move over here. It's enough in the open that you won't be missed. Though it's a shame to leave your body, I must say. You'd be a valuable asset to our research."

"But how lovely for me," Jaguar said, "to die right next to my namesakes."

"That will be nice for you," Clare said.

"It will remind me not to whimper," Jaguar agreed.

The silence of the room, the absence of breath in the presence of bodies that retained motion, reminded Alex of nightmares he'd had when he was in the army.

Somewhere in him he could hear Neri's laughter at this. *We love dead people. They're so quiet.*

He knew that the presence of death was seeping into him. No. Not death. In his two-year army stint, walking the streets of Manhattan and L.A. at the tag end of the Serials, he'd seen enough death to know the feel of it.

This wasn't death. This was absolute despair. He'd felt something like this in living people, primarily in children who had survived family abuse of some kind and who felt their lives enclosed by the absence of hope for change, for wellness, for love. A living death.

It seeped into him. He knew he had to resist it, but he wasn't sure how.

The man in the lab coat told him empathic contact would be a mistake. He could almost hear Jaguar laughing, and wished she was here to instruct him in the peculiar ways she had of blowing up technology. He hadn't her gift for it.

He looked around to see if there was anything like a source for the various hummings and buzzing and green light blips in the room.

There were laser-light pathways cast across the ceiling. There, in the corner, what looked like a proton generator, though what they'd do with a proton generator was beyond him. Still, it was something to focus on, and he focused.

Nothing.

He gave a grunt of frustration, made a fist, and remembered just in time not to pound it on the arm of his chair, because to do so would bring the man in the lab coat to him.

He sat and thought some more, keeping himself separate from the constant and profound flow of despair in the room. Somewhere nearby, he could hear music. Bach. A fugue, orderly and dispassionate.

"Bach," he muttered. "Now I *will* go mad."

What would Jaguar do to get rid of this machinery?

She'd told him once. It was a matter of looking beyond the obstacle and projecting yourself into the place you wanted to be rather than into the thing that stood between you and your goal.

All right, then.

Where did he want to be?

He closed his eyes and let the image of it rise to the surface of his mind.

Immediately, without any further effort, she was there. Long dark hair streaked with honey and sun. Long limbs and strong body. The smooth amber of her face, carved in the lines and angles of her people, wind-kissed, like the high desert land. Her sea-green eyes, welcoming him, inviting him in.

"Okay," he said to the image, "here goes nothing."

He opened himself to her, whispering her name over time and space, letting the empathic space be the only space he occupied. He would show her where he was, who was with him, what he knew if it killed him. He would open himself as fully as he could, and let the demons who waited be damned.

The image of her moved. Jerked her head up, startled.

Jaguar, I'm here. I'm—

Nonbeing filled him. Corpse occupied by soul but dead

the scent of nondeath. He was filled with it, filled with it. He felt it choking him, strangling him, hands around his neck like the hands of a man long ago no air no air. Then Jaguar and her body dead her soul in hiding from this outrage dead dead they were all dead falling on her dead but their hands cold clammy in her on her the soft sick scent of it like medicine like surgeon's gloves like urine she couldn't breathe could not breathe, her hands flying out, looking for something to grab like drowning and where's the straw to hang on to not there nothing there except this.

A searing pain burned itself across his consciousness, and instead of words, he gave voice to a long, high howl of agony.

They stopped in front of the cages, which were empty. Hecate and Chaos were out prowling.

She paused to consider this.

"Would you like the honors, or shall I?" the Looker asked Clare politely.

"I think," she said, "I'd like to watch."

Jaguar steadied herself to make one last try for her life, and as she did so a rushing of voice and image enveloped her, taking her breath away. A cemetery, and a house. A house filled with dead men, like the hollow place inside her. Hot and filled with pain and death and a voice.

A voice she knew. A voice that was alive. Alive. Painful and alive and marvelous and—

She blinked at Clare, at the Looker, and her smile was loud and clear.

"Alex isn't dead," she stated, grinning at them.

Clare shifted her vision from dreamy to attentive. "What?" she said.

"He's not dead," she repeated, ready to shout it now. "He's *alive. Alive.*" She howled out laughter, threw her arms wide, let her head fall back, and raised her voice to the night.

"*Hecate*," she cried. "*Hecate. Hecate.*"

Stunned by sound, the Looker hesitated, and the great golden cat leaped from the bushes, knocking Clare down and leaving a line of slashes across her face.

"Hecate," Jaguar called again, but she'd already turned toward her target, crouched low in front of him less than two yards away, tail sweeping the earth and eyes bright with watching.

"A cat," Jaguar said, "can look at a Looker."

He stood frozen for a brief second, and then his hand began to shake as the human and feline predator stared at each other, evaluating their chances. He tried to stop the tremors, control his aim, but when he moved his hand, Hecate's jaw's jerked open in a deep growl.

The Looker fumbled, dropped his weapon, stumbled backward, recovered himself, turned, and ran toward the dark cover of the shrubs.

Hecate followed.

Somewhere close by, Jaguar heard a high keening wail of pain, then silence.

At her feet, she felt the scrabble of movement and saw Clare, on the ground, face bleeding, her hand reaching toward the weapon the Looker had dropped. Jaguar stretched out her leg and placed her well-heeled foot over it.

"No, Clare," she said.

Clare's eyes grew wide, and her hand retreated from the weapon.

"I always promised myself I wouldn't whimper either," she said quietly.

Jaguar shook her head. "You don't understand, do you? You said my job was like yours, but it's not. I'm not supposed to kill you. I'm supposed to help you."

She kicked the weapon away from them both and knelt down on the ground beside Clare, taking her face in both her hands. "This is the Planetoids," she said. "This is what we do here. Face your fear and learn to live with it. Beyond it. In spite of it."

Clare's bloodied face showed eyes wide and absorbent as the sky. "There's nothing I'm afraid of."

"Yes there is," Jaguar said. "You're afraid to feel."

"No," Clare said. "I'm not. I only know it interferes with my work."

"No," Jaguar snapped. "You're afraid to feel anything, because then you'll have to feel everything. *Everything,* Clare. The last tingling terror of everyone you ever killed. Your father's loathing of you. Your mother's loathing of your father. The way they betrayed you. Raped you. That old feeling of your body, not yours. Owned and used by someone else as if you were no more than a corpse. The feeling of being a corpse under your father's hands. Knowing you could do nothing to stop it. Nothing."

Jaguar pressed her face closer to Clare's. "Do you remember that? That feeling of nothingness in your skin, and the deadness of it. He would come into your room and you'd just lie there, and he'd move you around, *doing* things to you, and they hurt. Do you remember what it felt like, Clare?"

"Is this true?" Clare whispered. "Is it? I can't *feel* it." She stretched out a hand, as if groping for something she could touch and feel and hold.

"You don't even know what it means to feel, do you? It's frozen down so deep you can't get at it anymore."

"How—how do you know? How do you know what it's like?"

And as Clare asked the question Jaguar knew, without any doubt, what she had to do to answer it. Going into her, trying to dig out the last glacial bits of who she really was wouldn't work. She could only give her what feeling she had, with no holding back.

Where is your darkness, Jaguar?

Let it shine. Let it shine.

She opened herself fully, a wave of light—faster than light—open to her. The charged air of the empath enveloped them, leaving them momentarily silent and motionless. She let it ride all the way, washing over both of them, letting the reflection of her own life be the mirror Clare could look into and see, at last, herself.

Here. This is how I know. This is what happened to me.

She was the mirror now. Her life, in this place she'd never shown anyone before. This piece of herself that she hugged back as if it was her life, though it was not who she was. She gave it to Clare. Let her darkness shine.

Clare. This is how I know. Remember? Remember? Like this.

The moment passed into them, and Clare clutched at her head. "Stop," she said. "I don't want to know this."

Too late. Here it is. All mine. All yours.

Clare groaned and curled in on herself, feeling it all. Feeling, at last, returned to her, painful and marvelous and alive.

Jaguar let the memory recede, slowly, allowing the tide to pull back to sea. Letting the wind breathe it away. Then, softly, under her breath, she began to sing, a night chant of her people, asking the darkness to pass into light, and the light into darkness, just the way it always had. Just the way it was supposed to. She pulled Clare's head onto her lap and stroked it, singing the heartbeat of the universe back into the horror of this night.

She took her time with this, trying not to think how ill she could afford to do that. She had to get this right with Clare before they could do anything about Alex or Adrian or the line of dead men. After a while Clare stirred, opened her eyes to stare up at the stars.

"I couldn't bear to feel. Father—" She stopped, then turned her head to look at Jaguar. "I couldn't bear to know how much I loved him."

"Love is always bearable," Jaguar said. "What you couldn't bear to feel was how much you had to hate him."

Clare sighed, breath leaving her like old pain. Old dust swept away. She remained silent, and Jaguar continued sitting with her, stroking her hair. She realized she was sweating when she felt the trickle run off her forehead. Clare would be okay now. She would be okay.

She had to start thinking through her next moves. She might still have time to make the shuttle, if she left soon. Should she should go look for Adrian, though? Or leave him and Clare behind and go on alone.

Her first question was answered when she heard the sound of someone crashing clumsily through the shrubs, and Adrian's somewhat battered face appeared. He came stumbling toward her, Nick's old gun in his hand, pointing this way and that.

"Christ," he said. "There's some kind of giant cat running around. Is that where you learned your tricks?"

She looked up at him wryly as he approached. "Some of them," she said. "Will you stop waving that gun around, please. You look like an old movie."

Adrian stuck it in the back of his pants, walked over to her, and put a hand on her shoulder. "Is she . . . alive?"

Jaguar nodded. "Just a face slash. She'll be all right. I don't know if she'll ever look quite the same, though. Can you help me with her?"

She pulled Clare up to a sitting position and slung an arm around her shoulder, indicating that Adrian should do the same. Clare was going in and out of consciousness, and would probably remain that way for some time. But they'd have to go on, and Jaguar was afraid she might need her help before the job was done. Clare would have to come along.

"We'll stop at the apartment and get some bandages—clean her up. I've got some medication there that'll put her right for a while. Then we'll have to get a move on, or we'll be late."

"Late?" Adrian asked, catching Clare under her other arm and lifting. "Late for what?"

"We've got a shuttle to catch," Jaguar said.

"Shuttle?" Adrian said. "You mean—"

"I mean," she said, "lift and walk, buddy. It's about to be a very long night."

14

ALEX FELT A ROUGH HAND PRESSING INTO HIS forehead. He opened his eyes and stared up at a familiar face.

"Didn't they warn you not to try that shit?" Terence said.

"Jesus," Alex said. "You were the connection."

Terence took a step back and scanned him for damage. "I guess you're still alive. For now, anyway. And surprised, aren't you?"

Alex said nothing. He could think of nothing to say.

"Yeah," Terence continued. "You thought I was just some old workhorse, picking up the organizational pieces for the people who mattered—Teachers and Supervisors. You thought I was just stupid."

"Actually," Alex said, "I thought you were a good record keeper. *Now* I think you're stupid."

Terence shook his head slowly, then, smiling, raised his hand and whacked Alex with the back of it. "You aren't in charge here. Remember that."

"Not likely to forget," Alex said, wincing. "Who *is* in charge?"

"For now, I am," Terence said. "In a while someone else'll be here."

"Is it that man with glasses who's been on the Plane toid?"

"That's him. The Looker, he's called. He keeps track o everything."

"Everything?"

"Well, this part of the organization, anyway. I don' think anyone knows who really runs DIE." Terence wavec a large hand around the room. "This is just a little bit o it. Research. They keep their people scattered. Like to move a lot, I understand."

Alex understood, too.

"Terence," he asked, "why haven't you killed me yet?"

Terence shrugged. "Not sure. I'm supposed to hang o to you until I get orders otherwise, unless something goe: wrong. Maybe," he added, "the Looker wants to save yo for his project."

Alex couldn't help it. He shuddered.

"Yeah," Terence agreed. "Pretty raw. I haven't spent lot of time here, and I hope I won't be. I'm hoping they'l put me in another facility. Somewhere where they're doing some computerized work."

"Why?" Alex said. "So you can be a record keepe again?"

"Hey, you can laugh, but these guys pay. Listen, I gotta go, but I'm gonna be back to check on you. Don't try any more of that shit again, okay? It makes a noise."

He walked halfway across the room, turned, and looked one more time at Alex. He seemed to be considering something. Then he spoke.

"Listen, I just gotta know. I mean, here you are, and you know you ain't coming out of this one, so you might as well tell me the truth."

Alex looked at him blankly. "The truth? About what?"

Terence shrugged. "Did you? I mean, just between us— did you ever sleep with Jag?"

Alex leaned back and closed his eyes. "Don't call her Jag," he said. "She hates being called that."

• • •

Jaguar thought they must look like a very decrepit crew.
Clare and her bandaged face. Adrian and the black welt
coming up fine on the side of his face. Her own uninjured
face showing signs of fatigue. She hadn't looked at herself
in a mirror to check on it, though. She didn't know that
she wanted to see a mirror again for a long time.

They stood in the doorway of the shuttle station, feeling
morose as well as injured.

They'd missed the straightline out, and had no choice
but to catch a terminal service run to the R-Station. Delivery vehicles and small passenger runs went to the R-Station
daily, but Jaguar knew the schedule of runs. Once they got
there, they'd either have to wait another twelve hours for
the next terminal service to the home planet or they'd have
to try and connect from another Planetoid with a straightline service. Which would take at least the same amount of
time, if not longer.

They had no trouble getting seats on a terminal-service
shuttle. Nobody bothered to ask who they were or where
they were going. All clearance passes were checked at either the R-Station or on the straightline run. Which they'd
missed.

She tried not to panic at the amount of time she was
losing. Panic wouldn't serve her right now. Think. She had
to think.

They got off at the R-Station and stood in the midst of
the foot traffic. People passing at fast clips, hurrying to get
to wherever they were going, bumping pieces of luggage
against each other's legs. She and Clare and Adrian seemed
to be the only people standing still.

"Shit," Jaguar said. "This is ridiculous. We have to do
something."

Anything. Keep moving. Keep moving.

She glanced around at the signs for arrivals and departures. She knew where she needed to get to. That was something. And she knew what she needed to get her there. A

fast, small shuttlecraft, capable of landing without a pod
Something that carried a minimum of crew and no cargo.

Her eye caught a sign that pointed to the charter docks
A charter shuttle. That was just what they needed right now
The docks were probably a mile away through confusing
halls and stairs that led nowhere. And what she'd do to get
one that was going her way, she didn't know yet. But at
least it was something to try.

"Come on," she said to the others.

"Where're we going?" Adrian asked. She took a good
look at him. His face was colorful, and he was subdued
but at least he wasn't whining. She didn't think she could
stand whining right now.

Then she turned her attention to Clare. She was silent
She hadn't quite returned to the present yet, and it might
be a while before she did. Jaguar let her be silent. Better
than whining. Better than noise.

They'd talked on the way over, because Jaguar had ques
tions that needed answering. She'd seen most of the im
portant items from Alex's brief contact. The place where
they held him was the center for the pseudogenics research
and they needed to get him out of there rather than going
in after him. Now she needed specific coordinates for the
house, an idea of how many guards would be there, how
many of them would be armed. Clare's answers were brief
distant, and precise. Jaguar knew where she needed to go
now she just had to figure out how to get there.

"That way," Jaguar said, pointing with her long finger
She picked up the pace, walking ahead in long strides
trusting Adrian to make sure Clare kept up. They wound
their way through the crowd of people trying for the lounge
which was in the same direction, then down the halls, where
the number of people began to dwindle to crew and luggage
carriers and security guards.

Security guards. Shit. That might be a problem.

The arrows for delivery vehicles pointed them down a
narrowing corridor, utilitarian rather than pretty. They

hadn't bothered to decorate here, or cover the pipes and transmitter boxes that lined the walls. Ahead of her she saw the sign for the docking gate.

Just ahead of that, another sign.

CLEARANCE GATE. SECURITY ENFORCED. Keep going.

But she felt a hand on her arm.

"Hey," Adrian called at her. "What's that mean?"

He pointed at the sign, and she saw, just below it, a view screen. She couldn't hear what was being said, but a very clear picture of her own face appeared, followed by a list of particulars about her.

She turned a grim face to Adrian. "It means we're up shit's creek, probably," she said.

Someone must have found out that Clare was gone. Or that the Looker was dead. Or maybe they found Nick's remains at the burn plant. Or maybe the warrant Nick had was still good.

"Tricky," Adrian said, watching the view screen, "but interesting."

"What the hell does that mean?" Jaguar snapped, and then, seeing that he didn't even hear her, seeing that he was busy ticking out some plot in his own mind, she grinned at him.

"Okay, con man," she said. "What's your idea?"

"Well," he said, "it might work to our advantage, actually. Do you have any papers on you? Like, passes from the Planetoid or something?"

"Of course, but—"

"Okay. Give them to me."

She reached into the deep pockets of her jacket and handed them over. She wasn't about to argue now.

"Now put your hands behind you, as if you're cuffed. Right. Like that." He pulled the weapon they'd taken from the Looker out of his own belt and held it at her back.

"You're my prisoner now," he said, grinning.

She smothered a laugh, ducking her head down.

"Cut that out," he said. "Look beaten. Or try for subdued at least."

"Adrian," she said, "what about Clare?"

He considered her, then wound his free hand around her elbow.

"Um—protected witness. Injured in the tussle to get you. Walk, lady."

"Clearly," she said, "you're enjoying this a little bit too much."

But he didn't hear her. He pushed them ahead and went right up to the security guard, flashing the papers quickly and then stuffing them in his pocket. "I need a vehicle," he said. "Planetoid business. Emergency status."

"Who the hell are—hey, isn't that the lady they're looking for?" The guard gaped at Jaguar, who leaned forward and growled at him. Adrian pulled her back.

"Better not," he said. He leaned in to the guard. "She bites."

"Jesus—listen, what're you doing with her?"

"We have to get her to the home planet. There's an emergency situation there, involving a prisoner."

"Yeah? Well, I got something going out. Just step through here—"

He passed them through the gate, and Jaguar felt herself sigh in relief. They'd passed the gate.

Walking now, past a line of docked vehicles, and her eyes checking for the right one. The one that looked like it might take her where she wanted to go. Livestock shuttle.

No. Too big.

Something she'd never seen before. Boxy and bulky.

No.

A small craft, sleek and shining. Lear shuttle. Private craft. Reserved for corporate use. A pilot entering the front of it.

That one.

She stopped, and growled. Adrian turned and shot her a

look. With her eyes, she indicated the dark exterior of the Lear.

"Hey," Adrian said, "how about that one?"

"That?" the guard said. "It's got a passenger list. I want to give you something empty."

Jaguar growled again.

"That one," Adrian said, over the hum of the vehicle warming up.

"Listen," the guard said, "I'm gonna give you what I got that ain't being used. Besides, I gotta run a check on this first, make sure you're all cleared. I'll need your supervisor's name, and—hey. What the hell?"

Jaguar growled louder, and Adrian turned the gun away from her, toward the security guard. He gathered the two women in front of him and began backing toward the vehicle.

"That one," he said again.

The security guard raised his hands high. Jaguar scooted herself behind Adrian and pressed the entrance button. As the door slid open she could see a cart full of men in suits riding toward them, ready for their flight.

"So sorry," she murmured. "Flight delayed due to terrorist takeover."

And they were in.

Hira Shilo was in command of the Board of Governors' emergency meeting, and everyone let her be. God knew somebody had to be, and she was the only one willing to take on a mess that could only turn out badly, no matter what happened next.

They'd been discussing ways of managing the press around the disappearance of Clare Rilasco, when they'd received a report that a prisoner from Planetoid Three had hijacked a Lear shuttle and taken a Teacher and someone else hostage on it. The Teacher happened to be wanted for questioning in a number of matters, including the disappearance of another prisoner—Clare Rilasco.

"Jesus," Tremont said, "now what do we do?"

"At least we know where they are," Hira said. "I suggest we negotiate."

"Great suggestion," said Paul Dinardo, whose zone this nightmare had grown out of. "How'll we get them to talk to us? I doubt they'll answer cabin communication."

Hira tapped a finger against the table. "We could break through the computer."

"Oh sure. The easiest thing to ignore. How about if we send out a cruiser and have it shoot them down?"

The other Governors murmured, whether in agreement with this idea or against it, Paul couldn't tell. Hira looked at them in disgust.

"That's loathsome. For one thing, these are our people, no matter what's happened. And for another, the publicity would be awful. Because this is going to come out. It's the Rilasco case. It can't be hidden. So all we can do is manage the publicity angles. And shooting them down is not a good angle."

Paul sighed in deep disappointment. "Well, I can't think of how to get through to them, anyway."

"That's because you don't want to get through to them. Anyone else?"

"Simple," Governor Tremont said. "Push the screen."

"I beg your pardon?" Hira said politely.

"We can push the waves on the lounge telecom view screen. They're always overpowered for these Lear shuttles. We'll at least be in their faces, even if they don't respond."

"Okay," Hira said. "How long will it take, and who do we need to accomplish it?"

In the murmur of discussion that followed, Paul got up and left the room.

"Don't worry," Jaguar said to the pilot. "We don't plan to wrinkle your shirt any. Just get us out of here."

The pilot, an older man with a distinctive profile and demurely graying hair, looked unconvinced. "I'm going to retire in six months," he said. "My wife and I are going on a European tour."

Jaguar sighed. She didn't have time to reassure him. "This is Adrian," she said cheerfully. "And Clare. I'm Dr. Addams. You are—"

"Um—Ross. I'm Ross. I'm going to retire—"

"In six months," she finished for him. "And you'll enjoy every minute of it, believe me. Right now I'm looking forward to taking my retirement someday, and I hope you'll help me achieve that goal. You have airlock control?"

"Yes, ma'am."

"Then take us out."

He hesitated, and she leaned over his seat, her hand resting on the controls, the tip of the red knife showing. She put her mouth next to his ear and whispered, sultry and low, "Take us out, Ross. Now."

"Yes, ma'am."

She turned and nodded at Adrian. "Stay here with him. Tell him where we're headed, and make sure we keep headed that way. Ignore any communications from outside, okay?"

"Right," he said.

Then, to the pilot: "You have computer hookup for your passengers?"

"Yes, ma'am. In the lounge area."

She left Clare with Adrian and walked through the sleeping cabins to the lounge, which was empty and quiet except for the humming of engines. A little time to think. To work through some possible next moves.

On a table nearby was a computer, and she opened the file to navigational aids, scanning for Leadville. When the map came up she stared at it, looking for the place she'd seen in Alex's mind, the place Clare told her about. A caretaker's house, in a cemetery. Caretaking the dead. Either they had a fine sense of irony, or they had all the sensitivity of amoebas.

She wanted to get as close as possible, as quickly as possible.

There. The Francis Duffey Memorial Park. The park was on the map. She'd want to come in a little farther out than that. She wrote out coordinates, then sat back and considered.

Get as close as possible. As quickly as possible. And then . . . what?

Her thoughts were interrupted by the buzzing of the telecom. She kept her eyes on the map. "Buzz off," she muttered, but it didn't listen.

"Are you receiving?" a female voice asked. "We just want to talk with you. Let you know we're willing to negotiate."

Dammit, they'd broken through. Couldn't raise a response on the cabin radio, so they were trying this. Breaking the lines.

Then Jaguar stopped and listened. She knew that voice. It was Hira, one of the Governors of Planetoid Three. She rarely dealt with her personally, but she was the face most likely to be put up front in a public crisis.

She walked over to the telecom and grinned into it. "Don't you know it's bad policy to negotiate with terrorists, Hira?" she said.

Hira's eyes widened, and then grew angry. "It's— Dr. Addams, what's the explanation of this?"

"Get Dinardo," she said.

"I asked you a question and—"

"And I told you the answer. Get Dinardo. I'll talk with him."

Hira's face disappeared, and was replaced in a matter of minutes by Paul's puffy and exhausted visage.

"Addams," he said, "what the hell are you playing at?"

"*Doctor* Addams," she said mildly as she took a seat, pulled out a pack of cigarettes, and lit one.

"That's illegal on a shuttle," Paul said automatically, as she knew he would.

"Not in a hijacking," she said. "It's in the codebook, under the etiquette of duress, smoking, and other bureaucratic nightmares."

"Right," Paul said. "Subheading Addams. Dr. Addams, whose ass is in an inordinate amount of trouble right now. What the hell makes you think you can go around just blowing things up?"

"I? I haven't blown up a thing recently. Not that I can think of, anyway. And my ass isn't in nearly as much trouble as yours is about to be. Certainly not as much as Alex's." She blew smoke at the screen. "Know where he is?"

"Home planet. Five-day personal leave."

"Wrong. Hostage. DIE."

Paul began to sputter, and she cut him off.

"I'm going to retrieve him. Couldn't wait to do the paperwork first, but I'll take care of it when we get back. In the meantime, could you clear airspace for a landing at the following coordinates?"

She gave them, repeated them, and then smiled.

"Gotta run, Paul. Alex and I hope to see you soon. If not, you have copies of our wills."

She flipped the off lever and walked out of the lounge. Then she stopped.

Something Paul said gave her the beginnings of an idea about how to handle this.

She made her way back to the cabin, where Adrian was keeping up an amiable patter to two silent people. He stopped when she came in, and she shook her head at him. "Nothing," she said. "I just need to ask Ross—does this craft have an autofunction?"

The pilot turned to her and blinked.

"Autofunction?" he repeated.

"Whatever you call it these days. Can you start it and set it for coordinates and have it get there without a pilot?"

"Well, sort of. I mean, as environmental conditions shift, you need someone on hand to shift the controls, so in fact a pilot is absolutely necessary for maintenance—''

"Don't get in a sweat," she said. "Your retirement is secure. I just wanted to know."

She took Clare by the elbow and led her through the sleeping cabins to the lounge, where she sat her down and took her hand, feeling it cold in her own. She was still in shock. From loss of blood and loss of illusions.

"How are you holding up?" Jaguar asked, massaging Clare's hands.

"I'm . . . afraid," she said, surprised at the idea.

"Appropriate." Jaguar grinned. "You're doing fine. Listen, I need you to do something for me."

Her eyes said anything you ask. Jaguar continued. "You have to contact whoever's at the Leadville house, and get Alex out of there. Have them meet us—somewhere we can still see the house. Would the Francis Duffey Park work? The house should be visible, but distant."

"It borders the cemetery. There's some woods in it that are fairly secluded, but close by."

"All right. Can you get through on the computer?"

"I should be able to. I'll . . . try."

They turned to the screen, and Clare started the code sequence for contact.

A standby command appeared. They waited.

"Come on," Jaguar said. "What the hell are they waiting for?"

"Probably for someone to tell them what to do. Without the Looker, I'm not sure who's in charge. I would think— oh. Here's something."

Jaguar couldn't read the code, and Clare had to take a moment to translate. Then she frowned, turned to Jaguar.

"It's Terence Manning."

"Terence Manning?" Jaguar repeated. "But . . . he's . . ."

"Your record keeper. He's been working for DIE for years. Apparently he's at the Research Center."

"Jesus," Jaguar said. "I should've cooked him when his bones were still soft. What does he say?"

"He says he's receiving messages."

"Okay. Tell him who you are, and that he's to meet you with Alex in the park. Give him the right location."

Clare did so, and they waited. Then, a response.

A click of motion on the screen. The code. "He wants to know why," Clare said.

Jaguar knit her brow and tapped a finger against her lips. "Tell him something cryptic. Something that sounds typical of Clare, the assassin."

"I know," Clare said, and sent back the message, "because it's prettier."

On the return, the message read, "I want the Looker. Give me the Looker."

"He suspects something," Jaguar said.

"He always does," Clare commented. "Don't worry."

"No. I have to worry. This has to be done right. I need Alex out of there before we move." She put a hand on Clare's. "How do we handle this? Does the Looker have a code?"

"Of course," Clare said, "but I know it. He stupidly shared it one night after a particularly interesting game of poker."

Jaguar shuddered at the thought of playing poker, or any other game, with the Looker. "All right. Put it in." She thought hard. How would the Looker respond? What would he say? "Okay. Try this—you know how to word it. Say there's psi-capacity interference. Get the empath out. Explanation to follow. Does that sound like it'll fly?"

"It'll probably do. Everyone listens to the Looker."

She transmitted the message, and they waited. Soon enough, the response came.

"Clear," it read. And that was all.

Jaguar felt the knot at the back of her neck unwind. "Okay," she said. "Okay." She spent a few more minutes going over the exact location of the Research Center building, then stood and turned to leave, but Clare's hand on her arm stopped her.

"Do you have a minute? I know you're working, and I know you're worried—"

Jaguar tried out a smile. It almost worked. "Actually, I have no plans between here and Colorado. What were you thinking of—a manicure?"

Clare's return smile looked as worn-out as she imagined her own did. "Just something I wanted to tell you about what happened tonight."

Jaguar patted her hand lightly. "Go ahead."

"First, you were right. I did want to get caught. I didn't know it at the time, but I couldn't—go on. Maybe it was the experiments. The pseudogenics. All those dead men. I don't know."

The dead men. Where Alex was. Rows of men, dead and not dead, their bodies being used, and their spirits trapped in that use. Jaguar shuddered.

"Yes," Clare said. "They reminded me of—of what happened to me. My . . . father." She brushed the palm of her hand in the air in front of her, keeping it out, away. "At any rate, I wanted to get caught. Wanted out. You were right."

"Thank you," Jaguar said. "It's nice to know."

"I thought you'd appreciate it. You're someone who believes in her work."

"I do," Jaguar agreed.

"And," Clare said, "there's something else. Tonight. When you knew Alex wasn't dead, and you smiled."

Jaguar nodded, waiting for Clare to continue, curious to know why she'd brought that up.

"Your face was so alive," Clare said, her hands soaring up and out, like the wings of a bird to express what she couldn't say in words.

"Alive," she repeated. "I'd never seen anyone so alive before. I wanted you to know, that made the rest possible."

Jaguar moved her hands over her face, brushed them

through her hair, and let them rest at the back of her neck. Tired. She was tired. "I'm not sure what you mean."

"Knowing you could care that much," Clare explained. "Knowing you could feel that, even after . . . the Serials. The Killing Time. I began to think there was hope for me, after all."

Jaguar let out breath, let her hands drop to her side.

"As I said," Clare told her again, "it might not be important, but I wanted you to know."

"No," Jaguar said. "It's important. One of the most important things I've heard. Ever."

She left Clare then, and went to find a porthole to stare out of. Somewhere she could sit and consider the stars and the vagaries of the human factor, for the remainder of the flight.

The pilot set the small shuttle down in a grazing meadow, much to the consternation of the sheep who had been quietly poking at the stubbly grass.

Jaguar patted him on the back as he turned to look at her questioningly. "Good work," she said. "Now, explain the automatic settings to me."

"The—what?"

"Tell me how to set the autopilot for a landing about three miles from here, due east," she said patiently.

"But the landing gear isn't equipped for that kind of quick start and stop. It'll—"

"I know what it'll do. Just set it."

He gulped once, and did as he was told, his nervous hands playing over the computer face clumsily. "Set," he said.

"Great. You can go now."

"I can . . . go? Where?"

"Anywhere you like," she said. "Disneyland. Only, do it quickly, please."

He scuttled out of his seat and was gone, looking behind him only twice.

Jaguar called to Adrian and Clare, and they appeared in the pilot's cabin. Adrian looked nervous, but Clare was cool as always.

"You know what to do from here?" she asked.

"I'm to go and meet Alex and whoever's with him. I'm to say the Looker sent me ahead, and have him turn Alex over to me. From there . . . I'm not sure."

"Events will occur," Jaguar said. "At least, I hope they will. Adrian?"

"I stay behind Clare, out of sight. Jump in only if there's trouble. But what about you?"

"I should be right behind you. If I'm not—the idea is to get Alex the hell away from here in one piece. Take care of any guards, and get him home. So whatever you have to do to accomplish that, whether I'm there or not, just do it. Okay?"

"But—" Adrian began to protest.

"Just," she said, "do it. Get out of here. They'll be waiting for you."

Adrian cast one last glance of concern at her, shrugged, and led Clare out of the shuttle.

They stood in a clearing. Alex, Terence, and a guard.

Clare approached them slowly, keeping her bandaged face held high.

"Is this pretty enough for you, Clare?" Terence asked, raising a weapon and holding it to Alex's head.

"Beautiful, Terence. I'll take him now," she replied.

"I don't think so, Clare. I'll need clearance first."

He nodded at the guard, who raised a weapon on the other side of Alex's head. Terence walked forward and turned his weapon toward Clare.

"Terence, the Looker sent me to take over. He's had to go on ahead to report to his people, and I'm to dispose of . . . the problem." She smiled through her bandages, adding, "You weren't hired on for that kind of work, were you?"

"Clare," he said, "I wasn't, and I'm not giving him up until I get the all clear from the guy I work for."

Clare sighed and spoke gently, patiently. "What's the trouble, Terence?"

"First, I don't trust you. I'm not even gonna ask what happened to your face, but it doesn't look good to me. Second, I don't trust the Looker. Third, holding on to Dzarny's the only protection I got right now. So what I'm gonna do is just walk away from here with him. Now. The guard can finish him off, and the Looker can catch up with me at his own convenience."

Clare shook her head sadly, and was about to speak again, when the shadow of an airborne vehicle passed over her, then him, then Alex. It was a large shadow, and Alex looked up at it.

Too large. Too low.

Terence paused. Peered at the sky, then twisted his head back toward the Research Center.

The flash of light and noise that followed almost drowned out his voice as he shouted at the guard.

"Kill him," Terence shouted. *"Now."*

"I don't think so," Clare said, and raised a gun from the folds of her dress, fired at Terence.

A tremor ran through the ground under them in the wake of the blast, and the guard struggled to maintain his balance.

Alex dove for the guard's legs and, as he did so, was aware that someone had joined him rather precipitously.

He felt the breath of wind as legs leaped over him, and heard a gasp. Looked up to see that Jaguar had the guard by the throat and was holding her knife against it.

"It would be wise," she said, "if you held very still while my colleague and I make arrangements to ensure our safety."

Alex took a moment to catch his breath, then scrambled over to her, grabbing the guard's arms and holding them behind his back.

"Hello, Jaguar," he said. "Didn't know if you'd make it."

"That makes two of us," she agreed, and stopped in her manipulation of the guard's arms to run her gaze over him. "You're okay?" she asked.

"Better now," he said. He looked over in the direction she'd come from and saw Clare Rilasco, sitting hunched over Terence's body.

"Clare," he said. "She's—"

Jaguar looked up and over at her prisoner, then nodded in satisfaction.

"Crying, I think," she said.

"Should I—"

"No," Jaguar said. "Let her be. She deserves her grief. She's earned it, God knows." She nodded at her belt. "Cuffs in there."

Alex removed them and secured the guard's arms. "Jaguar," he said. "I'm not sure what you did, but I thank you for it."

She stood and gazed back past the woods. Flames were rising in the distance. "You may be the only one to do that," she said, then turned a rueful grin toward him. "I blew up a shuttle."

"You—I beg your pardon?"

"Shuttle. Big. Go kaboom on Research Center. Get it, white man?"

Alex pulled the cuffed guard to his feet and bit back on a smile.

"A little overkill, wasn't it?" he asked.

"Maybe. But I needed a distraction, and I wasn't in the mood for taking chances."

She turned and gestured toward the center. "Your message came through loud and clear," she said, "though I don't doubt it cost you something in pain to deliver it."

Alex closed his eyes and thought about this. "So you saw . . . all of it?"

She walked around the guard and stood in front of Alex.

Her eyes said something to him that he couldn't quite read. Something about what she saw. How she felt about it. It would be a long and complex process, getting to know her. She had too many moving parts, and all of them spoke in whispers or screams, with not much in between.

"Yes," she said. "I saw everything. I know everything. I'm hoping that nobody else does."

The dead. They needed to be dead. It was wrong to keep the dead alive, like maggots under the skin. And no matter what official body found them, they'd just want to continue the torture, for scientific purposes, of course. She had seen, and chosen to end it. He approved her choice.

She turned away from the flames and saw Adrian walking across the field toward them. She held a hand out in greeting and flashed him a smile.

"Hey," she said. "Know anyplace I can pick up a shuttle fast? I want to go home."

15

DR. ADDAMS'S OFFICIAL REPORT ON THE COMpletion of her assignment was a concise written document that she transferred to Alex via computer. It included a commendation for the action Adrian had taken on her behalf, mentioned that Clare Rilasco had entered the rehabilitation phase of her program, and requested permission for a three-week rest leave. Alex had helped her find the right words to explain the untimely demise of the Lear, and apparently they'd said something right, because neither of them were being reprimanded.

An official apology and reimbursement had been sent to the corporate owners of the shuttlecraft. It was accepted after much grumbling. But the Governors' Board had done a good job of throwing their weight around, insisting that the move was a necessary part of a complex operation, and weren't they the ones who kept all the good people on the home planet from having to deal with things like prisons and recidivism and so on? And would the good people who liked to keep their suits clean and their businesses running prefer a return to the old days, the pre-Serial days, or even the Killing Times?

Grumbles had subsided. Brows had been mopped. Drinks had been ordered. Hands had been shaken.

All was well.

Clare agreed to testify at a grand-jury hearing into the operations of the Division of Intelligence Enforcement. Or, what was left of their operations.

By the time official warrants were sworn for various DIE employees, most of the homes and offices they occupied had been vacated. The rats had scurried off the ship, dispersing into a variety of countries across the home planet, choosing towns that barely had names, Alex was sure. He was also sure they'd reorganize. Find a new name to play the same game under. But this would certainly slow them down quite a bit. He thought it would be some time before experiments in living death were taken up again.

Clare couldn't testify about DIE's connection to NICA, because she knew nothing about it. Alex figured NICA would cover its assets and cut its losses on this one. Too bad.

Only some parts of the Looker had been found. An arm, chewed off at the elbow, and a broken pair of glasses. He hoped Hecate and Chaos had enjoyed a good meal. He sincerely hoped they had licked their plates clean.

In her report, Jaguar had said that she'd "instigated a therapeutic conversation" with Clare during the heat of the crisis in order to bring her program to a successful conclusion.

Alex knew what that meant.

She'd made empathic contact, and hit the mark. Whatever she'd done, it worked.

But she hadn't spoken to him about that, outside the official language of reports. In fact, outside of the necessary professional interactions, she hadn't spoken with him at all. Stole a shuttle and blew it up to save his life, and she wouldn't talk to him about it.

And she'd made no mention of Nick.

He'd be classified, officially, as a disappearance, and in the absence of evidence, the absence of a body, there'd be no investigation. That, Alex thought, was for the best.

There were some events that didn't fit protocol, no matter how you turned them, and it was better to let those events fade into obscurity. But he still wanted to know, for himself, what had happened. What she'd done with his remains, and how she felt about it.

It was late at night, two weeks and a day after Jaguar had saved his life, that he marked the assignment complete and transferred the file to the inactive folder. He stared out the door of his office, down the halls that were dark and empty. The case was closed.

He tucked his computer in for the night, closed up his office, and left the building. But he didn't go home.

He thought he knew where she would be.

Jaguar possessed the stage, and all the people who occupied the bar. They were, for once, silent and listening, eyes pressed onto her swaying, silk-clad form. When Alex walked into the Silver Bay, she was singing a song that used the upper range of her voice. He sat with everyone else and listened.

It was a song about the Serials. An old one, mourning the losses. Trust, hope, anything like a chance for beauty. Then, somewhere in the wavering notes of grief, a chance for the world to reweave itself, a pleading for the heart that heals and lives again.

Her voice was a thin ghost of a line carrying the blade of sorrow to his ears. He listened and waited, ordering a brandy that he sat twirling around and around in its glass and not drinking.

Between songs, he caught her eye. He signaled to her that he wanted her, and she tossed a nod at him. At the set break, she didn't stop to talk to the other band members, but walked right over to him.

When she reached him, she didn't say a word. Not hello. Not what are you doing here. Not how'd you like the song. Nothing.

She knew.

"Sit," he said, motioning to a chair. Then he leaned over close to her and took her face in both his hands, holding it very still. He leaned close, catching the scent of mint as he did so.

Anyone who saw them would think they were lovers caught up in a moment of intimacy. The moment of contact looked like that sometimes, though it could also seem as violent as fire, or soft as feathers, depending on the empath and the subject. Alex let his hands search, find the way in through this dear and unfamiliar flesh, even before his dark eyes washed into the deep green of her abundant sea, going in slowly, taking time and taking care as he went. She made no motion to escape his hold. She was letting him do this. Consenting to it. He hoped it was a good sign.

The first levels were easy. Just a simple slide across the surface. Here he found some tension. Not fear. Not yet, anyway. Just the tension of facing the unknown. Nothing he needed to deal with. Then there was something else. Something lovely and serene, still and holy, the quiet place of the empath. This was a place he rarely got to know in others, though he knew it from himself. He explored it, respectfully but thoroughly, and found no sign of the shadow sickness. No darkness. None of the ice, slippery and reflexive, that had been Clare's.

What he found here was all Jaguar. A pacific clarity, shining and fresh. If it had a scent, it would smell, like her, of wild mint under a bright sun. He recognized something he had always known about her, but had never been able to put into words. She acknowledged no discipline except that of her own spirit, but her spirit was perhaps the most principled he would ever know.

He continued moving unhurriedly, aware of both the fragility and the strength of what he touched. With no resistance, she allowed him access to the memory of what had happened with Nick. Easy to find her here. Easy to see what she'd done, and why.

Here, she had plunged the knife into his heart, with no remorse, no regret, and no guilt. Here, she'd said the death prayers, cleansed the shadow from his spirit as it left his body. Here, she let go of her final grief. They'd both been through hell, and now only one of them remained to talk about it.

He'd saved her, and tried to trap her, and she'd killed him before he could kill her. No remorse, no regret, but some grief for a world that mangles its children so badly. Most importantly, there was no sign of creeping shadow. She was well. That was all that mattered.

With relief, he moved on.

Now he found something cloaked and protected, though not closed. Not, at least, to him.

It was warm here. Warm and sweet. God, it felt so sweet, like good water after thirst, sun on your face after a long cold winter. He stopped and let it soak into him, a brief moment of unadulterated pleasure, unexpected and precious. He savored it, and she let him, trying for no defensive maneuver.

She just let him.

Then something sharp—here at the edge of this place—made him pause. Something like a fear. It darted away, and he let it. They were probably headed in the same direction anyway.

To the closed space.

What he wanted. Where fear and desire met, challenged each other. A place of all the most profound memories that told the story of who you were. The place she let no one walk except herself. He tested the strength of it with an initial push. Not a bit of give.

He pushed a little harder, his hands against her face, his eyes pressed against the back of her brain, and she gasped. He held her there, at the edge of it. Then he said, apologetically, "I have to, Jaguar. I'm sorry, but I have to."

Her breathing was rough, and her eyes wild. He took a moment to let her adjust, to make sure he had informed consent for this. "Jaguar," he said, "what you let Clare see—I want to know that. Who you are. Where you've been—that's important. Do you understand?"

Her hands clenched on the table. She took in a ragged breath. "Go," she said. "Just go ahead. I can't . . . help you with it."

He took a breath. Slow and easy. She could feel with him, the air entering his lungs.

More breathing. Keep it easy. Let the breath move the energy. Slow and easy. He waited until the rhythms of her breath flowed with his.

"Jaguar Addams," he said, "see who you are. Be what you see."

The worst thing about it was the smell, the pervasive constant smell of bodies left too long in the sun. The bodies piling up in the streets and the ambulances too busy to handle them all at first, then the drivers too frightened to answer calls.

Jaguar remembered the awful smell floating up to the fourth-story window of their apartment. She would open it and look out, and her grandmother would pull her back in, closing the window hard, but not soon enough to close out the smell of death.

Her grandfather gave her mint, showed her how to crush it to release its sweet sharp scent.

Mint, to cover the smell of rotting flesh.

"You shouldn't be down here," her grandfather told her as she stood in the lobby of their apartment building. "Not alone. Not anymore."

She had snuck down to the lobby to meet him while her grandmother was at a friend's apartment, having a cup of tea. Her grandfather looked frightened. She didn't understand. Death meant little to her, and when it became the norm, it seemed merely normal. Already, she'd seen a few people killed. She wasn't going to school anymore, and she heard her grandparents talking about arrangements to leave the city, at least get her out. But she didn't want to leave them. Didn't want to go live with people she didn't know. Why should she leave?

He knelt down to her level and put his soft hands on her shoulders. "Jaguar, it's not safe." He shook his head at her unblinking, uncomprehending eyes.

She rode on his shoulders, up the elevator to their apartment, and they entered it, laughing at a joke he had made.

"Why did the chicken cross the road?" he asked her. When she said she didn't know, he told her, "To show the raccoon it could be done." They both laughed. He unlocked the door.

The man with the gun stood on the other side, a smooth smile growing on his face as he brushed back his smooth, light hair. He wore a lab coat, a white, unwrinkled shirt, a dark tie. His hands were encased in the second skin of surgical gloves.

"I've always wanted to kill someone," he said politely, merely by way of explanation. "This seems like such a perfect opportunity, I'd hate to have it pass me by. So," he added, smiling from grandfather to granddaughter, "who's first?"

Her grandfather stood in front of her, pushing her back, trying to push her out the door.

It all happened very fast after that, with only a little noise, and a great deal of blood.

Her grandfather, shot twice in each leg, writhing in pain on the floor. Bullets spit out, the blood everywhere, this nameless man standing over him, looking into his eyes, saying, "How does it feel?" Her grandfather too weak to share even his pain.

She rushed over to him, hanging on to his neck and screaming. The man pulled her off him and flung her onto the couch. She remembered the feeling of flying through air, not knowing where she would land, like the dreams she had sometimes of flying, then falling.

The man pointing the gun at her grandfather's head. Then the man laughing.

"Maybe," he said, "I see another opportunity presenting itself. Another experience."

He came over to the couch and held the gun against her head. It felt cold, she remembered. His hands, made sleek by the gloves, ran lightly over her skin, caressing her, then tugging at her clothes.

She closed her eyes as he undressed her. Was he going to put her to sleep? Like they did to the dog? Put her in her pajamas first? She didn't understand. She heard her grandfather moaning, a scrabbling sound of his feet against the floor, the sound of a shot fired, and the scrabbling sound stopped. She opened her eyes and saw that more blood was coming out of her grandfather now, only this time from his chest. His open eyes stared at her.

The man turned to her. "I hope," he said, "he can still see."

He took off all her clothes, then pulled down his own pants.

He looked at her, examined her carefully, the cold of the gun brushing against her skin. She remembered his laugh, because it wasn't a laugh that said something was funny.

He laughed, and spoke. "I just had a thought," he said. "Maybe you'd like to have some fun, too?"

She stared at him, not understanding. He took her hand and pressed the gun into it. "Go ahead," he said. "Shoot me."

She stared at him more.

"If you don't, you'll be sorry."

She shook her head, holding the gun, heavy in her hands.

He sighed. "Okay, then. Have it your way," he said brightly, and took the gun back, pushed her hard against the couch, starting pressing himself into her and laughing. Laughing.

It hurt. It hurt. Like knives cold gun at your head. Like suffocating being strangled knives hands on your throat. Like surprise all of everything gone no way of knowing what what what. He hit her, twice, three times, more, and then there was a great darkness.

When she came to, it was to the sound of the door opening. She looked, and saw her grandmother standing and staring at her grandfather's open eyes. Her grandmother would do something. Her grandmother would know what to do.

The man in the lab coat was still there, sitting there as if he'd been waiting for her grandmother. He laughed, and pulled the trigger on his gun again. Again. Again. Again.

Her grandmother's face went white and her breath went ragged. She clutched at her chest and fell to the floor. More blood. More blood.

Then, the darkness. Then, waking to the sleek feel of plastic against her skin. Then, the feel of knives in her. Again.

Again.

Again.

She decided she was dead, and lay still, feeling nothing. Not even letting her skin know what was happening to her.

Again. Again. Again.

How long did he stay? Maybe just a day. Maybe a week. She didn't know, because she was already dead, and when you're dead there isn't any time. Isn't any body. Isn't anything to feel anymore. He moved her here and there, and the plastic against her skin became her skin as she became plastic, just plastic. Just dead.

Then he looked down at her and said, "This is getting boring."

And he left.

She lay still for a long time, wondering if she would stay dead. After a while the smell from the floor made her feel sick, and she got up, walked to the apartment door, and left. If she was dead, she'd go and be a ghost. If she was

alive, she should go and get someone. Go and tell someone
what happened.

She stumbled her way down the stairs, out the lobby,
and into the street looking for . . . what?

Help. Someone who would help. But everyone kept
walking. Nobody even looked at her. Like she was invisible. There was a guy up the street yelling at a woman. A
boy kneeling by the curb, crying.

Nobody looked at her. She sat down on the curb, next
to the little boy, but she didn't cry.

Instead, she sang a song her grandfather taught her, and
opened her arms wide while she sang.

All around her was the smell of rotting flesh. The smell
of mint, still lingering on her fingers. The look of fear as
it crowded her. The taste and touch and arms and legs and
face of it.

All around her were the fears, reaching for her. All the
fears, yellow and acrid smelling, soft and suffocating, sharp
and sudden, crowded around her. All the fears, and the
attendant weeping, the attendant rage. The fears of all the
people on the street. The fears of everyone with a gun. The
fear of every fanatic.

The emptiness of it, never-ending repetitious spirals of
dull sameness. The awful banality of it, dragging on from
day to day in the same acts of repetitive pointless violence,
petty or grand. The utter emptiness. The fear of every Wall
Street stockbroker and Madison Avenue adman. The petty
fears of the politicians. The things they should have been
afraid of, but weren't. The things they turned their faces
from out of fear. Fear in the dark and cold waters of refusal
to see.

She sang to them, and to her own fears.

Death and the shock of it. The surprise. Fear of aban-
donment. Fear of being separated from those who loved
her. Fear that losing their love would break her. Fear that
she would break. Fear of betrayal. Fear of the bogeyman.
Fear of exactly what did happen.

They clutched at her with bony fingers, reaching for her, wanting to touch her, and she opened her arms wide, sang them to her, welcomed them.

Thin and solitary, a little girl who was already a ghost because she had survived her own death, she opened her arms wide. She opened her arms to all the fears, yellow and acrid smelling, soft and suffocating, sharp and sudden. All the fears, and the attendant weeping, the attendant rage. She did the only possible thing she could to survive. She accepted her fears, holding them as her own.

She opened her arms to them, and when they rushed to her she held them, rocked them close as if they were her children, until she and they, spent from pain and weeping and rage, fell into a dreamless sleep.

Here, at last, Alex felt her pull away, and here, at last, if she chose to do so, he would let her go.

Alex dropped his hands from her face and breathed deeply in and out. He clenched and unclenched his fingers. The sounds of the bar—glasses clinking, people talking, the holodisk playing through the break—came back to them both.

"I'm glad I know," he said softly, "at least some of it."

She nodded, shifted in her seat, looked off to a far point across the bar, and began to speak quietly. "When I was very little—before the Serials, when we still lived in New Mexico—I was afraid of monsters," she said, her voice sounding long ago and far away. "My grandfather showed me how to chase them away."

She held her hands palm forward in front of her and pushed hard. "Out, out, out. Like that. We'd say it together, and the monsters would go away."

Alex suppressed a smile as he contemplated the image of a young Jaguar, eyes serious and intense, holding off monsters with her bare hands.

She continued speaking. "When he died, I was furious

at him, because he let the monsters get him. How could he
when he was such a strong man? Then I met Nick, and I
thought—''

She paused, shook her head. ''I don't know what I
thought. That he'd teach me what my grandfather didn't
have a chance to. How to push the monsters away. But he
couldn't. He couldn't live beyond the Serials. He died then,
and he never found his way back to living. I was angry at
him, because I thought he was stronger than me. Like my
grandfather.''

Alex understood. If Nick or her grandfather couldn't survive, how could she? But she had not only survived, she
kept her spirit intact, and Nick hated her for that. How did
she dare to think she could escape the darkness of her memories when he couldn't escape his. How dare she live,
whole and well, and what did that say about who he was?
He wanted nothing except for her to sit in the pit he lived
in so that he could justify staying there. Alex had seen it
before, in others who lived within the bitterness and rage
of their pain.

''He was shadowed,'' Alex said. ''Too far gone. Didn't
want anything except—except for you to be what he was.
I'm sorry I didn't see it sooner. And I'm sorry I doubted
you.''

''I doubted myself, Alex,'' she said. ''Nick . . . he saved
my life.''

''And he tried to kill you. If he had—'' Alex left the
sentence unfinished, tried another one instead. ''Jaguar, he
saved you, but he didn't want to save himself. It was too
hard. Too much work. That's not your shame. It's his.
Only, I wish you'd trusted me enough to tell me what you
knew.'' He let that sink in, and saw her acknowledge it.

Then he leaned back in his chair and brooded.

There was one thing left.

Something lingering in the sweet warm space he found.
It was a small fear, or a new fear. Perhaps a residual. He

wasn't quite sure how to place it, or what to name it. Or even if he should.

Professionally, did it make a difference? Personally, did he have to know?

The answers were, respectively, no, and yes.

She kept her face turned from him, but he could see it in profile, her gaze fixed on some distant point.

"Jaguar, there's another fear you carry. Something new," he began, but she anticipated him and interrupted.

"Residual fear," she said, waving it away. "Just . . . here."

"Name it, Jaguar."

Time passed with the slow and steady sound of her breathing, the continued patient beating of her heart.

"You," she said at last, her eyes glittering in the dark. "It's just you."

They sat for some time in silence, staying in the quiet place necessary before reentering a dangerous and unquiet world. Alex wondered what prayers she said, after the empathic touch. He knew that his would include the guidance blessing—the one that asked for help in remaining open to what would be.

When the band signaled her that break was over, she rose and returned to the stage. While she was singing Alex slipped out into the night, and found his own way home.

ROBERT A. HEINLEIN

THE MODERN MASTER OF SCIENCE FICTION